Pop Culture Magic 2.0:
The Evolution of
Pop Culture Magic

Pop Culture Magic 2.0: The Evolution of Pop Culture Magic

Taylor Ellwood

Megalithica Books
Stafford England

Pop Culture Magic 2.0: The Evolution of Pop Culture Magic
by Taylor Ellwood

Editor: Kat Bailey
Layout: Taylor Ellwood
Cover Design: Isis Sousa

ISBN: 978-0-9932371-2-6
MB0176

Set in Consolas and Book Antiqua

A Megalithica Books Publication
An imprint of Immanion Press

info@immanion-press.com
http://www.immanion-press.com

Dedication

To my daughter Kyra, for expanding my pop culture horizons with all of your interests!

Acknowledgements

As with all of my books, writing this one has been a team effort. Thanks to Sarah Lynne Bowman who pointed me in the direction of some key resources in pop culture studies on role playing games. Thanks to Erik, Victoria, Kelli, Kaia, Cate, Tony, Paerie, James, Melissa, Fred, and the rest of the Magical Experiments community for supporting my work. Thanks to Leni Austine for the occasional chats about pop culture magic. Thanks to Isis Sousa for coming up with a beautiful cover. Thanks to Storm Constantine and Immanion Press for publishing this book. Thanks to Emily Carlin for being another voice about pop culture magic. Special thanks to Felix Warren for writing the introduction to this book. Special thanks to Kyra and Kelson for being fantastic, interesting children and sharing what their own pop culture interests are. And a very special thanks to my sweetie Kat for her editing and her unconditional support and belief in me.

Table of Contents

Foreword

A little over eleven years ago *Pop Culture Magick* was published by Immanion Press. I felt it was fitting to publish Pop Culture Magic 2.0 (without the K!) 11 years (more or less) later to celebrate the original publication, as well share how my own work with pop culture magic has changed since I first wrote the book. What amazes me the most about the last decade is how much pop culture magic has been taken up by other people. Before I wrote *Pop Culture Magick,* the only magicians who'd written about it or worked with the concept were chaos magicians, and they'd only touched on it lightly. Since *Pop Culture Magick* was written, I've watched as people from a variety of magical backgrounds have starting utilizing elements of pop culture in their own work. I don't think this is solely due to my book, but I'd like to think that *Pop Culture Magick* has played a significant role in opening people to the possibility of integrating pop culture into their magical work.

I received a lot of criticism when I wrote *Pop Culture Magick.* I was told I was reinventing the wheel or that what I'd written wasn't real magic. Obviously, eleven years later, my critics are wrong, and I take a lot of satisfaction from that because it's good to be right about something (or many things!). There is an unfortunate tendency in many people to try and discourage creative thinking and critique of traditions. Anyone reading this book is likely not one of those people, but if you know such people you will find that they will do their best to discourage your creativity and vision because they feel threatened by it. Don't listen to them. They aren't worth your time or effort. If anything, do what I did and use their criticism to inspire you to keep working on your ideas.

When I look at the landscape of pop culture magic now, what stands out to me the most is the variety of pop culture magic practices. I see a diversity that is truly gratifying because what it demonstrates is how flexible pop culture is, and in turn how it can be applied to the essential principles and processes of magic. Whether you are someone who draws inspiration from *Harry Potter, My Little Pony,* various comic book universes, or other types of pop culture out there what is derived from such inspiration is a connection to magic and a connection to the culture of this time, the mythology of this era, which in its own way is as vibrant and powerful as anything else out there.

If you go onto Tumblr.com and do a search for pop culture magic or pop culture paganism, what you will see is a diversity of practices utilizing pop culture magic. Some of those practices are more traditional, involving the creation of spells and the use of specific components; while other practices are more along the lines of the empty handed approach to magic, using whatever is on hand in order to do magical work. What all of them have in common is a desire to weave elements of pop culture into the magical work.

Some may wonder why that is and the answer is simple: The pop culture practitioner resonates with those characters or ideas and recognizes how they can be applied to magical practices. They feel a genuine connection to the pop culture entities they are working with, or they get inspired by an idea in a book, show, etc. and decide to see if they can actually apply it as a magical practice. And provided they understand the underlying principles of magic, they find that pop culture magic works and suddenly the practitioner feels that they've found that missing piece of their spirituality. And they have, much like people into pop culture in general feel when they discover a show or comic or whatever else that really touches them emotionally and spirituality.

Even though pop culture magic is more accepted, there are still the inevitable critics and controversy. In the spring of 2013 some fundamentalist polytheists got up in arms because other polytheists were interested in integrating pop culture into their spiritual work. The fundamentalist polytheists slammed those people and pop culture magic in general because they felt threatened by the fact the other polytheists were taking spiritual concepts from those traditions and applying them to pop culture. On the one hand I can sympathize with the fundamentalists, who want to preserve their traditions as best as possible, and as such view anything that isn't of their traditions to be a threat to those traditions. On the other hand, such intolerance is what creates fundamentalism in the first place, and frankly Paganism and Polytheism can do without it.

There's nothing wrong with wanting to maintain a particular tradition as it is, but there's also nothing wrong with taking a concept from a tradition and applying it to something as part of a person's exploration of his/her own spirituality. I think that if clear distinctions are made it shouldn't cause problems, but the Polytheist blow up showed reactionary thinking that was intent on showcasing pop culture magic as ridiculous and fluffy, instead of trying to draw clear distinctions that could respect the work the other people were doing while also demonstrating why that work is distinctly different from their traditions. Unfortunately, all their reaction really showcased was just how intolerant the fundamentalist polytheists can be.

Eleven years ago I received similar reactions to *Pop Culture Magick,* but there wasn't really anyone else around doing it, or if they were they were underground. What was really ironic is that the knee jerk reaction I received came from chaos magicians, determined to dogmatically assert what real magic was or wasn't. Nonetheless their reaction, far from discouraging me, indicated that there was real value to this idea. I'd argue that any time you encounter such reactions from other people it's usually because you've discovered something genuine and they fear how it will change the status quo.

Genuine progress occurs when we are willing to draw on the traditions and disciplines that provide a foundation of practice for us, while also choosing to be creative and test that practice with new ideas with creative integrations of practices from different disciplines and traditions. Progress is inevitable and necessary for the evolution of humanity. When we stop being inquisitive, curious and creative, and instead cling to what is already known for the sake of tradition, what we are really doing is signaling that we're ready for extinction. Tradition has its place as a foundation for our evolution and as something to appreciate and honor in its own right, but it should never become more important than our drive to continually progress with the changing of the times.

This book reflects that understanding of this principle of evolution. What I wrote about pop culture magic eleven years ago isn't set in stone. What I write now isn't set in set in stone either. Both books are the representation of ideas, as well as magical theory and practice, but they are also temporary, as indeed everything else is. Someday, a long time from now, this planet won't exist and this book will likely not exist either. Everything is temporary, and what allows anything to continue being relevant and alive is the continued choice to evolve and change, to grow and learn, to challenge and take risks. When we destroy that initiative within ourselves, we are destroying our future. As such, the ideas and practices in this book should be tested by you. Don't take my word for it...instead test and verify to discover what really works.

Pop Culture Magic 2.0 is an evolution of the work I did in *Pop Culture Magick*, as well as an evolution of pop culture magic in general. It's a response to the changing technology as well as continued cultural changes that have occurred in the last decade, but it is also an evolution of my theories and practices. What it is not, however, is the authoritative text on pop culture magic. It is one text among many, and you may find you agree or disagree with my ideas on pop culture magic. Regardless of what you feel, what is truly important is what you choose to do with the information. My hope is that it will inspire your magical work and provide you some directions you can take your work in. It's also my hope that this book will continue challenge conventional thinking about magic in general.

There are three disclaimers I must make. One of the complaints that reviewers of *Pop Culture Magick* offered was that they were unhappy that I didn't draw on the pop culture that they were familiar with. Its nitpicky criticism and it annoys me to this day because they did not focus on the underlying concepts and applications but instead focused on the superficial aspects. So I say this to you dear reader: The examples I provide are based off my interests in pop culture. Please don't expect me to have the same interests as you have, and please don't critique my interests because they aren't yours. Whatever examples I draw on are used as just that: Examples.

Focus on the understanding the technique or process and apply it to the pop culture of your choice. It may not be the pop culture I'd use, but I'm okay with that. Just don't expect me to use pop culture you know. I will admit that much of what many other people find popular are things I don't find interesting or popular. In fact, I tend to maintain a skeptical distrust of what other people find popular, in part because I'm very careful about what I expose my mind to, when it comes to sources of inspiration and creativity. To this day I've read little of Grant Morrison's work (for example) and what I have read I've been unimpressed by. Other occultists can't get enough of him and love his work. I'm fine with that, but don't expect me to use his work as an example. I really wish I didn't have to include that disclaimer, but people get attached to their pop culture and I understand that.

The second disclaimer is that some people who've read my work have complained that I didn't include spells. I don't cast spells. I don't do the candles, incense, and various tools that people use. What tools I do use are highly personalized. So you won't find spells in this book. What will you will find is detailed, thoroughly researched exploration of the principles of pop culture magic, as well as experiments. You can take these ideas and fit them to your own style of practice, which may include spells. And if you really want spells, do a search on Tumblr as there are many people sharing pop culture spells through that site.

The third and final disclaimer is that I've taken sections from my book *Multi-Media Magic* and added them to this book, with revisions. *Multi-Media Magic* is no longer in print. It never did as well as I hoped it would, and so I've taken it and re-appropriated the text into what will be three different books, this being one of them, in order to make sure the concepts get the exposure they deserve to get.

Alright…with those disclaimers made, let's explore the evolution of pop culture magic. I'm excited by the possibilities and I hope you are as well.

Taylor Ellwood
July 2015

Introduction
by Felix Warren

I don't remember the first time I stepped into a story's world.

After all, like most pop culture fans, I loved pop culture from an early age. It's easy to love pop culture as a child. The toys for most children's pop culture are engineered to help the child interact with the story, be they props from the actual show or dolls of the characters. Such props encourage roleplay, and when you're playing the role of a character with supernatural abilities, you end up roleplaying using those abilities in this world.

Of course, that's all just child's play. Imagination games to keep kids busy until they get old enough to do something productive. With the exception of fringe culture members, it's assumed that adults don't engage in this kind of behavior, and if they do they become socially shunned. Adult behavior needs to be more distinguished and rational than child's behavior, according to mainstream assumptions, and so adults shouldn't have toys. Which is strange when you consider that the 'replicas' and 'memorabilia' for adults' shows are so similar to toys for children's shows in crucial ways. Props abound, each one more hyper-realistic than the next for the most discerning collector. ("Collector" is a much more dignified word than "fan" in our society, isn't it?) And in fact adults' toys get to be more immersive (and expensive) than children's toys, as if adulthood secretly rewards us with the ability to dive further into the stories we love... as long as we keep it on the down-low, keep it to "collecting" and "nostalgia." But who are we fooling? When someone sells a hyper-realistic light saber with sounds and special effects meticulously crafted to imitate the movies, they can make that kind of financial commitment on a high-end product because they know enough people out there want to become Jedi on some level.

I've had my pop culture toys as a child and as an adult. I acted out plenty of fantasies as a kid, but it's hard to tell if I ever seriously meant to do magic with the props I was playing with. Sure, I tried shouting a few spells or other incantations ("Beetlejuice Beetlejuice Beetlejuice!") to see if the movies and shows would cross over into real life, but rarely with real intent or belief that it would change anything. I wasn't applying the real mechanics of magic yet.

It would take a long time until I'd pull part of a story's world into mine.

It wasn't until I was a grown adult that I picked up my children's toy version of the Moon Wand from Sailor Moon (purchased at an age a few years over that indicated on the box) with the deliberate intent to use it to replace my ritual magic wand. Pretty as the wooden wand that was gifted to me was, it was too traditional for my style of magic, and it didn't fit my personality at all. A shiny piece of plastic that made music and flashed lights when I pushed the button was more my speed. My magic improved and I wanted to do magic more often - I was personally attached to it now via a powerful pop culture artifact, and from then on anything seemed possible.

This story was privileged information at one time. I was embarrassed. I thought people would think I was childish for using the Moon Wand to construct serious magic. Sometimes I was right, too. There's a strong pressure in most of today's society to be normal, and that carries over even into subcultures. Not every fan of Sailor Moon would appreciate what I do with the Moon Wand, nor are they guaranteed to respect it. Overall, people viewed what I did as interesting or funny, but in many people's eyes I was taking things a little too far with a kids' cartoon or "not getting serious about magic."

In 1999 when I was first experimenting with pop culture magic via the Moon Wand, it was hard to find another person doing what I did. Within a couple years I escalated my pop culture practice--I started building a religion based off of the demon pantheon in the anime Slayers. I found little support in the Slayers community for these endeavors, because most fans weren't also practitioners of the ceremonial magic arts that the show's demon pantheon was inspired by. I could find ceremonial magic practitioners who would take me seriously when I'd describe my research into the alchemical symbolism overtly inserted throughout the story. I was encouraged to go straight to the source texts instead of watching an anime, and was told that a cartoon wasn't going to have magical information or structure of any substance or accuracy.

I did what any grown adult would do - I hermited myself away from outside commentary and worked on my pop culture craft by myself, telling myself I'd check back into the community in ten years or so. That was around 2003. Social media wasn't part of society's chemistry yet, and certainly wasn't part of my life. Ten years later, we would have all sorts of networks to connect people with the same interests, even really specific interests.

Ten years is a long time to go without any peers beyond your closest confidantes, and it's long enough for your confidantes to have learned all your stories about pop culture magic and gotten a little tired of them. So in 2013, I joined tumblr with the intent to tell people all I'd learned about demonolatry, about how it connected to Slayers, about pop culture magic in general. Basically, I was going to write about my entire list of "topics people always fought me about." I started publishing my work on those topics to a blog called Merkavah Party Van (google it). I braced for the flames to start up again, but told myself it would be worth it if I could find a few people out there who cared about this kind of magic and spirituality.

Well, that didn't work out like I planned. Instead of finding a few readers, my work found hundreds, then thousands. These people left their feedback and sometimes made their own posts and works based on my work or our conversations. I started basing my work off of their input and theories. On tumblr I had found a rich and supportive community of pop culture mages and pagans, and other magic-using and pagan peers willing to discuss theories and structures with me. There are some users on the site who are opposed to pop culture magic (or really any topic) and may start an argument about it, but there are also candid discussions where each side calmly weighs out the reasoning of the other side.

This can happen because social networks connect so many people now. I don't have to sift through hundreds of people to randomly find another pop culture magician. I can tag my post "pop culture magic" and, through the seeming-magic of taxonomy searches, you can find my work. So can others with similar mindsets, and I can find their work when I search for "pop culture magic." It's so easy to connect now, and that ease of connection in and of itself can be used to fuel magic... if you start thinking unconventionally.

As you'll learn more in this book, pop culture magic is all about thinking unconventionally. Taylor draws from years of experience with pop culture magic to explain the many structures it can build and sustain. He explains the many ways pop culture can change us and the ways we can change it and also use it as a force for change in our lives. Reading it reminded me of the beginning years of working on my pop culture craft, when I wondered if what I was trying to build was even possible. If I had found his book in 1999, then it could have saved me a bit of gruntwork and also helped me connect with others of like minds. Sadly by the time he published *Pop Culture Magick,* I'd stopped looking for peers, so I missed out. You, however, don't have to miss out. I'm happy that you can read this book now, wherever you are in your path. I look forward to how many more people might pull a pop culture's world into their own, and the future conversations we can have.

Felix Warren
August 2015

Chapter 1: A New Definition of Pop Culture Magic

When I wrote *Pop Culture Magick*, I defined pop culture as: "Pop culture is defined by what it does. Pop culture resists the mainstream blah culture. It possesses and represents different value systems, which clash with the values of mainstream culture" (Ellwood 2004, p. 17). I went on to define pop culture magic, as a form of magical practice that draws on contemporary culture, its icons, and even its depiction of spiritual practices as a valid form of magical practice. I also explained that pop culture magic was defined in part by the attention and belief that people gave to a given pop culture entity.

In the ten years since I defined pop culture and pop culture magic, my consideration of what pop culture is or isn't has become more nuanced, influenced in part by what I've observed other magicians doing and my own experimentation, but also by my continued research into pop culture studies. While I think the original definition can still be a useful one I wouldn't apply it to my own practices, and as such this book is a departure from that original definition, as well as a redefining of pop culture magic. I don't expect anyone to go alone with it…it's simply the evolution of my own practice- but I do hope that what I share in these pages is as useful, if not more so, as what I'd shared previously in *Pop Culture Magick.*

I no longer consider pop culture to be something which resists mainstream culture. Rather I see it as an extension and expression of mainstream culture, but also of subcultures that don't overtly fit into mainstream culture. Such subcultures can include corporate and alternative cultures, but can also include cult of personality subcultures as well. The various subcultures and mainstream culture do have core values associated with them, and those values inform not only how people act in a given culture, but also how they use cultural artifacts in their lives, work, and spiritual practices. It's important to recognize that pop culture plays an important role in how we conceptually understand and navigate the modern realities of our world. George Lakoff and Mark Johnson point out that:

> The concepts that govern our thought are not just matters of the intellect. They also govern our everyday functioning, down to the most mundane details. Our concepts structure what we perceive, how we get around in the world, and how we relate to other people. Our conceptual system thus plays a central role in defining our everyday realities (1980, P. 3).

Pop culture influences the experiences of every person exposed to it- even if the influence is negative. To ignore how pop culture helps us to conceptually understand and mediate the world around us is to ignore a fundamental tool of humanity, as well as magic. In contrast, by learning to apply magic to pop culture we consciously mediate the pop culture influence and concepts into useful tools that allow us to understand the world in which we live.

I also defined pop culture magic in context to how popular something was in mainstream culture, arguing that the more popular something or someone is, the more energy is going it, and the more viable it is for pop culture magic workings. I reasoned that the attention of lots of people made pop culture entities more powerful because the attention served as a form of belief. While I think that this principle is still valid for pop culture magic workings, I also think some revision is in order.

What I've discovered is that anything which is meaningful to someone can be a form of pop culture magic. In other words, I might be the only person who finds a particular television show to be meaningful, but so long as I find it meaningful and can apply it to my life it is a valid form of pop culture magic. It may not have the same "oomph" that some other more popular pop culture has, but it can still be worked with effectively for magical purposes. It's important to recognize this distinction so that we don't unnecessarily limit ourselves to whatever is considered currently popular. For example, when I wrote *Pop Culture Magick, Buffy the Vampire Slayer* was very popular because it was on television. Now you can watch it on Netflix, but it's not receiving the same attention and/or belief that it got in its heyday. Nonetheless for someone who really identifies with that show and the characters, it could still be a viable form of pop culture magic.

Additionally, I don't think that defining pop culture magic solely in terms of entertainment really captures what it is. While entertainment is certainly form of pop culture, so too is corporate culture. For that matter you also have people creating their own fandoms (subcultures) out of pop culture, which speaks to the fact that for those people a particular version of pop culture is much more than just entertainment. Pop culture magic can take a variety of forms. It's an adaptable form of magic that is shaped more by the individual's connection to what s/he considers pop culture to be than any other kind of standard: "Convergence occurs within the brains of individual consumers and through their social interactions with others. Each of us constructs our own personal mythology from bits and fragments of information extracted from the media flow and transformed into resources through which we make sense of our everyday lives" (Jenkins 2006a pp. 3-4). Pop culture magic is, in many ways, the creation of a personal mythology around the cultural artifacts that resonate with the life of the practitioner. There is a variety of pop culture magic practices that demonstrate the diversity and identification that practitioners have with pop culture and speak to how specific pop culture mythologies have meaningfully touched the lives of the practitioners.

As we'll explore later in this book, pop culture is also an appropriation of older cultures. Pop culture is rooted partially in older mythology, and although it's fair to say that contemporary society is continually creating new myths, it's also important to note how much older cultures and their own pop culture continue to influence our versions of pop culture.

When I wrote *Pop Culture Magick* social media hadn't been invented, and that has its own effect on pop culture magic. I personally find it gratifying that social media has helped to spread the concept of pop culture magic, with many adherents enthusiastically practicing it as a result. The technology, in and of itself, offers potential avenues of experimentation with pop culture magic. While I wouldn't call pop culture magic a mystery tradition in the sense that other forms of esoteric practice are labeled, I do think that it is a field of magic that is becoming increasingly more viable as more people experiment with it using both contemporary technology and the culture of our times.

Pop culture is a continually changing phenomenon. What is popular now may not even be a buzz word or interest for people a year or two later, but I think that if we revise our definition of pop culture magic what we find is not only a plethora of potential pop culture resources to draw on now, but also a variety of such resources to draw on from the past.

So What is Pop Culture Magic?

Pop culture magic is the application of the process and principles of magic to change reality, utilizing pop culture as a creative and expressive medium. To put it another way, pop culture is a tool that helps the magician conceptualize and apply magic to reality. Pop culture magic uses contemporary culture as the creative medium for applying magic to a given situation.

Pop culture magic can take many forms, because it draws on every expression of contemporary culture. In this sense contemporary culture, with all of its different media, provides more flexibility than what could be found in older cultures. For example, up until relatively recently corporations didn't exist, so you won't find an older cultural tradition that involves working with a corporation. With pop culture magic, if you want to work with or against a given corporation you can because it's part of the culture and something that we can understand in the context of our culture.

Pop culture magic also mediates older cultures. I've noticed, with some fascination, how an older culture's myths (or pop culture) are appropriated and adapted into contemporary culture. What is derived is the contemporary culture's perspective of the older culture, as well as a mediation of the older cultural icons in a way that makes that context specific to contemporary culture, but nonetheless still allows for a genuine connection with the entities from the older culture. That connection will be different from how someone who is a reconstructionist would approach said entities, because the reconstructionist is a trying to connect via the original culture medium. In contrast, a pop culture magician is connecting through the mediation provided by contemporary culture.

The cultural aspect of pop culture magic is particularly important because it acknowledges that culture plays a role in our experiences that can't be denied. Culture is always with us, and I'd argue by extension that pop culture is also always with us. Lakoff and Johnson explain the following about culture: "Cultural assumptions, values, and attitudes are not a conceptual overlay which we may or may not place upon experience as we choose. It would be more correct to say that all experience is cultural through and through, that we experience our 'world' in such a way that our culture is already present in the very experience itself" (1980, p. 57). Pop culture is an expression of the cultural assumptions, values, and attitudes we carry with us; and it can come out in various ways, such as when you sing, whistle or hum a tune that you've overheard, or reference a pop culture icon in conversation. Understanding that culture is part of our everyday experience allows us to choose what cultural influences we choose to work with, but with that said, it should also be understood that you can't escape the rest of your culture. For example, if you're a Polytheist you might argue that you'll just expose yourself to the particular pantheon and culture of that pantheon, but by virtue of being raised in modern culture, you will always bring modern culture to your experience. Instead of demonizing this, I would suggest embracing it as a form of cultural exchange that can add value to your experiences, because you consciously recognize it and adapt it to your practices. Pop culture magic needn't threaten the sanctity of a given magical tradition, religion, or spirituality, and if anything may provide alternate perspectives that can be drawn on to better understand the distinction between a given magical tradition and/or practice, and pop culture magic.

What makes pop culture magic so important is that it critically examines what magic is, and what magic can be. Edward Schiappa pointed out that:

> Definitions represent claims about how certain portions of the world are. They are conventional and depend on the adherence of language users. Definitions function to induce denotative

> conformity, which is another way of saying that definitions are introduced or contested when one wants to alter others' linguistic behavior in a particular fashion. A successful new definition changes not only recognizable patterns of linguistic behavior but also our understanding of the world and the attitudes and behaviors we adopt toward various parts of that world. (2003, p. 32).

Definitions alter more than just linguistic behavior. Definitions alter the very way we conceive and understand the world, ourselves, and how we interact with reality. Pop culture magic challenges what magic and a given spirituality or magical tradition can be. Naturally there are those who are opposed to pop culture magic because they feel it dilutes from what magic is, but if anything the debates about pop culture magic have helped revitalize magic and make it more approachable for people who might otherwise not engage in it. Pop culture magic challenges the understanding of magic and how we practice it, which is necessary in order for magic to continue to evolve as a discipline.

While some magicians will try and treat pop culture magic as a psychological or intellectual approach to magic, I don't consider it to be a psychological or intellectual approach at all. Instead, I'd argue that pop culture magic can provide a magician genuine and deep encounters with the spirit world, provided s/he is looking for those experiences. Much as with any other type of magic the magician, in part, makes pop culture magic what it is or isn't. With that said, even someone who prefers a psychological approach to magic can occasionally be surprised when s/he discovers magic is much more than something that is in your head.

Pop culture magic is the intersection of identity and culture, which are two significant concepts that shape each and every person. With pop culture magic, we can use contemporary culture to shape our identities, or use our identities to change contemporary culture. This mashup of identity and culture allows us to uncover patterns of possibility and reality that are meaningful to our lives and spiritual work, as well as the world at large. We use pop culture to make meaningful connection with the inner worlds, because what pop culture provides us is the contemporary context that helps us understand those inner worlds from our own cultural lenses. R. J. Stewart noted:

> Many Innerworlds are intentional structures built through group visualization, linked to specific life-energies. They are given their stability not only by the beings that occupy them, but by the active co-operation of humans...Most of the Innerworlds that we can enter are reflections of patterns that appear, or have appeared, or will appear, in our outer world. Some act as matrices for creative energies, which mould the generation of the outer world, both social and environmental. (1990, pp. 39-40).

Inner worlds are worlds accessed through specific media such as story, myth, or song. The characters in myths, stories, and song are symbolic, but also represent an energetic connection to the inner world that a person can use to bring meaningful change into his/her life. Pop culture presents us with patterns that appear in our world and provides us a way to meaningfully interact with those patterns both in the outer world and in the inner worlds of our imagination and spiritual journeying. Additionally, pop culture is a creation of intentional structures through group visualization, albeit using more than just pathworking and meditation techniques. Modern media is also brought into play in order to create a narrative that involves not just the writers and artists who initially create what is engaged with, but also the viewers and readers who end up making it their own via their imagination. In some cases this can lead to the continued creation of the pop culture narrative, or appropriation of it for their own means (fan fiction is an example of both continued creation and appropriation of pop culture). Some pop culture narratives even manage to endure long enough to achieve significant cultural influence, and as a result also create an inner world which is more meaningful because people continue to interact with it. *Star Trek, Star Wars, Batman,* etc., are examples of such narratives that have rich inner worlds that can be worked with because they have sustained a level of influence that has evolved them beyond the initial fad interest.

It should be noted as well that an older culture doesn't automatically provide a more legitimate inner world than a given pop culture provides. In truth what determines how meaningful an inner world can be is the active participation of both the human and spiritual sides of the equation. If I have a meaningful encounter with a "fictional" pop culture entity, and it is one which is continually sustained on both sides, I think that speaks to the efficacy of that inner world and how it impacts my spiritual practices, as well as how I apply the lessons to the outer world and the patterns revealed to me in that outer world. A genuine experience is made genuine by the willingness of the person to open up to that experience, and if pop culture is how someone opens up to the spiritual aspects of the world it shouldn't be judged as being of less value because it draws on contemporary culture.

Part of what determines a connection to the inner worlds is how a person engages with the doors to that inner world. Typically the doors to a given inner world are found via the symbols that relate to the inner world. Pop culture is replete with such images, ranging from corporate logos to graffiti, from super hero symbols to the covers of books, from television commercials to songs on the radio. All of the symbols create a rich environment, but too much information can overload us. We need to pick what we connect with in pop culture with care because what we're connecting with is as much a cultural influence as it is a spiritual presence.

Another reason we need to pick our connections with care is because we don't want to fall into the trap of intellectualizing the experience. Stewart observed:

> An intellectual interpretation of a symbol is by no means identical to experiencing the energy embodied by the symbol, particularly when the interpretation involves offhand alterations of basic meaning in respect or relevant words that should describe the subject matter accurately...a magical image, by way of contrast, may or may

> not have similar attributes to any specific psychological archetype, which persists in the innerworlds or shared imagination for immense periods of time. (1990 P. 36)

This is an interesting quote from Stewart and one I found useful for understanding pop culture magic from a different perspective. I've never favored the psychological approach to magic, and neither does Stewart. The experience of a symbol as magical doorway that leads into a narrative is not anything new, but pop culture takes it into new directions via the different forms of media it provides. Grant Morrison's *The Invisibles* explores it in terms of using the characters to reveal the inner world of London, but also to examine the Beatles, especially John Lennon, as a viable contact to a type of godhead that again allows another way to contact the Hidden London. You can also see it with other pop culture and even corporate culture. Storm Constantine and I have worked with this concept via the Wraeththu series, and I've also used it with the Harry Potter universe. Imagination is the key to the doors that lead to inner worlds, and it is also what brings to life the characters that people interact with.

Pop culture can be viably present within inner worlds the magician can explore. The reason they are viable is because they are part of the cultural consciousness and are supported by people interacting with them. Thus Harry Potter, as an example, is a viable Inner World that can be worked with in part because so many people already have invested some belief into it, and also because the characters have become real for people. They may not be real in the same sense as you and I are, but on some level they exist and when people interact with them they are also able to interact with the meanings associated with the characters. There is intentional visualization associated with such worlds, even if that intentional visualization is only to interact with those worlds via one's imagination.

I find that the longer a given form of pop culture exists, the more viable the inner world becomes. This is especially true if you encounter the pop culture across various media outlets. As an example, you can experience the Star Trek universe by watching shows and movies, but also read books and comics and play video games. The same is true with *Batman, Star Wars, Superman,* etc. As I write this book Marvel is currently boosting a lot of its characters through a cross media campaign that includes all of the media I mentioned above, but it also has a substantial pop culture history to draw on.

The logo for a corporation can also be a gatekeeper to the inner world of that corporation. Corporations can have an inner world because of the investment of the people that work in them and the consumers that buy from them, and even by the people and other corporations who are against a corporation. Such interactions are a form of intentional visualization that is sustained by the commercials and brand activity, as well as by how people participate in the corporations. They can be worked with on a magical level, though caution should be applied. A corporation is always out to get more from you than it is willing to give in return.

A magical tradition might not look at pop culture as a viable representation or means of magical work, but the methodology of a magical tradition can be applied to pop culture and it'll work, because pop culture, and even corporate culture, are to some degree formulaic. The themes we find in older cultural traditions can be found in newer culture as well, and such themes can be used to provide a meaningful structure for an inner world to be worked with. Identifying such themes can take some research, but they aren't hard to find precisely because they are formulaic. One might question why a person would even look to pop culture for spiritual inspiration and practice, and in my experience it comes down to what is relevant to a person and will help him/her learn and grow. If *Harry Potter* is more relevant to someone than an older tradition, it doesn't make it less magical for that person. What *Harry Potter* provides is a context and inner world which that person can use to meaningfully connect with the themes and patterns present in that pop culture.

A magical tradition might also argue that pop culture characters aren't "real" spirits, and as such question whether legitimate connections can actually be established. However, I think that the spirit world is a nuanced and sophisticated realm in its own right and that it's entirely possible for spirits to change with the times in order to establish a contextual connection that enables a deeper relationship to happen (Harpur 2002, Harpur 2003, Ellwood 2004, Ellwood 2008, Harpur 2011). There is also something to be said for the fact that genuine belief can make a fictional character real for the person connecting to that character. If we "nay say" the idea that a pop culture entity could be real, we might also critically examine whether any spirits are real. What makes them real, in part, is the interaction we have with them and how that interaction influences our lives.

Exercise

What pop culture do you feel a spiritual connection with? What are the inner worlds of that pop culture and who are the spiritual guides that can lead you to that inner world? How are you integrating this pop culture into your spiritual practice?

The Impact of Culture on the Magician

The methodology of the pop culture magician is shaped by the opportunity to circulate the pop culture magic into different forms of media that serve as tools. These media enable communication and connection, while also providing new venues through which reality can be manifested:

> This circulation of media content — across different media systems, competing media economies, and national borders — depends heavily on consumers' active participation…convergence represents a cultural shift as consumers are encouraged to seek out new information and make connections among dispersed media content…Convergence occurs within the brains of individual consumers and through their social interactions with others. Each of us constructs our own personal mythology from bits and fragments of information extracted from the media flow and transformed into resources through which we make sense of our everyday life (Jenkins 2006a, pp. 3-4).

The personal mythology that is created is highly individualized in some contexts, and yet in others is shared via knowledge communities the magician participates in. In knowledge communities the personal mythology can be tested against other people's experiences and/or available cultural material to verify if the personal mythology is valid for more people than just the person who experienced it. This verification also demonstrates an important aspect of culture that is sometimes ignored in our zealousness to be individuals.

Examining the underpinnings of culture and how it affects people shows that what is culturally drawn upon to practice magic isn't as important as acknowledging the fact that culture has an impact on people. Even the choice to resist a particular form of culture is a result of such an impact. What we choose to do with that impact and how we choose to accept it determines the empowerment we get out of it. This principle is illustrated in the example below.

One magician I know is currently doing an intensive ritual working with the character of Tyler Durden. He has made collages with pictures from the movie and random writings that still pertain to the idea of *Fight Club*, as well as making sacrifices of his blood, spit, nails, etc. to Tyler Durden. And he's had a response from the entity of Tyler, and consequently has acted differently than he normally would. In other words, his devotion has caused Tyler to have more of a presence in his life, and change it for the better. What you work with will have an impact on you, and this applies to not only pop culture magic, but also to more traditional approaches. This happens because you shape the context of your workings with what you find personally and culturally meaningful; that context establishes the efficacy of your magic. The specifics vary from person to person, because although all of us exist in a cultural collective based around a particular society, what is most meaningful to an individual is based on the values that s/he chooses and/or is raised with.

This means that even though culture has some impact on our chosen values, each person still decides what values work for him/her. This occurs through testing the validity of those values. Pop culture presents alternatives and raises questions, and also presents new cultural interfaces for people to use as they interact with each other and the archetypal entities that people happen to believe in. So, as an example, the character of Tyler Durden is an interface for not only the attributes and characteristics that Tyler Durden represents, but also the cultural force that embodies the concept of the trickster. He is another form of that archetype, just as Loki and Coyote and Bugs Bunny are.

It's easy to fall into the trap of believing that you make everything up and manifest reality to your will, to the point that nothing else exists unless you created it. But such a solipsistic view of the world is unreal and delusional. After all, can you really justify getting hit in the face by another person as something you created entirely on your own? It's true that you participated in making that happen, but the other person involved also had to do something to make that reality manifest.

Culture of any form has an effect on you. When you choose to dress up in a business suit and go to an interview, you are agreeing to certain cultural norms and societal expectations that you will fulfill a particular role at the interview and, if chosen, the job. The very choice of wearing a business suit, as opposed to something less formal, is a choice that you may not even knowingly make, beyond having an awareness that wearing a bathrobe would cause you to look less professional and in most places cost you the job. And when you add to the mix the various entities/forces that you interact with, those also have an impact. Such an entity can be the pet you have at home, but can also be a nebulous concept such as "god." Both of these entities will have an impact on you. The pet provides a source of physical and emotional (and perhaps spiritual) contact, and likewise "god" in whatever form can provide a spiritual, emotional, mental, and even physical contact. The people you choose to interact with have an impact on you, and while this may seem very obvious to you, how those people have an impact isn't always as obvious. The behavior patterns that a person exhibits are often based on similar patterns their parents, siblings, or friends demonstrated. That person might not even realize that s/he is acting a particular way because it's a way s/he has been indoctrinated to behave.

At the same time, we need to recognize that we have agency. Agency is both the assumption of responsibility for yourself and the awareness that you knowingly and unknowingly have an impact on reality. For the majority of people the impact is, for the most part, unconscious. These people haven't assumed agency and are directed by the cultural influences in their lives. For a minority of people agency is assumed and used to not only be aware of being shaped by culture, but also become aware of how culture can be shaped to their purposes.

Culture isn't wholly shaped by humans, but is also shaped by the various mythologies, beliefs, etc., that are integrated into it. While these mythologies come from humans, they do take on a life of their own that lasts beyond the original context and explanations that were first used to create them. You have some control over those archetypal forces and you exert that control when you make associations and connections and invest meaning into the cultural paradigm you choose to believe in and use.

Part of that control is brought about by choosing the entities you work with. Working with pop culture entities is a choice that draws on what is current, but comes with a recognition that you are working with the latest cultural aspect of something more primal. In my earlier example, Tyler Durden is both the entity Tyler Durden, but also a representative of the trickster[1]. The choice to work with Tyler Durden occurs on a number of conceptual levels. The first level is your perception/understanding of that entity. The second level is the entity's awareness of itself and you. The final level is that of the trickster, which inspires the connection made via a person's choice to work with Tyler Durden. This inspiration occurs as a result of looking for particular characteristics that embody a need you have to change something about your reality, which may be found in that particular archetype. Of course, my perception of Tyler Durden as a trickster is subjective, which means other people may associate other archetypal forces with him, or perceive him to be a singular and separate entity from the trickster. Regardless, choosing to work with him is

[1] It's important to note that archetypes are just one theory to explain the prevalence of the different types of patterns in mythology. For some people, the mythology of a given culture is perceived to be a literal truth about literal entities. They would argue that Tyler Durden is a separate entity from the trickster. I personally believe that while an entity like Tyler Durden can be an individual entity, it can also be an aspect of the concept of the trickster. I think it really depends on the paradigm that an individual practitioner adopts when working with such entities.

acknowledging that he will have an impact on you, even as you work with him to have an impact on reality. He will affect you in ways you don't expect from him because he is not limited to your or my perceptions, just as we are not limited to his. By consciously acknowledging that you aren't only shaping reality through culture, but also are being shaped in turn, you can purposely direct the way you are shaped toward what's most useful for you. You claim agency for yourself.

The reason it's important to note this aspect of culture and how you interact with it is so you have a much more conscious approach toward what you use for your magical workings. Pop culture may not be what you want to use, but it does have an impact on you, and noting that effect allows you to determine whether or not it should carry over into your magical and spiritual lifestyle. At the very least, by realizing that you are not the sole arbiter of reality, you come to realize that magic is much more than just about shaping reality to your will. It's also about interacting, learning, and evolving with an open mind. It's an understanding that though you can't escape culture, you can choose how to purposely mediate it. Magic involves learning from the reality you shaped and accepting that you will be shaped by it as well.

Pop Culture and Identity

In order to fully understand pop culture, it's useful to explore how identity intersects with it, and with culture in general. Everyday our identities are shaped by the cultural influences that we take part in. In this modern age of media we have more exposure to different cultural influences than any previous culture has had. Technology allows us to access a variety of cultural resources across the world and engage in both cultural appropriation and cultural exchange. All of this in turn influences a person's sense of identity.

We use identity to situate ourselves in context to the world around us. In *Multi- Media Magic* I explained, "Identity is central to the practice of magic. In choosing an identity, a person provides him/herself foundation. The identity may change as a result of magic, but it gives magic something to act on and from. It is the basis by which a person forms an agreement with the universe, as to his/her place within it" (Ellwood 2008, P. 155). Identity is the foundational cultural construct that we create in order to relate to the world around us. An identity can be changed because identity is not a static expression of reality, but rather an on-going negotiation with the experiences that a person has.

Identity is also metaphorical: "We use ontological metaphors to comprehend events, actions, activities, and states. Events and actions are conceptualized metaphorically as objects, activities as substances states as containers (Lakoff & Johnson 1980, P. 30). In fact, we use ontological metaphors in order to integrate various experiences, events, activities, etc. into our identity, where they serve an additional function of defining how the identity is expressed. What's equally fascinating is that we also apply identity as a metaphor in our interactions with nonhuman entities, in order to humanize them, but also situate them in context to our own identity (Lakoff & Johnson 1980). What results is an interactive experience with reality, wherein a person attributes aspects of personality to his/her environment (or recognizes those aspects) in order to more effectively engage the environment s/he is in: "They [The authors are referring to personifications as examples of ontological metaphors] allow us to make sense of phenomena in the world in human terms - terms that we can understand on the basis of our own motivations, goals, actions, and characteristics" (Lakoff & Johnson 1980, P. 34). This making sense of phenomena is essential to being able to interact with a given environment, and what better way to do it than make the environment and what's in it an extended part of our own identity, or if nothing else an interaction of our own identities with the identities we perceive the environment to have?

In *Magical Identity*, I further explored identity:

> If identity is the basis by which a person forms an agreement with the universe, such a basis can only be established by understanding that identity is the active agent by which someone can work magic. Identity is central to magic, because it is through your identity that you define your life. Identity is formed by your

> action and activities, and by the cultural, sexual, and moral beliefs and ideologies you adopt to define your senses of self. Identity informs every action you perform, every rationalization you come up with to explain why you've done what you've done (Ellwood 2012, P. 15).

Identity is the fundamental expression of ourselves and in one sense can even be thought of as analogous to culture because like culture it is something you can't escape. Your identity is always with you and, like culture, it plays a role in how you navigate the various challenges and triumphs of your life. I find that culture and identity are interwoven because culture has so much bearing on a person's identity and how s/he conceptualizes the environment in which s/he is interacting. This brings us to how pop culture and identity are connected.

Because identity and culture go hand in hand, it is useful to consciously work with identity as a form of pop culture magic. In fact, you see this type of work occurring every day with celebrities, musicians, actors, authors, etc., all of whom are aware (on some level) that they have a pop culture persona that is an idealized version of their identity. That persona is the intersection of pop culture and identity, and as we'll explore later in this book it's entirely possible for anyone to create a pop culture persona. Pop culture influences our concept of identity every day through the cultural artifacts we engage with. The books you read, the shows you watch, the music you listen to, the games you play, and the clothes you wear are just a few examples of how pop culture shapes your identity and influences your interactions with the world.

To illustrate this consider how you and other people label you based on certain characteristics. If you're a board game player you might be labeled a geek or a nerd. If you like wearing designer clothes, you might be labeled a snob or preppie. If you enjoy playing sports, you might be labeled a jock. These labels, right or wrong, are used to categorize people, amongst other things. Your characteristics define you to a certain extent, and often it is through your characteristics that other people will label you. However, you also have control over that labeling, in the sense you can actively shape your identity to whatever you want to be. Your interests are part of how you shape your identity, but they aren't the only indicators of identity and you can choose to actively work with them in shaping the identity you want to establish.

Another way that pop culture interacts with identity is found by how you integrate pop culture into your life. Some of these interactions are conscious, but many of them are also unconscious. For example, if you find yourself thinking of a song you heard, it's likely an unconscious interaction with pop culture. The same is also true if you play a video game or watch a movie or TV show that makes a vivid impression on you. In fact, watching TV or playing video games put you into an Alpha brainwave state of mind, which is when your mind is most receptive to advertising influences (a good reason to carefully filter the media in your life).

Exercise

Spend a week tracking all of your pop culture interactions and media usage. In other words, track what shows you watch, what games you play, what music you listen to, advertisements you notice etc.,. As you track these different forms of pop culture ask yourself how they influence you and your identity. How do they show up in your life (both on a conscious and unconscious level)? How do you integrate them into your sense of identity? Why are you interested in those particular forms of pop culture?

This exercise can help you understand how pop culture influences your identity. As you examine the various pop culture influences that are in your life, ask yourself how those influences carry over into your actions in general, and your spiritual work in particular. You may find that pop culture is much more a part of your life than you've realized, and that it plays a role in how you conceive of your magical work.

The Relevance of Magic in Pop Culture

One of the reasons pop culture magic is becoming more prevalent is due to the fact that the paranormal is increasingly showing up in pop culture. Whether it shows up in reality TV shows focused on ghost hunts or in television serials, or in other various forms of pop culture; magic and the paranormal have become part of mainstream society in a way that I think is ultimately beneficial to Paganism because it increases awareness and acceptance of magic. Annette Hill noted the following about the prominence of belief in the paranormal:

> There is a paranormal turn in popular culture. Beliefs are on the rise in contemporary Western societies. Almost half of the British population and two-thirds of American people, claim to believe in some form of the paranormal, such as extrasensory perception, hauntings and witchcraft...The paranormal in popular culture is distinct from research into the scientifically inexplicable. It is paranormal matters purposely shaped within an entertainment and communication environment...Fascination with the dead, a desire to see the unique, and a search for unusual experiences, suggest a strong narrative of spirits and magic in society (Hill 2011, P. 1).

While she only focuses on British and American audiences, it's interesting to note how relevant the paranormal has become and how pop culture has become a medium for expressing the paranormal. People want to know more about magic, want it to be more accessible, and pop culture ends up being a gateway to that effect: "The paranormal as it is experienced within popular culture involves seeing an audience not as spectators or viewers but as participants. People co-perform and co-produce their individual and collective experiences" (Hill 2011, P. 2). When audiences become participants they bring with them their collective desire to believe in magic, but more than that, they bring with them a desire to make magic become part of their lives.

What the Pagan and Magical communities, in general, have failed to grasp is how pop culture presents an opportunity for us to challenge the stereotypical beliefs held about the paranormal and magic. While there is admittedly some sensationalism in the various depictions of magic in the media, this leads to is a fascination and interest in learning more about magic and a desire to discover what it really is, as opposed to what people have been told about it. Pop culture magic, in particular, presents an opportunity for people to take their pop culture interests and turn it into a genuine spiritual practice:

> The move from the margins to mainstream in paranormal beliefs and ideas in popular culture highlights the irreducible complexity of cultural forms and our engagement with them. Spirit communication was once an unorthodox religious engagement with them. Spirit communication was once an unorthodox religious practice within the modern spiritualist movement, but it quickly became part of entertainment and communication industries. Today paranormal matters invade primetime, TV Psychics are celebrities, historical buildings are famously haunted and magicians exploit paranormal beliefs. There are recurring themes then and now. These themes include the re-imagining of historical spirit forms or folk legends for contemporary times; the search for evidence through personal experience; mind, body and spirit practices that unite various paranormal beliefs, ideas and practices are less associated with religious thinking and more about lifestyle trends. There is a cycle of culture where new products, services and events connect with a never-ending search for a unique, alternative, and extraordinary experiences (Hill 2011, p. 12).

The popularity of the paranormal in pop culture creates an awareness on the part of the audience that there is more to life, more to the spiritual and existential realities of this world than what is presented via mainstream education and religion. Not surprisingly, the audience wants more of the fantastic, mythological worlds they've been exposed to by modern media.

Pop culture magic is a participatory practice. It allows the audience to become the magicians, to interact with the characters and mythology that has meaning to them while drawing in ritual practices and processes that are part of the occult. This formalization of pop culture into magical work is not just a form of entertainment, to be passively experienced, but rather a performative experience that allows the person to experience real magic through the lens of their favorite pop culture. This same experience allows people to explore their spiritual connection to the world, while also asking questions and getting answers that may not be found in traditional spiritual paths. Consequently what can be crushing to someone who practices pop culture magic is the denial that their spiritual path is as valid as the spiritual path of a Polytheist or traditional Pagan (never mind that those same people face similar discrimination from more mainstream religions).

Why Pop Culture Magic is Attacked

When a pop culture magic practitioner tries to share their practices with other Pagans, Polytheists, or occultists they either are considered to be eccentric or attacked because such beliefs and practices are considered to be inauthentic. When I first wrote *Pop Culture Magick*, I shared some of my own experiences where people tried to discourage my interest. In the decade since, while more pop culture practitioners have shown up, there is still a fair amount of hostility directed toward them. In response to a Tumblr post I made about the history of pop culture magic, one of the respondents shared the following:

> When I made the mistake of mentioning pop culture magical correspondences to 'friends' in college (specifically my connecting each of the TMNT to an element representation), I was viciously attacked, both online and off. I never mentioned it to anyone else ever again, and the whole experience sent me back into the broom closet for YEARS. I doubted everything that had ever happened to me as a child, all my experiences and revelations, everything I had

> felt was right and correct in my heart now felt WRONG. Which meant I was WRONG. How could I be a true witch or magician with these strange associations? A few years ago, I found the Pop Culture Magick and Grimoire on amazon and ordered them immediately. I even paid for 1 day shipping! The moment I read the first chapters, I nearly burst into tears of joy! I wasn't "crazy" or "wrong" in my connections and beliefs! I wasn't alone anymore! The feeling of VALIDATION was unlike anything I'd ever experienced. I wanted to contact the jerks from college and rub the books in their faces! (PVWitch - Personal Communication, October 10, 2014)

This person was not the only person to share such experiences. Other people also shared similar experiences where they were aggressively attacked for having such beliefs. The question that arises is why pop culture magic and those who practice it are attacked by other people in the Pagan community.

One of the reasons pop culture magic is so aggressively attacked is due to how the mainstream treats interest in pop culture. People who like anything that doesn't fit the mainstream notions of acceptable culture are typically labeled as geeks and nerds, and while the label of geek has, in recent years, come to be a bit more popular, it nonetheless has negative associations with it. Someone who shows interest in pop culture, particularly science fiction, fantasy, anime, and other forms of fiction is considered to be someone who is socially out of touch with what is considered to be proper tastes. And not surprisingly, there is a tendency to attack anything that doesn't fit with notions of what is considered to be of good taste. It should be no surprise then that this extends even to the Pagan/Polytheist/occult communities, which have their own notions as to what is considered acceptable or not acceptable.

We can look at this conflict in terms of the concept of good taste, which is a guideline to what is considered culturally acceptable:

> Concepts of 'good taste,' appropriate conduct, or aesthetic merit are not natural or universal; rather, they are rooted in social experiences and reflect particular class experiences. As Pierre Bourdieu (1979) notes, these tastes often seem 'natural' to those who share them, precisely because they are shaped by our earliest experiences as changes, and rationalized through encounters with higher education and other basic institutions that reward appropriate conduct and proper tastes. Taste becomes one of the important means by which social distinctions are maintained and class identities are forged. Those who 'naturally' possess appropriate tastes 'deserve' a privileged position within the institutional hierarchy and reap the greatest benefits from the educational system, while the tastes of others are seen as 'uncouth' and underdeveloped. Taste distinctions determine not only desirable and undesirable forms of culture but also desirable and undesirable ways of relating to cultural objects, desirable and undesirable strategies of interpretation and styles of consumption (Jenkins 2013 p. 16)

This notion of taste applies to pop culture magic in the sense that pop culture magic and its practitioners are treated in a way that is reflective of such standards. The pop culture magician has the bad 'taste' to utilize pop culture as part of their magical and spiritual practice. Because pop culture magic doesn't align to a specific tradition or mythology it's perceived as a threat. It is new and different and is considered to threaten the values of more established traditions and practices. Pop culture is perceived as having a corrupting influence that distracts the magician from focusing on their spiritual practice, because s/he is looking to pop culture as an inspiration instead of adhering to standards of good taste (Stewart 2006, Jenkins 2013).

Another reason pop culture magicians and Pagans are pathologized is because of how fans are portrayed in mainstream culture. The movie, *The 40 Year Old Virgin,* is an excellent example. The main character is portrayed as a fanboy who is out of touch with mainstream society, its norms, and sex, until the person he hooks up with convinces him that letting go of his fan interests will get him laid and accepted by mainstream culture (Jenkins 2013). Such depictions of fans, of people interested in pop culture, create a social stigma about pop culture and people interested in it in a manner that is deemed obsessive. Unfortunately this kind of attitude can be pervasive, and I think it can partially account for the antagonism shown to pop culture magicians and Pagans as well as why pop culture isn't considered to be in good taste.

Pop culture magicians and Pagans focus on applying magical and spiritual practices to pop culture, treating pop culture as something which deserves the same attention and appreciation that is given to canonical culture practices and beliefs. But those people engaged in a traditional practice don't see it the same way: "Fan culture muddies these boundaries, treating popular texts as if they merited the same degree of attention and appreciation as canonical texts. Reading practices acceptable in work of 'serious merit' seem perversely misapplied to the more 'disposable' texts of mass culture. Fans speaks of 'artists' where others can only see commercial hacks, of transcendent meanings where others find only banalities, of 'quality and innovation' where others see only formula and convention" (Jenkins 2013 p. 17). This devaluing of pop culture by people outside of it is nothing new, but what it should teach us is that there will always be people who take exception to the practice of pop culture magic because they feel that such a practice threatens their own spirituality. In a sense, there is a competition occurring between pop culture and mainstream culture, between pop culture magic and other spiritual practices, and that competition ultimately boils down to a sense of what is considered authentic culture vs. what is considered to be temporary. The problem with such a competition is that it ignores the deeper currents of cultural practices and consequently fails to recognize that pop culture magic is a natural evolution of spiritual practices that will evolve to meet the needs of the time period in a manner that is relevant to people who need a spiritual connection but cannot find it in more established spiritual and religious practices.

The people who critique pop culture magic do so because of the cultural biases that are already present and in place against pop culture. Additionally these people suffer from a case of imagined subjectivity, which Matt Hills defined in the following passage:

> Imagined subjectivity, we might say, attributes valued traits of the subject 'duly trained and informed' only to those within the given community, while denigrating or devaluing the 'improper' subjectivity of those who are outside the community...The real problem is that despite consistently failing to measure up to the 'good' imagined subjectivity of the rational self, this idealization continues to carry such cultural power and effectiveness. By regulating what counts as the 'good' subject, i.e. the authorized and competent self, this highly limited version of imagined subjectivity acts as an extremely powerful cultural device. It can be used to restrict and pathologize specific cultural groups, while promoting the achieved 'normality' and 'legitimate' authority of others. Imagined subjectivity is hence not just about systems of value; it is also always about who has power over cultural representations and cultural claims to legitimacy, and who able to claim 'good' and moral subjectivity while pathologizing other groups as morally or mentally defective (Hills 2002, pp 3-5).

The pathologizing of pop culture magic and Paganism is done as a means of reinforcing the legitimacy of the critics and their particular spiritual paths at the expense of pop culture magic practitioners. However, the authority these critics hold to is ultimately suspect because it is biased and based on their perspective as to what constitutes genuine spiritual experiences. By applying cultural models of good taste to spiritual practices, what they demonstrate is the very intolerance they complain about when people come down on them for their spiritual practices.

I've also come across an intriguing argument that may provide another explanation for the antagonism that pop culture magicians and Pagans experience. The anti-fan argument states the following about anti-fans:

> The anti-fan is the person who hates the fan object of another fan for the simple reason that object is in direct, straightforward, or historical competition with his/her own object of admiration. This way, an anti-fan is always a fan. I would like to suggest that binary oppositions between fan objects are a precondition for such cases of antifandom. The two competing objects have to be in an outright rivalry with each other. Often, this means that the competence and skills of the two objects, which are in direct competition, are near equivalent (or perceived to be near equivalent) and it is this equivalence that makes the opposing fan object a threat to the fan's object and makes him/her an antifan (Theodoropoulou 2007 P. 318).

While it may seem odd to label Pagans, Polytheists, and occultists who are anti-pop culture magic as anti-fans, I don't think this argument misses the mark. In some cases it seems that the hostility directed toward pop culture magic comes about because there is a perceived threat over the interest some people have of applying magic and spiritual tradition practices to pop culture. Pop culture magic is perceived as a threat because people utilizing it are seen as appropriators of specific tradition and practices that are not originally part of the culture. In a sense, there is competition because people practicing pop culture magic are presenting a way to practice magic or work with specific traditions that draw on contemporary culture while possibly using practices from other traditions. On the one hand, this is a valid concern and one we need to acknowledge by being respectful of the traditions and practices that are already there. On the other hand, no tradition exists in a vacuum. We stand on the shoulders of those who came before us and yet we also change what we practice based on the exigencies of the times. The solution, in my opinion, is to do the research and respect the various traditions and practices out there, while also developing a practice that speaks to who you are and how your spiritual connections show up. My own approach to pop culture magic draws on relevant resources, but I always make it a point to acknowledge what I'm drawing on and make a clear distinction between the actual tradition and what it is I'm doing.

Many Polytheists, Pagans, and occultists will still continue to denigrate pop culture magic and those who practice it, but there are many who are open to the idea as well and supportive of people discovering their own spiritual path. Fortunately there are more pop culture magic practitioners now and this consequently helps to establish a community for those of us who seek it. In the next chapter we'll also explore how fan communities can become useful supporters of pop culture magic and Paganism, as well as provide a way to bring other people to the practice of magic.

Pop Culture Magic and Pop Culture Paganism

When I wrote *Pop Culture Magick*, the term pop culture Paganism was not being used. I didn't know of anyone who identified as a pop culture Pagan, and while some of my spiritual practices are focused around pop culture, I never thought to label myself as a pop culture Pagan. Nonetheless in the last eleven years pop culture Paganism has started up and I suspect there will be more pop culture Pagans over time.

On a post on Tumblr by The Pagan Study Group, the following distinction is made in regards to Pop Culture Magic and Pop Culture Paganism: "It's important to first make a distinction between Pop Culture Paganism and Pop Culture Magic, as they are two different things often confused for each other. Just as not all Wiccans are witches and not all witches are Wiccans, not every Pop Culture Pagan practices PC Magic, and not all PC Magicians practice PC Paganism. One is a spiritual and/or religious practice while the other is a type of magical practice and they don't always go hand in hand" (2014). This distinction isn't unique to pop culture magic and Paganism. In Paganism there are people who identify as Pagan and don't practice magic, but nonetheless treat their Paganism as a spiritual/religious practice. Nonetheless it's useful to know that such a distinction is present in pop culture spirituality.

Pop culture Pagans don't see pop culture as just something to be utilized for magical purposes, whereas someone who is a pop culture magician may look at pop culture through the lens of how a given pop culture can be applied to magical work. This distinction is important because it shapes how pop culture is engaged with. A pop culture magician may move from one pop culture mythology to another (much like chaos magicians), or may choose to stick with particular pop culture mythologies, but nonetheless be concerned with how those mythologies can be practically applied to magical work.

The pop culture Pagan, on the other hand, is primarily concerned with forging and deepening a spiritual relationship with the chosen pop culture mythology that s/he identifies with, and will develop a system of worship around that mythology as well as integrating aspects of Paganism such as the major Sabbats and Esbats. For example, Storm Constantine and I developed the system of Dehara, which is based on the *Wraeththu* fantasy series. In Grimoire Kaimana, we created holidays based on the Pagan calendar, but with Deharan names and deities.

Pop culture Pagans may worship specific pop culture characters as deities, with the understanding being that such a character is deified by the belief the person has in the character, or because the character exists independently and inspired the pop culture that featured the character, or that the character is a mask of sorts that represents an older deity (Ellwood 2004, Ellwood 2008, The Pagan Study Group 2014). Pop culture Pagans also draw on the pop culture variants of older mythology, in part as a way to connect with the older mythology and spirituality it represents, and in part because the pop culture variant is something the pop culture Pagan can relate because of the contemporary cultural context the pop culture variant is situated in. For example, the characters of Thor and Loki, while originally derived from Norse mythology, nonetheless also have pop culture variants that show up in Marvel Comics, movies and cartoons. While it can be argued that these variants are not accurate representations of the original mythology, they nonetheless can be spiritual presences that a pop culture Pagan connects to. When this occurs, it is important for the pop culture Pagan to recognize the difference between the pop culture variant and the original mythology. The pop culture variant is derived from the original mythology and does have a connection to it and the traditions that are part of it, but that connection is a gateway to those traditions as opposed to an accurate representation of them.

Sometimes pop culture Pagans also worship the personas of celebrities or other famous people, either alive or dead (The Pagan Study Group 2014). They aren't worshipping or working with the actual person, but rather with the persona which is an embodiment of the attention, beliefs, and energy put toward that person by their fans. The persona is separate and distinct in the sense that it lasts beyond the actual person and can become deified, but while the person is alive the persona is connected to the person (Ellwood 2004). In my opinion, much of the craziness occurs with your average celebrity is due to the attention and energy directed their way, so it's important to be cautious if you choose to engage in this type of spiritual work.

Pop culture Paganism will continue to become more prevalent as more people learn about it. What makes it appealing is that it provides people contemporary, contextual spiritual connections and practice, which is essential not all people will be drawn to older traditions and spiritual practices. I identify primarily as a magician and so what I share here is primarily focused around an integration of pop culture magic and pop culture Paganism. Some of what I share will be of interest to pop culture Pagans who don't practice magic, but nonetheless are interested in developing deeper ties with the pop culture communities available to them.

The Role of Participation in Pop Culture Magic

In pop culture studies, participation is a central concept which explores how fans participate in pop culture, both in terms of enjoying it, but also in creating and spreading it. Fans aren't just passive viewers, and for that matter neither are pop culture magicians or Pagans. Our participation in pop culture can range from something as simple as watching a show to something as complex as filming a show utilizing pop culture themes or characters. When you add magic into the mix, you introduce a spiritual element to the participation. Participation is defined as the following: "Participation...is shaped by the cultural and social protocols. So, for example, the amount of conversation possible in a movie theater is determined more by the tolerance of audiences in different subcultures or national contexts than by any innate property of cinema itself. Participation is more open-ended, less under the control of media producers and more under the control of media consumers" (Jenkins 2006a, p. 133). Participation is the fan activity around a given pop culture artifact or mythology. It's important to note that participation is fan-based activity. We differentiate fan-based activity from the activity of the company that produces the original pop culture artifact or mythology because there are different goals driving the activity.

The goal of a company is to spread pop culture in order to realize a profit. The company seeks to make money, and the cultural expressions a company uses is primarily in that vein. The participatory activities of fans are driven by a desire to share something the fans love with other people. What they share is derivative of the original pop culture artifact or mythology, and is personalized by the fan to reflect their own love of the pop culture they work with. I feel that pop culture magic primarily falls under the participatory activities of fans. It's done by fans as a way of connecting with the mythology as well as with other fans. I suspect most companies would actually be uncomfortable with a spiritual angle applied to the mythology, but there's very little that can easily be done to regulate it.

The reason participation is important to us is that it open the door to new ways to participate via pop culture magic, as well as discover how we can make pop culture magic a more meaningful part of fan communities in general. Pop culture magicians and Pagans may already be part of specific fan communities, but the question that we should is ask if we've really reached out to those communities to share pop culture magic and Paganism as a way fans can participate in their favorite pop culture mythology. I don't think this has occurred yet in fan communities to the extent that it could, and for the pop culture magician it may be quite useful to get more involved in such communities, both in terms of getting inspiration for further pop culture magic and for finding acceptance outside of the Pagan, Polytheist, and Occult communities.

Exercise

Who are the fan communities you can reach out to? What activities can you do with them, which introduce pop culture magic to them?

Conclusion

I've presented a new definition for pop culture magic. As I wrote at the beginning of the chapter, this definition is not meant to replace what I wrote in *Pop Culture Magick,* so much as present a more nuanced understanding of what pop culture magic can be. I feel that pop culture magic is here to stay, and that it has evolved beyond just being a toolset or series of techniques that chaos magicians could use. It is becoming spiritual paths and traditions for people who want such things and yet can't find what they are looking for in existing magical traditions. Pop culture magic offers us a way to mediate contemporary culture with spiritual practices, and as a result make sense of the experiences in our everyday lives. In the next chapter, we'll explore fan identity and fan communities in further depth in order to understand their connection to pop culture magic and Paganism. We'll also explore the concept of participation in further depth in order to understand how it can be applied to our interactions with the fan communities we are part of.

Chapter 2: Creating a Pop Culture Identity

As I've observed and participated in pop culture over the last eleven years I've noticed something interesting occur, which I think has only occurred recently because of how people are approaching pop culture. Over the last eleven years people have moved from being strictly consumers of pop culture to being creators of pop culture. Now it could be argued that this has been happening for longer than eleven years (and I'd agree with that argument), but in the last eleven years, it has become increasingly prevalent and part of our culture. Social media has greatly contributed to this, because of how much control it provides people in sharing the creative content they develop. But creating content isn't where it ends. If anything, it's just the beginning.

What people are creating, beyond content, is an intersection of pop culture with their identities, and in the process they are changing their identities. This occurs through various mediums and what's truly fascinating about it is the potential it offers to magicians who want to experiment with it. In *Pop Culture Magick* and subsequent works I touched on this concept, but even I didn't fully recognize its relevance until recently. The recognition of this intersection of pop culture and identity provides the pop culture magician a way to consciously change their interactions with the world via the identity work they do. While I've already briefly touched on the topic of identity and pop culture in chapter 1, we'll explore it in further depth here so that we can effectively use it in our magical work.

Understanding Identity in Pop Culture Magic

The intersection of pop culture and identity can be conceived of as experience taking, wherein a person matches their own behavior, actions, and thoughts to a character they strongly identify with (Ellwood 2004, Ellwood 2008, Grabmeier 2012). Experience taking enables you to merge your own life with the identity of a character, but also learn skills from the character. Experience taking isn't just limited to reading a book and identifying with a character, but can occur via other mediums such as television, social media, or video games (Gee 2007, Gee 2013, Jenkins, Ford, & Green 2013). Experience taking occurs to people all the time, often without those people consciously recognizing or capitalizing on it, but as magicians we can consciously choose to use the identity of a pop culture character to learn skills. In my opinion, experience taking is essentially invocation. You are invoking the character into you and allowing that character to influence your interactions.

Experience-taking can also be a form of mediumship, where the pop culture character possesses the person. This can result in both positive and negative circumstances. For example, the recent Slender Man stabbings are, in my opinion, an example of experience taking, where the two girls became mediums of expression for Slender Man. They wanted to be like Slender Man and even insisted they were getting instructions from Slender Man to stab their friend. What that incident highlights is how important it is to be careful with what pop culture you identify with. Taking a pop culture character on as part of your identity can bring with it all the flaws of that character, unless the magician is careful to filter out what isn't needed. Fans who have experience being a medium of a pop culture icon know how important it is to maintain an awareness of their own identity, to avoid the psychic danger of over-identification with the pop culture character they are identifying with (Henderson 1997, Hills 2002). They will develop a strategy, such as imagining a switch, which they can turn off the invocation with the pop culture character they identify with.

The formation of identity isn't just rooted in experience taking, but also in identification as a fan of a particular pop culture mythology (or more) and in the interaction the magician has with the community that shares the same interests. Your sense of identity is also grounded in the various inanimate objects you interact with every day, including your clothing, pop culture artifacts, and other related materials that part of your fan interests (McCloud 1993). Identity also includes the values and beliefs of the cultural community that identity endorses. Fan communities, which are forums for people who like a particular type of pop culture, are also knowledge communities. Knowledge communities provide fans ways to negotiate with media producers, including corporations. At the same time such communities often incorporate pop culture into their lives, critique it, write about it, and even create new stories for various favorite characters (Jenkins 2006a). Identity plays an important role in the identification a person has with being a fan. This is doubly so for anyone who makes their fandom part of their spirituality, because the fandom becomes an expression of their spiritual practice.

It's important to recognize that your identity is a flexible concept in some ways, and in others ways it is set. For example, your race is a set aspect of your identity and brings with it specific experiences that are unique to your race. A white person will not have the same experiences that a black person has, and a black person won't have the same experiences that a Latino person has. Pop culture interests, on the other hand, are flexible aspects of identity, self-chosen by the person as part of their identity.

Choosing an identity involves becoming part of the community with its various practices and ways of interpreting experiences. We learn to experience the world through the lens of the identity we've taken on. The learning we do isn't just about learning skills, but also learning how to integrate the new aspect of identity into the rest of our identity (Gee 2007). This occurs through a combination of community interaction and the personal choice to identify that aspect of identity as something meaningful to your life. Etienne Wenger notes the following about identity:

> Our identity includes our ability and our inability to shape the meanings that define our communities and our forms of belonging….I will use the concept of identity to focus on the person without assuming the individual self as a point of departure. Building an identity consists of negotiating the meanings of our experience of membership in social communities. The concept of identity serves as a pivot between the social and the individual, so that each can be talked about in terms of the other…it does justice to the lived experience of identity while recognizing its

> social character - it is the social, the cultural, the historical with a human face (1998, p. 145)

Identity isn't just a sense of self, but also a sense of connection with the communities you are part of. You are always part of some type of community, but how you choose to participate in that community is shaped by your identity. Where the magic comes into play is through the recognition of the fact that you can use your identity as a magical expression of the community, but also a personalization of your role in that community, as well as a mediation of the magic and whatever spiritual contacts are found in the interaction you have with the community. Pop culture magic is a mediation of the pop culture you identify with, bringing that pop culture into this world as a viable spiritual connection for yourself and other people.

Exercise

What pop culture do you identify with? How do you make it part of your magical and spiritual work? How do you share it with other people?

Pop culture magic and/or Paganism becomes truly effective when you integrate the pop culture of your choice into your identity. While some practitioners will approach pop culture magic from the chaos magic perspective of using anything that works, but only using it while there is a need, I think that there are more pop culture magicians and Pagans who are actively incorporating the pop culture of their choice into their lives as a viable part of their identity. For us, pop culture magic isn't just about meeting a specific need and then moving onto some other paradigm. Instead, the pop culture of choice is something meaningful enough to us that we've made it a significant part of our lives and have integrated it into our spirituality, because that pop culture of choice allows us to connect meaningfully with the universe through the medium of that pop culture.

Fans and Pop Culture Magic

When I wrote *Pop Culture Magick,* I didn't use the word fan in the book, but in retrospect I wish I had because pop culture magicians are fans of the pop culture they use in their spiritual practices. The word fan does bring some baggage with it. When you think of the word, do you think of someone obsessed with a particular celebrity, show or character? Do you think of someone who can provide lots of information about their interest, and essentially nerds out when they meet someone with a similar interest? Often this is how fans are depicted in mainstream culture, and while there is some truth to it, as always stereotypes are exaggerations that miss out on the realities of what it means to be a fan (Hills 2002).

Fan culture plays an integral role in pop culture magic for a variety of reasons. First, fan culture is a celebration of pop culture, as well as an acknowledgement of how that culture has changed the lives of the fans. In the documentaries *Jedi Junkies* and *Bronies,* the fans of *Star Wars* and *My Little Pony: Friendship is Magic* have been strongly impacted by their interaction with those shows. And those are just two forms of pop culture. Harry Potter, DC and Marvel comics, anime, etc., all have their fandoms, their conventions, and their communities. Henry Jenkins defines fans as poachers who want to share their pop culture of choice with other people:

> Fans…see unrealized potentials in popular culture and want to broaden audience participation. Fan culture is dialogic rather than disruptive, affective more than ideological, and collaborative rather than confrontational…poachers want to appropriate their content, imagining a more democratic, responsive, and diverse style of popular culture. (Jenkins 2006b, p. 150)

Pop culture magic and Paganism can be considered a form of poaching, in the sense that like any other fans pop culture magicians and Pagans want to share their love of the pop culture of their choice. Additionally, they want to personalize the pop culture into a magical and spiritual practice that is relevant to them.

The second reason fan culture plays a role in pop culture magic is that it can provide access to practices, materials, and resources that helps the pop culture magician with his/her practice. Additionally fan culture provides a sympathetic audience that resonates on some level with what the pop culture magician is doing. Having an audience that isn't hostile and may even want to participate in pop culture magic is essential to the proliferation of pop culture magic as a viable magical medium. Fan culture provides access to fan traditions and creates works that are derivative of the pop culture that inspired those works and yet nonetheless complements that pop culture (Jenkins 2013). Pop culture magic is part of that derivative work and part of the cultural artifacts that create a tradition and sense of community for people who are fans of that pop culture. This is important to us because those cultural artifacts and traditions provide the necessary grounding needed to develop a truly comprehensive spiritual practice, alongside what is learned in traditional magic and Paganism.

The third reason fan culture is important is because of the values that fan culture embodies:

> What's so important about fandom, surely, is that, yes, we can believe in certain values, but we could find those values in any number of different stories in our culture. What's important to fans, however, is that these values are found in a very specific set of texts, which implies in a sense that those texts are elevated, that they are numerous. These texts hold the fans' attention in a certain way; they compel fan attention, and therefore the faith that the fan would feel in a certain narrative universe is very much fixed on that universe (Jenkins 2006b, p. 18)

As a fan of a given pop culture you identify with the values and beliefs that embodied in that pop culture. Claiming that is essential for pop culture magic because it fuels the magical work you do. This is why a chaos magic approach to pop culture magic doesn't work very well. The chaos magician isn't invested in the pop culture or the fandom the way a true fan is. A true fan genuinely believes in the pop culture mythology they are into and makes it a part of their lives, because the values present within that particular pop culture speak to the fan in a way that nothing else does. Likewise the characters and overall mythology resonates deeply with the fan, and at the same time invites participation and active engagement with them. They want deeper connections with the people who work with them and they will find those deeper connections in fans. Fans interact with pop culture than someone who casually enjoys it. A fan is invested in the pop culture, and not only in the original pop culture texts and artifacts, but also in how they appropriate and make the pop culture part of their lives:

> The fans' particular viewing stance, at once ironically distant, playfully close, sparks a recognition that the program is open to intervention and active appropriation. The ongoing process of fan rereading results in a progressive elaboration of the series 'universe' through inferences and speculations that push well beyond its explicit information; the fans' meta-text, whether perpetuated through gossip or embodied within written criticism, already constitutes a form of rewriting. This process of playful engagement and active interpretation shifts the program's priorities. Fan critics pull characters and narrative issues from the margins; they focus on details that are excessive and peripheral to the primary plots but gain significance within the fans' own conceptions of the series. They apply generic reading strategies that foreground different aspects than those highlighted by network publicity (Jenkins 2013, p. 155)

What fans focus on in pop culture is the relationship they have with the characters, concepts, and values that are meaningful to them. Understanding this about fans helps us also understand the potential for every fan creation to be a part of pop culture magic. Fans are so invested in the pop culture that what they create in relationship to it becomes part of that universe and can become a viable form of magic, dependent mainly on if the fan practices magic and applies principles of magic to the pop culture and their own creations in it. For example, the *Wraeththu* series by Storm Constantine eventually morphed into a magical system, which is continuing to be worked with to this day and at the time of this writing is being expanded on by fans of the series (myself included). In later chapters we'll explore in more depth how pop culture can be turned into viable systems of magic, but what I share here speaks to the simple fact that being a fan, truly believing and being invested in the pop culture, plays a significant role in that process.

Another reason fan culture is significant to pop culture magic is because fan culture brings with it an identity rooted in how a given form of pop culture has endured and become part of the cultural mythology of our times. Both *Star Trek* and *Star Wars* are good examples of fan cultures that have lasted beyond the initial showing, and have ultimately transformed into a multi-media phenomenon, which provide fans a variety of ways to interact with the mythology (Hills 2002). *Harry Potter* is another possible example of this type of fan culture. All of these fan cultures have not only had multimedia creations of the original pop culture artifacts, but have also had fans create their own stories as a way to interact with that fan culture. Whether it's fan fiction stories, homemade movies, or the creation of a pop culture system of magic, what has been produced has been used as a way to allow the fan to participate in the fan culture they identify with:

> I want to suggest that fandom is not simply a 'thing' that can be picked over analytically. It is also always performative; by which I mean that it is an identity which is (dis-) claimed, and which provides cultural work. Claiming the status of a 'fan' may, in certain contexts, provide a cultural space for types of knowledge and attachment...what different 'performances' of

> fandom share, however, is a sense of contesting cultural norms. (Hills 2002, pp. xi -xii).

The contesting of cultural norms is a challenge to what is considered normal by mainstream culture. In the case of pop culture magic, it's a challenge to what is considered normal by Pagans, Polytheists, and Occultists who don't practice pop culture magic. Pop culture magic doesn't fit cultural norms because people choose to worship and work with "fictional characters," and insist that modern cultural narratives have as much validity as traditional cultural narratives. People who ascribe to the traditional cultural narratives disagree, in part, because they see pop culture magic as a threat to the cultural norms they are trying to maintain.

Part of what creates this friction is the fact that in some cases, Fan culture can treat pop culture as form of religion or a cult. For example, *Star Wars* has generated enough of a following that some people in the U.K. have identified their religious beliefs as Jedi. Likewise *Harry Potter* has inspired Hogwarts like Schools in Paganism such as the Witch School and Grey School. Additionally some Pagans have created spiritual systems and practices around pop culture, which to the casual observer seems ludicrous. The usual knee jerk reaction is to dismiss these practices as invalid, with the argument that fictional characters can't be treated as deities and that pop culture can't produce viable practices because it's based on fiction. The problem with this argument is that it takes a rather linear and categorical approach to spirituality and what it can and can't be.

What we need to consider is that fans do engage in behavior that could be considered to religious or spiritual practices. Additionally we need to understand that a fan culture is a subculture with culture specific practices and discourse…a cult-like culture if you will, without the negative aspects of being a cult (Collins and Porras 2002, Hills 2002). What must also be understood is that fan cultures inevitably will integrate aspects of religion and spirituality into the culture:

> Religious discourses and experiences are re-articulated and reconstructed within the discursive work of the fan cultures, meaning

> that cult fans cannot ever 'cleanse' cult discourses of religious connotations, but neither can fans use of religious terminology be read simply as an indication that fan cultures are fan 'cults' or 'religions'. Between religiosity and discourse - between cult and culture - there lies the dialogism of the media cult's neoreligious devotion. Cultic in the sense that its fan objects are perhaps ultimately arbitrary, fandom is also cultural in the sense that it seeks to account for its attachments by drawing self-reflexively and intersubjectively on discourses of 'religiosity' and 'devotion' (Hills 2002, p. 129).

The religious and spiritual discourse that shows up in fan culture is reflective of the fact that people find specific types of meaning within whatever is meaningful to them. To dismiss that meaning because what the fan is focused on spiritually is derived from fiction is to miss the something essential about spirituality itself: Spirituality finds us as much as we find it. If Harry Potter is spiritually significant to someone, we shouldn't dismiss it automatically or the person, but instead should ask ourselves what makes something like that so significant. The answer isn't hard to uncover. What qualifies a given pop culture into a form of spirituality is the personal connection a person makes to the characters, which leads to a spiritual journey and discovery of practices that help that person connect even further with those characters. This is not different from more traditional spiritual and magical practices. The process is similar. The only difference is who/what reveals itself to the seeker.

At the same time it is worth noting that fan culture and pop culture magic is distinct from more traditional cultural religious and spiritual practices in that there is a continual creation of content around the fan culture that evolves as a result of how people engage the practices (Hills 2002). People engaged in specific tradition based spiritual practices tend to focus on keeping those practices as intact as they can because they want to preserve the tradition. Pop culture magicians and fan culture in general don't have this same concern. This is because of how pop culture changes due to the creation of different media and artifacts by both the original creator of the content, and fans who have developed an interest in that content and want to participate in creating more.

Fan culture and pop culture magic reinforce the identity of the fan while also providing a variety of ways to express that identity both within and outside the fandom. Fan culture creates an identity for the fan rooted in the culture, and pop culture magic provides an expression of that identity as one that can affect not just fan culture, but the world in general. Fan culture enables the fan to manage their identity as a fan in a setting which is supportive instead of hostile to the fan interest. This is important to us as pop culture magicians and Pagans because the spiritual identity that is part of our practices can possibly find similar support in the fan culture communities we become part of. It also provides us with a continual source of inspiration for our pop culture spiritual practices, because we are drawing on and contributing to the fan culture we are part of.

We've explored the relationship of fans and fan culture to pop culture magic. While a lot of what I'm presenting in this chapter is not focused on actual spiritual practices, it's important for us as pop culture magicians and Pagans to ground ourselves in communities that will support our interests in integrating spirituality into pop culture. That support won't be found in the Pagan community or other alternative spiritual cultures, at least not to the extent that we need it. Looking elsewhere can help us find allies and support for our practices.

Exercise:

What is your fan culture? What are some events you can go to meet other fans? How does your fan culture inspire your spiritual practices?

Community and Fans

In this section, I'm going to explore the concept of community as it relates to fans. In *Pop Culture Magick* I didn't touch on community at all, but it's clear to me that community plays an integral role in pop culture and the proliferation of pop culture magic. My exploration of these topics is done with an eye toward the future of what pop culture magic and Paganism can become. The previous section of this chapter grounds this exploration of community within fan culture by recognizing that fan culture provides the basis for community to be established and sustained.

The word community brings with it a variety of meanings and associations. For the purposes of this book and pop culture magic in general, I think it's important to recognize that community can take shape in a few different ways. There is the temporary community of a convention, which lasts for a specific period of time and has specific activities built into it for all of the people attending. There is also the community found with a dedicated group of practitioners that are focused on working within a particular tradition or in our case a particular pop culture. Community can also be a recognition that you are part of a specific subculture, such as labeling yourself a Pagan or a Brony. What I share here are types of communities, and these are just a few types, but to actually understand community and employ it as a tool for our purposes means understanding what community actually provides us. To some degree, we've already explored some of the facets of community in this chapter, so the following definition of community should come as no surprise to you:

> Community is constructed symbolically as a system of values, norms, and moral codes that provide boundaries and identity…One locates community by recognizing boundary construction. He [the author is referring to someone he is citing] writes that the construction of symbolic boundaries is an oppositional act. Boundaries are constructed in relation to some 'other,' not to something fixed or absolute. While some boundaries may certainly be material or biological, most are symbolic – constructed through the communication of shared symbols and meanings. (Grabill 2001, p. 90)

We've already discussed identity at some length, but it should be clear from this definition why identity is so important. Identity enables us to connect with the communities we identify with, which in turn provide us community practices that further reinforce the identity we've chosen. At the same time, a community by its very nature also provides boundaries and those boundaries also inform your identity within that community. For example, if you identified as part of the Goth subculture, you might note part of the identity and boundary of the Goths is the clothing they wear. The clothing simultaneously asserts the identity of the Goth and also acts as a boundary which tells you if someone is or isn't part of the Goth subculture. Boundaries are more than just clothing types though. You may find that certain behaviors are encouraged or discouraged that set up specific boundaries in relationship to being part of the community. Think of some of the communities you've identified with. What are some of the boundaries in those communities? How do you know what is or isn't a boundary within a given community?

In *Magical Identity*, I also explained that identity is made up of your family, ethnic, racial, gender, and other aspects. The same can be said of community. Your race, gender, country, ideology, etc., all play a role in situating you within specific communities (Grabill 2001). However, part of what also makes you part of a community is your own interests. In the case of fan communities, what makes someone a member of a fan community is their interest in the source material and how they take and apply the concepts shared in the material in their lives. However, there are different levels of participation as well. A casual fan will not have the same level of knowledge or interest as someone who has made the fandom an integral part of their lives. And a fan community isn't automatically peace and harmony. Different fans will have their own interpretations of the fandom they are part of, which may or may not fit with what other people think of the fandom (Jenkins 2006a). This is only important to us because not all fans may welcome pop culture magic or see it as an appropriate form of the fan community you identify with.

Fan communities provide a level of information and practices around specific fan interests that can be useful for a pop culture magician or Pagan because of the resources and research provided, as well as the strong interest of the fans in producing new content related to the fandom:

> Organized fandom is, perhaps first and foremost, an institution of theory and criticism, a semistructured space where competing interpretations and evaluations of common texts are proposed, debated, and negotiated and where readers speculate about the nature of the mass media and their own relationship to it…the intimate knowledge and cultural competency of the popular reader also promotes critical evaluation and interpretation, the exercise of a popular 'expertise' that mirrors in interesting ways the knowledge-production that occupies the academy. Fans often display a close attention to the particularity of television narratives that puts academic critics to shame. Within the realm of popular culture, fans are the true experts; they constitute a competing educational elite, albeit one without official recognition or social power (Jenkins 2013 p. 86).

Fan communities provide expertise, but to truly belong to a fan community involves participation in the community. A casual fan will not understand the fan practices and participation in the way a dedicated fan will. The distinction is important for us because as pop culture magicians we are choosing to involve ourselves in fan communities and need to be respectful of how we interact with those communities. We should not take the approach of a casual fan with only a minimal interest, but rather should have a deeper appreciation and more active role in the fan community so that we can learn and integrate the practices and participatory activities that in turn can be used in our pop culture magic workings. Fans create work that focuses on building the communities they identify with, as well as representing the values of those communities and what they love about the pop culture they are into (Jenkins, Ford, & Green 2013).

Exercise

What fan communities are you part of? How do you participate and interact with these communities? How do they shape your identity?

Social Practice, Participatory Culture and Pop Culture Magic

In culture studies, the terms participatory culture and social practice are used to denote the activities that people engage in within their subcultures of choice. The majority of this book will explore pop culture magic from the perspective of participatory culture and practice, so it's worth exploring the theoretical underpinnings of those terms so that we understand them in relationship to pop culture magic and how it interfaces with fan communities, as well as with our own spiritual development.

Participation, as a concept, plays a key role in the practice of pop culture magic, because we are not just practicing the magic on our own (though many of us may be solo practitioners), but are also practicing the magic in context to the backdrop of the actual pop culture we are drawing from as well as the fan community that already has a relationship with that pop culture. Etienne Wenger defined participation as follows, "Participation here refers not just to local events of engagement in certain activities with certain people, but to a more encompassing process of active participants in the practices of social communities and constructing identities in relation to these communities" (1998, p. 4). Participation is the active engagement in specific practices that enable you to connect with the fan community, pop culture, and with your identity in relationship to both. When we perform pop culture magic we aren't just doing it for our own benefit, but also for the benefit of the pop culture we draw from and for the benefit of the fan community, in the sense that we are creating more acceptance for that pop culture as a viable form of mythology and spiritual transmission.

In cultural studies, participatory culture is grounded in identity and social practice. We've already discussed identity extensively, but social practice goes hand in hand with identity.

Social practices focus on the specific ways an individual or community engages the world, through everyday activity, but with a recognition of the social systems that such activities occur in (Wenger 1998). For example, when you practice magic you are performing specific activities for the purposes of connecting with spiritual forces, but also with other people, events, and things in order to achieve specific results. This would be considered a social practice even if you are doing the ritual work on your own, because what you are doing still affects your interactions with other people. Think about your daily routines and behaviors. Who are you interacting with and how do your activities adjust to the social circumstances of each situation? The answer is you are taking part in social practices that are part of the given community you are interacting with. Those practices help you become part of that community or identify you as someone who isn't part of the community. We engage in these practices every day, often without recognizing how they affect our identity or sense of connection with others. When we step back and examine the practices we engage in we discover that it's not just about doing something, but also about the historical and social contexts of the activities that provide specific structures and meanings for what we do. Practice, as activity, is about what we say or don't say, do or don't do, what we make explicit and what we assume (Wenger 1998).

Social practice is important to us as pop culture magicians and Pagans because the pop culture we draw on is also informed by social and historical contexts. Fan culture is an example of social and historical context in relationship to a given form of pop culture. Star Wars, for instance, has a specific history and social context it draws on and is situated in. That history includes the personal history and motivations of George Lucas and everyone else who created the original Star Wars films, but also includes the history and motivations of the fans. For someone interested in practicing pop culture magic using the Star Wars mythos, the context can be important because it provides a history and tradition to draw on. Likewise, the magical practices and rituals we draw on also have a specific social and historical context which needs to be recognized because it can provide valuable insights on the magical work we do.

Social practice is also about the meanings we derive from our experiences. A practice inevitably becomes a production of patterns of meaning. The meanings we derive from our practices help us engage with each other and the world. I also think that we imprint our meanings on reality in order to turn possibilities into reality. Meaning plays an essential role in participatory culture because it provides the participants a way to connect their identities with each other and with the community they are participating in. Participatory culture, in context to fandom, enables us to see how we as fans can interact with other fans, the corporations that have produced the pop culture and the world at large, and maintain our own meanings and identity in the process. The social practices we perform are part of that process. Acknowledging that allows us to understand that pop culture magic and spirituality is one of the social practices we use to connect with the pop culture we derive meaning from, and a way for us to participate with the fan community that pop culture is attached to. We aren't solely practicing pop culture magic or spirituality as a way to achieve specific results (though that may be part of the practice), but also as a way to establish identity and community in relationship to what we identify with on a spiritual level.

As you read the rest of this book and look at your own magical practices, think about your own pop culture magic work. How is that pop culture magic allowing you to connect and participate in the fan community? If you aren't connecting to the fan community, why aren't you and how might your practice benefit from connecting with other fans? These questions can help you situate your identity as a pop culture magician or Pagan in relationship to the fan communities that are into the pop culture you are into.

Conclusion

This chapter has been a mostly theoretical exploration of identity and pop culture. The majority of this book will focus on the practical applications of identity and pop culture magic, but I think that for pop culture magic to evolve we need to have a strong theoretical foundation that includes the disciplines of culture studies and social practice. Far too often what I see in books on magic is a tendency to isolate magic and treat it as a tool or something done separately, when in fact there is a social and ontological aspect to it that needs to be understood in order to effectively integrate it into our lives. When you add pop culture and fan communities into the mix, I see possibilities for pop culture magicians and Pagans in terms of being able to share pop culture magic and also being able to find a level of acceptance that has not been found in the Pagan, Polytheist, and occult communities. When I originally wrote *Pop Culture Magick* I had limited exposure to culture studies and social practice. Consequently, so much of that book is focused on an approach to pop culture magic that doesn't recognize how entwined pop culture is with fandom, and how that can be a significant source of inspiration for your pop culture magic work, as well as contribution to the fan communities you are part of.

Your identity as a fan may not seem all that significant, but I think if anything it plays a very significant role in the activities we engage in, which can include magic. So much of my magical work has been inspired by pop culture and by my identity as a fan that ignoring this aspect of identity seems shortsighted. The pop culture magician and Pagan isn't someone just using pop culture as a way to get practical results for problems. Instead, the pop culture magician and Pagan is someone who recognizes that pop culture can be a viable expression of their spirituality and connection to the world. Practical magic is still part of pop culture magic, but we also need to acknowledge the spiritual and social foundations that can inform the creation and practice of pop culture spirituality.

Chapter 3: Fan Culture, Corporations and Pop Culture Magic

One aspect of pop culture magic which has typically been touched on lightly by various people (myself included) is the relationship between fan culture, corporations, and pop culture magic. However, this relationship is important to examine for a couple different reasons that can affect what we consider pop culture magic to be, as well as how we work with it. While some people have focused on this topic, it's usually been in relationship to how magic can be performed as a way to subvert corporate interests. In my opinion, this is only one facet of how corporations can be worked with or against.

Corporations and fan culture exist in an uneasy space with each other. On the one hand, corporations create or provide a platform for the creation of pop culture. On the other hand, corporations can also discourage independent creation of pop culture, viewing such creation as an infringement on their "property" and potential profits. At the same time, corporations recognize that fans play an essential role in generating the profits and, as a result, they sometimes are supportive of fan culture and what occurs in it because of how it promotes the pop culture the corporation has helped to create. Fans have also learned how to leverage their interests to get corporations to back down or support a particular cause the fans are interested in, but the ability to do this is to some extent limited by the nature of the relationship between consumers and corporations: "Not all participants are created equal. Corporations - and even individuals within corporate media - still exert greater power than any individual consumer or even the aggregate of consumers. And some consumers have greater abilities to participate in this emerging culture than others" (Jenkins 2006a P. 3). As fans sometimes discover it's not always easy to get to a corporation to back down, especially if there is a perception that fan activity will endanger the bottom line. Recognizing this relationship can help us also recognize that pop culture magic may be perceived as a fan activity that is either considered harmless or considered to be a potential infringement, with all the issues that come with such an assessment.

We must also recognize that while the balance of power is typically slanted toward corporations, it isn't always that way. Fans have power and can create resistance to corporate interests by providing different perspectives that deviate from the sanctioned perspective offered by corporations. As an example, when the Warner Bros studio tried to get *Harry Potter* fan sites shut down, the fans reacted by hiring lawyers and eventually got the studio to rethink its policy (Jenkins 2006a). In this case, mainstream culture was forced to conform to a subculture. Granted, this occurred because the financial interest of the corporation was threatened by fan reaction, but this example proves that pop culture isn't entirely a mainstream phenomenon and that people involved in it aren't sellouts.

Pop culture magicians can also choose to work with corporations or do magic to subvert corporations. One detail which must be kept in mind in choosing to do magic work in relationship to a corporation is that you are dealing with an egregore that has its own agenda which may not be favorable to you. It's important to do pop culture magic with or against corporations carefully because you are dealing with a spiritual entity comprised of the intentions and beliefs of employees and customers and that entity may have more oomph behind it than you realize. Let's explore why this is the case by defining corporations in context to magic.

What are Corporations (Magically)?

From an occult/magical perspective, corporations are companies that produce specialized media which represents the corporate egregore. Intel, Microsoft, Vesta, Boeing, etc., are not just names of companies. They are corporate labels used to embody specific types of economic goods and services. The various logos, slogans, and symbols that corporations use, such as Nike's Swoosh, are symbols which embody a specific culture that is developed by corporate egregores to continually produce media and other goods, so that they can not only stay alive, but thrive in the minds of people. Even the products are a form of media in the sense that they are representative of the company and an embodiment that the egregore of the company can be worked with.

The corporate world has its own reality and culture, as reflected in the cartoon *Dilbert*, which simultaneously makes fun of and celebrates the corporate environment. The characters in *Dilbert* are pop icons that embody the terminal frustration that any white-collar worker feels, because s/he knows that s/he is giving away his/her life to work for someone else, and often deal with the sometimes meaningless and petty politics that occur in any business setting. It's a sad fact that the cartoon, while probably meant to be a parody, is often an accurate reality of the corporate world and the lack of empowerment it offers to people working in such environments. At the same time it also represents how such companies interact with people who aren't part of the company, but nonetheless are affected by it, such as fans.

For some occultists the way to deal with corporations is to strike back at the corporate world, devising memes that sabotage the corporate advertising, or using subversive magical practices that undermine the stated focus and goal of a particular organization (Arkenburg 2006). On the other hand, there's also something to be said for using the corporate system for other purposes beyond subversion. In a few different cases, I've used corporate media and the systems they represent for purposes that aren't necessarily at odds with the corporation, but nonetheless benefit me and the causes I believe in. The use of such a system can be beneficial in other ways, and you don't even need to sell out to work with the corporate systems and what they represent.

I presume that most of my readers work at a job in a corporate system. When I define such a system, I'm not merely referring to big businesses such as Microsoft, or media empires such as 21st Century Fox. Although those companies are legally incorporated, that alone, to my mind, doesn't make a company a corporate system. A corporate system is any business, small or large, that employs people and expects specific behaviors and norms to be followed. An academic university is a corporation. Employees are expected to publish and present papers, teach classes, work on committees, and train other workers for other university jobs. There's an expected code of behavior and each person that works at a university is giving some of his or her time away for this entity they work for. Government organizations such as the post office are also corporations in their own right, for similar reasons as I described above. A person who works at a power company is also a corporate employee. The same applies for any fast food worker. A corporate system incorporates a person into its structure in order to sustain itself. There are several other definitions of corporations, which are useful in understanding the exact nature of what we're dealing with:

> Despite their non-corporeality, corporations are able to display a wide range of behaviors in a conceptual framework of legal reality. Disconnected from the material plane, except in the way their influence is manifested, these entities grow, absorb each other, competing, altering their identities, renaming themselves, creating and losing capital, sway political parties, own and oversee property, pay taxes, sue, and be sued. Yet because of the nature of their existence, they cannot be imprisoned, physically coerced, or killed. Immortal legally, corporations as they are currently, are something of an egregore brought into being through the collective vision of the founders, an egregore that manifests through the collective will of the governing body and given qi, given energy through the financial investment of its stockholders. (Wu 2004, www.technoccult.com)

The perspective that a corporation is an egregore is fairly accurate in the sense that large pools of people give their time, energy, and resources to the corporation in return for jobs and/or financial security. Although stockholders invest in the egregore, they don't own it. If anything, it owns them because they rely on it to sustain their financial security. Certainly it's not in the interest of the egregore that they withdraw their resources from it, but in the end the egregore will likely outlast the stockholders and/or find new stockholders to sustain it.

A different perspective on corporate egregores is that they are multi-dimensional beings comprised of the resources and ideas of the people that sustain it:

> The modern corporation is far more than a building full of people that creates a product or manages resources. It exists in data space and aetheric space as well as physical space. It is an amalgam of will and imagination committed to self-preservation, growth, and profit. It wields media to establish its presence and identity in our age of global trade. The corporation is unified in its focus, and manipulates resources in accordance with that intent. It is, in many ways, an individual composed of many cooperative cells that are continuously recycled. The structure persists by its own intent and inertia. It can move, disperse, and distribute itself through data networks. It behaves with a single will, informed by the will of the corporate collective, bent towards the same end: maintaining the existence and continued growth of the corporate entity (Arkenburg 2006, p. 203).

This definition is similar to Wu's in that the egregore is identified as a being that acts to preserve itself and uses its resources to do so. The various people, places, etc., that are associated with it are all part of the lifeline that keeps the egregore alive. At the same time, Arkenburg makes an interesting distinction, namely that the entity works with data. This distinction is important because it acknowledges that corporations are intimately tied to the dispersal of information, especially information that increases their presence. Information is an essential reality of everyday life and corporations capitalize on that in a variety of manners. The commercials we hear on the radio and see on TV and the internet are just the most obvious method of interaction for corporations. Other forms of information dispersal involve charity work, construction of property in the name of the corporation, and of course just having products from the corporation in your home.

The downside of corporate reality for every worker is that s/he is giving the corporate entity life energy and time. For some of us this isn't an ideal reality. When you factor in that most, if not all, corporations also vie for our free time, the situation gets worse. All the advertising in different forms of media is created to constantly put us in touch with these corporate existences and the brand products they offer. Even an academic institution is offering a brand product, namely the education that people go to receive with the rather vague promise of a job at the end of your time of studying. Jenkins made an excellent point about corporations:

> Successful brands are built by exploiting multiple contacts between the brand and consumer. The strength of a connection is measured in terms of emotional impact. The experience should not be contained within a single media platform, but should extend across as many media as possible. Brand extension builds on audience interest in particular content to bring them into contact again and again with an associated brand (2006a, p. 69).

The result is advertisement bombardment, but also an attempt to get the energy and life of a person focused on feeding the corporations vying for your time and life. The more contact you have with corporations, the more you give your life over to them. Your life is a resource and corporations need resources to exist. But where does that leave you and what can you do about it?

This question is one pop culture magicians should consider carefully in their own magical work, because to some degree or another we are connecting to corporations and their egregores through our own work. This doesn't mean we should stop doing pop culture magic, but instead that we should recognize what else it can expose us too. With that said, corporations are a reality of life and likely aren't going away anytime soon, and they can be useful for us in our magical work.

Let me share an example of how corporations show up in pop culture. Let's you say you wanted to do a working with a Disney character. You aren't just working with the Disney character; you are also, to some extent working with the corporate spirit and culture of Disney and that needs to be factored in your working. If you want to work with a Disney character, what needs to be considered is how that character is simultaneously its own entity, and an extension of the corporate entity of Disney, as well as the culture of Disney. In the game *Kingdom Hearts,* which is an amalgamation of Disney and Square, the character of Sora is told by Donald and Goofy that he has to be happy in order for the gummi ship to work, because the ship is fueled by happiness and laughter. Sora does his very best to embody that and off the characters go, but let's think about the connection to Disney embodied in that exchange.

If you've worked for Disney as an employee, you know that one of the expectations is that you come to work happy. Any problems you have need to be left at home. The Disney experience that people expect at a Disney theme park is one where the employees are cheerful and happy. Walt Disney made it very clear that he expects that people working at Disney will help create and sustain the magic of Disney by being happy whenever there is a possibility they could interact with a possible client. This cultural vision shows up in the various cartoons and other products that are part of Disney. It is part of the spirit of the Disney egregore and as such it will also show up to some degree in the various characters.

If you want to work with a Disney character, you need to consider how the corporate spirit of Disney might show up in the working. For example, if you are working with a Disney character while unhappy, how will that affect the working, if at all? I suspect there would be some effect because of how tied in the corporate spirit of Disney is to the characters, right down to how people portray those in the Disney theme parks. My point in bringing all of this up is that when doing a magical working involving a corporation or an entity linked to the corporation it's a good idea to understand the actual culture of the corporation, to get some sense of the spirit of it and recognize how that might show up in the magical working you are doing.

Exercise

What corporations is your pop culture connected to? What is your relationship with corporations? How do they affect your life? How, if at all, have you worked with a corporation magically?

The Relationship between Fans and Corporations

Fans and corporations have a relationship which is sometimes harmonious and sometimes rocky. Pop culture is the intersection where fans and corporations meet. Corporations have a vested interest in the pop culture becoming something which is popular enough that it will help sell product in the form of various types of media such as toys, books, movies, shows, posters, costumes, etc., and fans have a vested interest in the story and narratives of their pop culture and wanting to see them continued. However these vested interests of both parties don't always go hand in hand.

The corporations are interested in the bottom line, while fans are interested in the story and being a part of it. At the same time the relationship fans and corporations have with each is one of an implicit contract, where there is an expectation on the part of the fans that the corporation will keep the pop culture going, while the corporate cultures expects that fans will simultaneously support and keep their hands off the pop culture. It's ironic, because in some ways corporations want fans to support what they love and in other ways they don't. The problem with implicit contracts is that they are based on subjective experiences, which inform whether or not those contracts are fulfilled. And while corporations can resort to legal action in some cases, often they end up relying on how they market the pop culture of choice, as a way of responding to fandom (Austin 2013).

The fans can and do respond to the corporation breach of an implicit contract by either expressing dissatisfaction through disengaging with the pop culture the pop culture they enjoy, while also complaining to the creators, or boycotting it altogether (Austin 2013). The other way fans respond is to actively support the pop culture version they agree with and push back on the marketing that the company has put out. Because fans have a community to draw upon, they are able to work together to stand up to corporations and provide their own perspective on the pop culture they love (Jenkins, Ford, & Green 2013).

The reason this is relevant to the pop culture magician is because we aren't practicing pop culture magic in a void. There is a context that can and does inform our practice with a given form of pop culture. Understanding fan culture and its relationship with corporate culture can provide some ideas for how to work with pop culture, but can also help us understand how to co-opt or work again corporate interests that are behind the production of pop culture. I also think that pop culture magic isn't just limited to your favorite characters or shows or games but can be derived from a variety of sources including both fan and corporate culture, but if we choose to work with those sources, we should know what we are getting into.

It's important to understand that fan communities and corporations aren't always at odds with each other. Corporations do work with fan communities, in part because fan communities help build the fan base that buys the products. The social capital of fan communities can't be underestimated because of how fans build a community that supports and sometimes parodies the fan interests they have, creating short and long term value for the pop culture they support (Stribling 2013). Additionally fans become part of the marketing effort corporations (Jenkins 2006a). For example, if you're a fan of Assassins Creed and wear a T-Shirt with the AC logo, you are marketing that series as well as Ubisoft. The same applies to any other pop culture you can think of. Corporations recognize the marketing value of fans and are certainly willing to capitalize on that as a way of continuing to create the pop culture fans love, while also getting new fans because of the way current fans are marketing a given pop culture product.

Yet fan communities also bring their own input and creativity into the pop culture they love. The community has a variety of resources available to it outside of just what is produced by the corporations. Visit YouTube and you can easily find fan created movies and shows based on the pop culture they love. Corporations can try to dictate how the fans present what they create, but they can't entirely stop fans from creating and producing their own narratives of pop culture:

> Audience members are using the media texts as their disposal to forge connections with each other, to mediate social relations and make meaning of the world around them. Both

> individually and collectively, they exert agency in the spreadability model. They are not merely impregnated with media messages, nor are they at the service of the brand; rather, they select material that matters to them from the much broader array of media content on offer. They do not simply pass along static texts; they transform the material through active production processes or through their own critiques and commentary, so that it better serves their own social and expressive needs. Content – in whole or through quotes – does not remain in fixed borders but rather circulates in unpredicted and often unpredictable directions, not the product of top-down design but rather the result of a multitude of local decisions made by autonomous agents negotiating their way through diverse cultural spaces. Similarly so-called consumers do not simply consume; they recommend what they like to their friends, who recommend it to their friends, who recommend it on down the line. They do not simply 'buy' cultural goods; they 'buy into' a cultural economy which rewards their participation. And, in such an environment, any party can block or slow the spread of texts: if creators construct legal or technical blocks, if third-party platform owners choose to restrict the ways in which material can circulate, or if audiences refuse to circulate content which fails to serve their own interests. (Jenkins, Ford, & Green 2013, p. 294).

What this indicates to us is that pop culture isn't something we passively watch or read, but rather is something we actively co-create. Pop culture magic is one such expression of co-creation, even as there are others which may have nothing overtly to do with magic, but nonetheless in their own way contribute to bringing to life the characters and concepts that make pop culture into something more than just a commodity. Pop culture becomes a form of engagement that fans have with corporations, each other, and how they experience the world at large (Jenkins, Ford, & Green 2013). And in pop culture magic, pop culture becomes a mythology that connects us to the spiritual aspects of the characters we work, and allows us to derive a spiritual path based on the contemporary times we live in, the situations we deal with, and everything else that is relevant to us in this time we live in. That mythology is created by all of the fans and it consequently provides the magician an unprecedented amount of material to draw on in their pop culture magic workings.

At the same time, we can't discount the companies or their marketing efforts. Any given company seeks to create its own narrative through its marketing, typically known as a brand. The brand is the identity of the company and the pop culture, but also the interaction the company has with people interested in the brand. Companies recognize that people form social bonds through their interest in pop culture and in the brand established in the marketing of pop culture (Jenkins, Ford, & Green 2013). Companies focus on creating brands that are 'lovemarks' and simultaneously inform and entertain people about the brand. These companies recognize that people live in an interactive environment, where they can potentially help spread the word and meme (message) of the brand (Jenkins 2006a). Nonetheless, this isn't a one way relationship: "Members of 'brand communities' are often vocal about customer service issues and critical about business decisions the company makes, feeling that their passionate support of a company's products makes them an active stakeholder in the brand" (Jenkins, Ford, & Green 2013, p. 164)

A brand of a company is focused on creating a specific, context oriented message about the brand that calls attention to the product, and engages the desired audience in wanting to associate with that product and brand (Halloran 2014). This both works for and against the brand. It works for the brand in creating a conversation about the brand and company, but it works against it when people perceive that the brand is no longer focused on their interests. When marketing companies develop a brand, they focus on finding the emotional opening that a potential audience has, so that they can create specific content that addresses the emotional needs of the desired audience. While this isn't overtly magical, if we examine this from a magical perspective, what a company is trying to do is get the emotional resources of a given audience in order to sustain its own life through their continued engagement and interest in the brand.

I've chosen to focus chapter 3 on companies and their relationship to pop culture, so we'll explore how to actually develop pop culture magic around branding, but I hope that by taking some time to explore the relationship fans have with companies, it helps you examine your own pop culture magic workings in context to not just the pop culture itself, but also the influences and vested interests that help create that pop culture.

Brandscapes[2]: How to work with Corporations Magically

A brandscape is the entirety of the marketing of a brand as well as the fan response to that marketing. It's also the spiritual landscape of a brand, accessed through pathworking or other methods of magic as a way of working with a brand directly. Finally, it is also part of the corporate entity. When we interact with a brandscape, we are interacting with the corporate entity as well. The brandscape is the entity.

The easiest way to access a brandscape is through the logo of the business. Each business has a logo and the logo is representative of the business both in terms of its design and its colors. For example the logo for Nike (a fitness apparel company) is the Swoosh symbol. There is no specific color associated with Nike, so that wouldn't be a necessary for interacting with the Nike brandscape or the entity. Nivea (a skin care company), on the other hand, uses colors to make its logo distinctive. It's a blue background, with the word Nivea in white, which means that if you wanted to work with Nivea, you'd want to include the colors of blue and white.

It's important to recognize that corporate entities and the brandscapes themselves are ultimately focused on the success of the corporation. If you are going to work with a corporate entity or work with the brandscape, you need to remember that one of

[2] Diego Rinallo, while taking a class I offered on Pop Culture Magic, coined the term Brandscapes.

the agendas of such a being/environment is encouraging you to buy the services and products of that corporation. This makes sense, because a corporation is ultimately kept alive by the people that choose to spend their money on the services and products of the corporation.

Even if you are an employee of the corporation, this principle still applies. In some ways it applies even more so because you are working for the corporation and there is already an implicit expectation that you will be loyal to the corporation by using the products and services the corporation offers. Additionally, as an employee, your life and energy is already bound to the corporation.

The logo of the corporation can be used for different purposes. You can use it to evoke the corporate entity, like you would a sigil of a demon, angel, or other type of spirit, or you can use it to invoke the entity. You can also use the logo as a doorway to access the brandscape of the corporation. If you use the logo for the purposes of invocation or evocation, you might create your own replica of the logo or use an object that already has the logo on it. Additionally you might consider creating an invocation/evocation chant that integrates the slogan of the company, as a further way to attune you to its energy. For example:

Nike: Just do it!
Swoosh into me (or into the world)
Nike: Just do it!
I call on you to help me just do it with my sports activity.
Take away my fear and help me swoosh!
I want to just do it!

This is an improvisational chant of a possible invocation or evocation chant to Nike. You could probably come up with a better one if you wanted to work with Nike, but note how I've integrated both the swoosh and the slogan of just do it into the chant. If you were doing a working to Nike, I would suggest wearing Nike shoes and apparel (don't wear Reebok or Adidas! Or you'll offend Nike) and of course think of the context of the working: namely you'd want to do it in relationship to sports activities. If you want to invoke Nike you would call for Nike's essence to go into you, and if you want to evoke it you would want to send it out into the world.

In the case of a pathworking involving the brandscape of Nike you would still want to integrate the logo and the slogan. However, what you would be doing is creating a virtual brandscape or pathworking composed of the essence of Nike. To do this you would memorize the logo of Nike and then do a meditation where you would use the logo as a door to access the brandscape of Nike. Optionally, you might continuously chant Just do it as you were focusing on the logo and using it to access the brandscape. When you reached the brandscape visualize appropriate imagery, feelings, smells, etc. In the case of Nike it would be bright athletic colors, the smell of sweat, relevant sports related imagery, as well as shoes. The purpose of going to the brandscape is to access the corporate energy of Nike in order to learn more about Nike, to enlist Nike as an ally, or even to try and work against it. You can take this same approach and apply it to any corporation you want to work with or against. Simply get the logo and slogan and then create magical working around them, with the understanding that the logo and slogan are keys.

Exercise

Pick out a corporation you'd like to work with or one that owns your favorite brand. Get the logo and/or slogan if there is one by doing some research on the corporate website and related marketing materials. Now create your own version of an invocation chant, an evocation chant and a brandscape pathworking. Try all three out and record your results.

If you actually work at the corporation you are doing the working for, then it may be useful to do a brandscape working in order to create a stronger connection to the corporate entity or for the purposes of creating an entity that is part of the corporate energy but is focused on helping you with your career. As an example of this principle in action, I took the corporate logo from one of the companies I contracted with and slightly altered it to personalize the logo into a sigil that represented the company, but also represented what I wanted the corporate entity to do for me. In this case, I wanted it to protect me from any office politics, but also from prying eyes in the cubicle. Because most people can look over your shoulders at what you're doing, it can be quite frustrating to get work done that isn't official corporate work during downtime. On days where there isn't much work, but you still want to be paid, it's equally frustrating to pretend to work and constantly worry that someone will report you for surfing the internet or working on a personal project. I turned the corporate logo into a watchful eye that would help me be aware of what other people were doing, while shielding me from them noticing what I was or wasn't doing. While I do focus on getting a job done when the work is there for me to do, I don't want to be penalized when there's no work to be done. The corporate eye logo protected me from that fate, while at the same time putting the resources of the corporation to work for me.

Another technique I've used has involved getting training to do the job well. At my first contract position as a tech writer I had very little experience doing tech writing and because I was a contractor, my boss had no interest in investing time or training for me for any of the related duties I might have to do. I was expected to learn while doing the job. However, this approach was frustrating for both him and me. He had documents he wanted to have published, but the writing he was receiving wasn't up to his standard. I wanted to write the way he wanted, but the feedback I got wasn't really useful. To get around this problem, I decided to use magic to create an entity.

I took the acronym of the project I was working on and created a sigil that would serve as a programming symbol for the entity of the project. I then did a working to the corporate spirit of the company, where I took the sigil asked the corporate entity to give it life so that it could serve the corporation and help me. The role of this entity was to help me improve my understanding of the goals of the project, improve my technical writing ability, and improve my grasp of the technology I had to use. Shortly after I created this entity both my boss and I noted a dramatic improvement in my skills and in my participation in the group. For the duration of my contract that entity continued to help me learn new skills that would be useful for me to have not only at that job, but also future jobs. At every other job, I've since taken the acronyms of the projects and turned them into sigils. The entity of a given project connects with me and helps me do really well at my task. Each time, I've gotten the corporate entity to participate in the creation of the job entity so that I have the corporation backing my efforts.

Another way I've used corporate entities is to help smooth out issues between myself and other workers. While I get along with most of the other workers, there is the rare case where personalities conflict. In one case the team lead I worked with tended to get very stressed out due to other circumstances, but would end up taking that stress out on the rest of the team. To alleviate that, I put some energy in his cubicle that would cushion and dissipate his negative energy and also had the project entity smooth obstacles in his path, which consequently made him much easier to deal with. This was a case of making the corporate entity actually help its resource out, which was useful because then the entity was working for us instead of just using us. The energy I used also helped the entity understand how it could remove obstacles for the team lead.

The example above illustrates how you can take the resources the corporation has and put it to work for you. I learned a lot about how to do layout at my technical writing jobs, which helped me with the publishing business I help run. In each case, my goal has always been to do a good job, but also to take the corporate resources and use them to my advantage, instead of just being used and discarded by the corporation. I've continually focused on creating an entity that won't so much do my job for me, as teach me how to do it better and acquire skills I can use in other parts of my life.

Exercises

Try working with a corporate entity to gain new job skills or create an entity to help you navigate a job situation. Do you find that you learn the skills quicker? For inspiration for this exercise check out my book Manifesting Wealth where I discuss career magic at much greater length.

Working With Your Own Brand and Logo

If you own a business, you can also take these concepts and apply them to working with your business. I discuss this at length in *Manifesting Wealth,* but I'll touch on it here in the interest of being thorough. When you own your own business, you essentially are creating a corporate entity. The logo and slogan you come up with is part of that creation process, as are your daily business activities. Another part of that creation is also the description of the core values of the business, which answers the question of why you are in business and what is the calling that informs your actions. Finally, your business plan and your marketing plan are also part of the creation process. All of these elements form the DNA of the business and establish the brandscape that can be worked with.

Magically, the very actions I've described help with the creation of your business as a spiritual entity, but as a final touch I like to do a working using the logo and tagline of the business as a form of evocation, similar to the Nike one I mentioned above, where I bring the business entity to life. If your shop is based in a physical location, you would do the working there. If it's a business you run out of your home, then you can do the working in your home.

Once you've created your business entity, you can work with it at any time. You are the business owner, so you have an intimate connection with it. Additionally you'll have the logo and tagline on your business cards, your website, and other marketing material, which serves as talismans that you can use to call on your entity. Your reason for calling on your entity could be to help you land a sale, or inspire your business practices or any number of other activities, all of which I've mentioned in *Manifesting Wealth.*

I'll admit this isn't exactly what most people think of as pop culture magic, but in a way it is, because you are creating a brand with your business, which is a form of pop culture, albeit one that may only be relevant to a specific segment of people that need your services. It's important to remember that pop culture magic isn't just working with something that someone else has created, but also our own creations.

Anti-Corporate and Brand Magic

In some cases, you may want to work against a corporation. One way to do this is to sabotage a corporation. To sabotage Fox News, Arkenburg adopted the idea that information is available everywhere and that all entities are information patterns and its possible to access and modify those patterns: "I would reprogram my own local relationship with the spirit of Fox News, magically assault the corporation and inject a love bomb into its memestream, inspiring truthful awareness and rebellion in its acolytes" (Arkenburg 2006, p. 205). By injecting a love bomb into Fox News, it was his hope that he could sabotage its inner workings. Arkenburg notes that the culmination working coincided with the Bill O'Reilly lawsuit (2006). However, any gains he made utilizing that working didn't last for very long. Fox is still running strong and O'Reilly still has his own program. A corporation will protect its own resources, so long as those resources can continue to make it strong. The decision to sabotage a corporation magically should factor that in, and focus on poisoning the relationship enough that the corporation no longer gains sustenance from its asset. For example, if Arkenburg had focused his magic on finding some way to bring to light some controversial information about Bill O'Reilly that would make it hard for Fox continue to support him, then that would be an effective example of corporate sabotage.

The problem with the subversive approach is that the magician is dealing with an entity that can draw on its own resources and is an expert on drawing on others' resources, including people who work against it:

> Working with corporate egregores with the intent to subvert and/or otherwise disperse that manifestation is toxic magic, and certain steps are important in such work to protect the worker. Egregores such as these that are purely profit-driven are a kind of energy vampire, existing through the energy put forth both by those that work within the corporation, its investors, and its consumer base. If called into a hostile environment into a spiritual presence, it would not hesitate to drain an

> attuned magician of all available energy as well, for that is in its nature. (Wu 2004, www.technoccult.com)

A person who chooses to attack a corporate entity is dealing with a being that's used to being attacked by other corporate entities. This being could have much more power than a magician might have. While a sustained subversive magic attack can do some damage, the corporation can heal quickly.

I've also tried to subvert corporations, although my technique has been more subtle. I usually take the spam I receive in emails and cut it up into spam sigils. I'll also take advertisements found in magazines or even sound clips from radio and T.V. advertisements and make them into new cut-ups with the intent of turning the corporate entities against each other. A magician who's talented in technology could also create DVD or Youtube cut-ups which take advertisements and other corporate materials and sample them in random manners, while putting sigils in the background (Unsane 2007). Spam sigils tend to be more passive. They still infect the memestream, but don't directly attack the corporate entity, so much as subvert the messages it sends out. However the subversion of those messages subtly turns people against the brand and corporation, because they see it in a different light.

One example of such corporate sabotage involved the creation of parody videos of the Old Spice commercials. In the Old Spice Commercials produced by Kennedy-Weiden (an advertising agency working on the Old Spice brand), the Old Spice guy is an extremely handsome, intelligent, buff, adventurous man that every other man wants to be because their romantic partners will be more attracted the Old Spice guy. He can't help them with that, but what he can do is give them access to Old Spice, which will supposedly convey at least some of his desired traits upon them if they use it regularly. In response to these commercial, men of all body shapes and sizes created similar parody videos of themselves to showcase realistic men that your man could smell like. These parody videos were shared on YouTube as a way of simultaneously hijacking the Old Spice commercials and representing the interest of the average man (Jenkins, Ford, & Green 2013). While I don't know if a magician worked on these videos, the principle is similar, and an enterprising pop culture magician could create a similar video with the purpose of spoofing the brand while drawing on some of the attention it gets, as a way of charging his/her own magical workings.

Again, however, it's important to recognize that a brand will respond and sometimes do so in a manner designed to take over the subversive narrative and re-appropriate it toward the goals of the brand. Kennedy-Weiden, for example, did shoot some response videos and had the Old Spice guy respond to some videos as a way of keeping the brand message central to the videos. Marketers recognize that as a brand's message is spread and diverted and changed, it becomes diluted, so they continuously reinforce the original message to keep the focus on the brand and the corporation (Halloran 2014). It's important to note that a brand is built on the basis of the following principle:

> Successful brands are built by exploiting multiple contacts between the brand and consumer. The strength of a connection is measured in terms of its emotional impact. The experience should not be contained within a single media platform, but should extend across as many media as possible. Brand extension builds on audience interest in particular content to bring them into contact again and again with an associated brand (Jenkins 2006a P. 69).

If your purpose is to sabotage a brand, that's probably the last thing you want. However, it's also important to recognize that a brand and the corporation behind it isn't all powerful. Industries assume that they create brand and fan communities around their products, forgetting that if anything it is the fan who creates such communities on the basis of their own interaction with a brand. The people in charge of marketing may join the conversation, but they usually are reacting to a conversation that's already happening. The magician can utilize this to his/her advantage and start specific magical workings using modern media and magic to change the message of the brand, "they [The authors are referring to marketers] must think about what happens as content travels across cultural boundaries, sometimes stripped of its original context, creating 'impure' texts which are not simply distributed from culture to culture but - in the process - often bear the mark of audiences that remake, reinterpret, and transform content" (Jenkins, Ford, & Green 2013, p. 296). Because audiences can bring their own interpretations and messages into the mix, such as occurred with the Old Spice commercials, the brand must react and those reactions are not always in favor of the corporation.

So how do we magically go about subverting or sabotaging a corporation, if that is pop culture magic we want to work with? First, we must integrate modern media into the working. The use of pictures, text, logos, video and sound can all be useful tools for helping to create a subversive working. Additionally, we need to define the goal and results of such a working. Are we trying to destroy the company, change how the target audience responds to the company or something else altogether? Whatever it is we want to do, it needs to be a measureable goal, something that can actually be defined and determined.

If I were to do such a working I'd focus on a mass media magical working, where I'd create a collage poster that I could print out with images of the brand and behaviors that were different from the desired outcome. I'd create video narratives where the brand was spoofed in a humorous way that wasn't overtly hostile, but nonetheless would ideally raise a question in the minds of the viewer. I'd also inject a sigil of some sorts or work with a spirit that would be a counter to the corporation and would consequently be invested in helping to undermine it.

You can certainly come up with some interesting workings in this vein if it's something you choose to do. I think the key to making this working successful is to use multiple channels of communication, much like a corporation would use and to take up some type of action in your mundane activities that further supports your goal to undermine the corporation, such as boycotting the merchandise or protesting what the corporation does in other parts of the world.

Conclusion

One aspect of pop culture magic I've tried to call out in this chapter is that pop culture magic does deal with corporations to one degree or another. Corporations fund and produce pop culture, as well as patronize the artists and writers who create the content. If you are uncomfortable with the idea of working with corporate energy, then pop culture magic probably isn't for you because corporations are always a part of pop culture and are invested in pop culture as one way to make their bottom lines. However, if you can accept that then you can actually put that reality to work in your magical workings and make them even more powerful. And as I've noted above, fans also play an integral role in the creation of pop culture and can be a potent source of inspiration as well.

Chapter 4: Retro Pop Culture Magic

Pop culture magic isn't magic focused on whatever is the trendiest or most popular show, book, etc. currently occurring in media, although some expressions of pop culture magic can work off of such trends. What makes pop culture magic powerful has a lot more to do with the attachment a given person feels to their pop culture choices. The connection you have to your pop culture of choice is what drives the pop culture magical work you do. It's not surprising then that for some people the pop culture they work with is pop culture from decades ago. It's the pop culture they grew up with and it continues to play a role in their lives, including their spiritual practices.

Ironically, at one time, companies treated shows and other forms of pop culture media as a one-time event that people would lose interest in after having perused it once, or because program ratings were declining (Jenkins, Ford, & Green 2013). The episode film stills of the original *Dr. Who* series were thrown out because the BBC didn't think that that people would want to watch them again. This rather short sighted approach to dealing with pop culture materials resulted in missing episodes of the original series and other episodes that were only recovered because fans of the show at the time happened to record them. Pop culture may not always be popular to lots of people, but someone will find it interesting and find a way to keep it alive:

> The British cultural critic and theorist Raymond Williams suggests that cultural change occurs at variable rates. As a result, we can be influenced by things - experiences, practices, values, artifacts, institutions - long after they have lost cultural centrality. Ultimately, Williams asserts that how culture operates can only be fully understood by looking at the ebb and flow of cultural influences rather than taking a static snapshot of specific content or groups. (Jenkins, Ford, & Green 2013, pp. 95-6).

If you look at a pop culture phenomenon over the long run you'll find that it tends to come and go in waves. Consider the *Teenage Mutant Ninja Turtles*. Originally they were created for a comic book series, and then were eventually were picked up for a cartoon series. This was followed by movies, then for a while the cartoons and movies were shown as reruns. Then *Teenage Mutant Ninja Turtles* came back in another cartoon series, and at the time of this writing a new movie was recently released. *Ghostbusters* is another example where you had movies followed by a cartoon show, then reruns, and now there is talk of creating a new movie. Pop culture becomes popular, then fades, then becomes popular again. It never dies because it becomes part of the popular consciousness. Other examples include *Star Wars, Star Trek, G.I. Joe,* and the list can go on and on.

What retro pop culture also brings about is a focus on collecting pop culture artifacts. In the documentary *Jedi Junkies,* several collectors were featured who'd collected multiple versions of Star Wars characters. Enthusiasts collect the pop culture artifacts because they want them for nostalgic purposes or for potential monetary value down the line. However, for the pop culture magician, the value of collecting pop culture artifacts has more to do with how you will use them in your workings. You might find the original packaging interesting and you might even keep your collectibles in that packaging, but if you plan to use those figures for magical purposes, you won't want them in the packaging. The same applies for any other pop culture artifact you get. For the magician, collecting isn't about keeping something in pristine condition[3], but about integrating the pop culture artifact into the magical working.

You can take action figures and dolls and use them as housing units for the pop culture entities they represent or for an entity you create. They will be empowered by people noticing them. Old action figures stand out; they are perceived as collectibles. The entity can be derived from the actual character the action figure depicts, but alternatively the entity could be one you made up. For instance, there are a couple of G.I. Joe characters who are doctors. You could create a health entity and house it in one of these. When I create an entity and bond it to an

[3] Unless that fits the purpose of your magical work.

action figure. I think of the character's attributes and purposes and try to relate those to the entity, and synthesize the associations I have about the entity and character. One exercise that can be really fun is to use the action figure to challenge common assumptions about reality. Dressing a G. I. Joe figure in Barbie doll clothes and summoning an entity that represents subverting the dominant gender paradigm is a creative way of using pop culture to challenge mainstream ideas.

It may be preferable to work with the actual pop culture character instead of creating an entity, for the reason that the existing pop culture character already exists and performs a function relevant to what you might create an entity for. The G.I. Joe characters who are doctors can also be useful health entities to work with. Their purpose, after all, is to keep the other G.I. Joes healthy. Additionally, there is the potential issue that trying to map a created entity to an embodiment of an existing pop culture might not work or might produce consequences you don't want to deal with.

Part of what makes retro pop culture and pop culture artifacts valuable to collectors is what that pop culture embodies: "Old brands retain value simply by being old: the value of nostalgia, the so-called retro appeal. There is also value in the communal or cultural relationships that the brand has built over its lifetime. Finally, there are values on an individual level that relate to the former two other values" (Kozinets 2013). That value is a potent source of pop culture magic because it's shared across the consciousness of every person that has been exposed to that pop culture, and more importantly, because of what it evokes from people.

Retro magic is powered through nostalgia, the sentimental feelings that you may feel if you look at a game of Candy Land you used to play, or a G.I. Joe "action figure" that you imagined shot rays of light at C.O.B.R.A. commandos and miraculously always emerged victorious. This feeling of nostalgia, of memories past, can be used to empower your pop culture workings. When pop culture artifacts are included it provides a tangible means of connecting with those memories and drawing them as a source to fuel your working. You aren't just drawing on your memories, but also all the attention and memories of other people who have ever loved that particular pop culture, as well as with how they identify with that pop culture.

Retro pop culture sometimes takes the form of a cult focus, with a dedicated group of people retaining interest in it (as an example, old school *Teenage Mutant Ninja Turtles*), or it can be a pop culture technology such as the original Lite Brite or Atari 2600, which brings back nostalgia for those who had such toys as a kid. You also see this with cult films such as *Rocky Horror Picture Show*, *Firefly* and the *Serenity* movie, *Dr. Who*, or *The Big Lebowski*, which have cult followings that not only watch the show or movie, but also seek to reenact it through costume play or through holding events related to events that occurred in the shows. These reenactments serve as a form of ritual that connects the people involved to the pop culture they love. It can also be a source of pop culture magic, as I'll explore further below.

Admittedly new forms of *Lite Brite*, *G.I. Joe* and *Teenage Mutant Ninja Turtles* exist, but the pop culture magician who is picky doesn't need to work with the new forms[4]. The use of older, more established forms of pop culture is a way of steeping yourself in power structures that have a bit more permanence than current pop culture has. Hardcore fans of the original Transformers cartoon series, for instance, will write fan fiction about characters from that show (ignoring the other series), in a continuation of the tradition of the Transformers. However, even a continuation of older traditions mutates and changes, being more than meets the eye. Fan fiction writings deal not with the black and white universe of the Transformers series, but rather gray issues, giving more depth to the series and fleshing out the development of the characters. Naturally, fan fiction such as this is useful to plunder when creating pop culture entities or working with pre-existing ones, as it enables you to see how the fans (the believers in the entity) perceive said entity. Being a fan also helps and may create some intriguing interactions for you, particularly because as you change the pop culture entity, it will likely respond and interact with you on a deeper level.

---

[4] Not to mention that the newer versions just may not quite capture the spirit of the original versions.

Besides steeping yourself in pop culture past there is also the advantage of raising nostalgia in the everyday person. People who happen to have an original Lite Brite can easily incorporate it into pop culture workings. You could use it to create a sigil, setting up a shape with specific colors that could be turned on and charged by both the electricity and nostalgic attention people give to the Lite Brite. Alternately, you could use the Lite Brite to evoke a goetic demon or some other type of entity, again using both the electricity and the attention people give it. To empower your working, place it in a window where people can see it and watch as people stop to look at the design, reminiscing over the past, giving attention and power to the magic you've employed with the aid of old technology. Or if you're doing a group ritual, put the symbol at the center of your working. The nostalgia that people who remember Lite Brite feel will help power the ritual, and charge the symbol on the Lite Brite.

You could also put pictures on your website of "classic" pop culture that you've chosen to use in your workings. For example, you could create an altar to specific pop culture characters you are working with, such as the *Teenage Mutant Ninja Turtles,* and then take pictures of it to share on your website, tumblr blog, or wherever else you post[5]. The pictures can be used to evoke a sense of nostalgia from other people when they view your site, which will feed the intent of your working. At the same time, creating such an altar can also be useful for working with the pop culture entities you are working with, as well as charging specific workings you are working with them on.

Another magical practice you can do with retro or current pop culture characters involves writing fan fiction hypersigils. Hypersigils are narrative stories that also function as magical workings by incorporating the magician's desire into the story, or other creative process being used, and essentially use the writing (and peoples reading of it) to manifest the desired result into reality. William S. Burroughs is probably the most notable

[5] Make sure you pay attention to copyright law when putting pictures up on the web. While most companies generally don't care about a few pictures on a noncommercial website, some, such as Disney, have been known to go ballistic over small details.

user of hypersigils, though the term wasn't in use at the time he used writing for magic. He would create cut-ups and write stories that manifested possibilities into the world and into his life directly, using phrases, characters and events that evoked what he wanted. Grant Morrison, who coined the term, created a hyper sigil with his series *The Invisibles*, and you can find similar narrative workings in the works of other writers, sometimes intentional and sometimes not. The hypersigil writing is done as a way to interact with characters and craft a narrative reality that embodies the magical working you seek to manifest.

Write a fan fiction hypersigil that blends your favorite retro pop culture characters (or current pop culture characters) into your magical practice using a combination of words, images and video, or just words alone. A fan-fiction based hypersigil allows the writer to interact with characters in a meaningful and magical manner, manifesting the characters and motifs into the life of the writer. One person I know writes Dr. Who fan fiction extensively and has, as a result, interacted with the numerous incarnations of the Doctor through his/her writing. S/he has encountered them as entities that can be worked through the medium of her writing. S/he's even noted that the people s/he tends to date usually have a similar clothing style to a particular version of Doctor Who and adopt similar mannerisms in their actions and words. Clearly the writing has opened a path of manifestation for Dr. Who to show up in this person's life.

The hypersigil allows the writer to create a narrative working with the character(s), setting and plot that s/he wants to use. With a retro magic hypersigil you'd want to be fairly creative and focused on mixing in the purpose of the hypersigil with the story. While some authors try to adhere to canon (i.e. established protocols about the history of the character(s) and the universe they are in), others are more speculative, so feel free to push the boundaries as needed, though not so far as to lose all connection to the pop culture in question. Post it on an appropriate fan fiction site and let people reading it charge the hypersigil up.

You don't need to limit hypersigils to writing, and for that matter you don't have to limit them to retro pop culture characters. There is plenty of fan fiction out there on contemporary characters and you could create a hypersigil out of whatever content you produced with those characters. My reasoning for including hypersigils in this chapter is because I find that some of the ways older pop culture is kept alive is through how fans choose to create their own content. And the creation of that content is in and of itself, a magical act. Nonetheless pop culture magicians can actually use the content to charge and fire their own workings, as well as continue engagement with characters they love that have established a meaningful relationship with them.

Premakes

One of the interesting ways that people create retro pop culture content is through premakes. Premakes are videos made as if they were from the 1940s or 50s. They typically take current or recent movies and remake them into older trailers with actors from the 40s and 50s. It's an interesting approach that combines themes and pop culture with beloved actors from the past, and in the process creates new characters in familiar pop culture settings. The premake a fan makes could be another example of a hypersigil, where a narrative is created around the characters and themes the fan chooses. You could even insert the name of an entity or sigil into the premake as a way to get people to charge and fire your magical working.

The difference between premakes and Hollywood's latest retro rebranding trend is that what fans are creating is not an attempt to start the brand anew for the purposes of making money, but rather a way to fit cherished actors into movies and themes that they were never in, but which fans wish they had been in. Nonetheless corporations understand the value of drawing on the past:

> Hollywood remakes and refreshes old franchises just as old brands are continually extended and renewed. Alongside, popular consumer culture and fan culture merge effortlessly one into the other, their possibilities continuously expanded and technologically accelerated. Old comic book characters become refreshed into new motion picture characters—

> think of the Joker in The Dark Knight as a prototypical entertainment retrobrand. Characters such as Heath Ledger's Joker become the basis for new action figures with Ledger's face, new puzzles with his form, new trading cards and games in which his image of the Joker becomes the Joker (of this time, just as Cesar Romero was the chillingly antagonistic Joker of another, now bygone, era)... The example simply shows that the true retro revival is never over. This refashioning and revaluing, if successful, continues just as the gift continues to circulate—ever added to, never put down for very long. It may stop and rest, but it is ever subject to rediscovery. In our contemporary culture, the main source of energy and invention is in the past. And, in the moment of rediscovery itself, there is value (Kozinets 2014).

Pop culture is continuously recycled and recreated. Even the various themes that show up across shows, movies, comics and other media are repurposed from other content and remade as a way to capture the imagination of the people while at the same time keeping the brand and characters alive. And the act of rebranding can interest people in the older versions of pop culture characters, which is one of the aims of rebooting a franchise. It simultaneously creates new content for fans and inspires interest in the older content.

If you were to create a premake video as a retro pop culture magic working, you might do it with the purpose of stirring up nostalgia for the actors, the characters, and the themes in order to use that nostalgia as a source of power for your workings, or as a way to connect to the actors/characters involved in order to work with them as entities. Alternately, as I mentioned above, you might create a hypersigil out of the narrative story as a way of manifesting specific possibilities into reality through the narrative and people's interest and participation in it. Your magical working would start with the creation of the film, which in the case of a premake often involves taking clips from existing films and splicing them together to create a trailer or story of sorts. In a later chapter we'll explore how hypersigils can be applied to other types of fan films, but what's fascinating with a premake is that you are already drawing on pre-existing material and appropriating it for the purposes of a new story, which is essentially layered over the story the content was drawn from. As you would get ready to create a premake, you would align your intention to connect with the characters and story with the manifestation of a specific possible and then use the act of creation to start the magical work, while using peoples' attention, comments, likes, etc., to fuel and fire the magical work.

Retrogames

Retro games is another phenomenon of pop culture that has shown up in recent years. Retro games are video games created in the style of the 8 and 16 bit video game graphics that were used for games in the late 80's and early 90s or are the actual video games, now available on the latest platforms in their original formats (Jenkins, Ford, & Green 2013). In *Pop Culture Magick* I discussed how video games could be used for practical magic. You could use the attention and focus as well as the pushing of buttons as a form of practical magical work, if you were trying to charge and fire sigil. That is just one application of video game magic, and with retro games we have another possible avenue to explore.

Much as with any other retro pop culture magic activity, when you play a video game from long ago you are tapping into the nostalgia associated with the game, as well as the energy of all the other previous players who focused on trying to win the game. Additionally you are connecting with the characters in the games, which have their own identity. Even if you are playing a game that has been created in the retro game style, there is still a connection that evokes that period of game play. You can work with that connection, with the energy of the previous players, as well as the characters.

If you're working with the characters, then you'll work with them in a similar manner to how to you would work with any pop culture entity. In the case of tapping into the energy of all the other players, plus your past memories, you can set the working up so that when you play the game, you draw on your memories and the energy of the players and set it up so that when you win the game, the magical working is released. You link the specific desired result to the game and use the combination of your own effort and the effort of others to put power into the manifestation of the result. Each push of the button, each interaction with character, each battle feeds the magical working. The winning of the game releases all of that effort into the manifestation of the result.

Conclusion

Retro magic allows us to access the fun of being a child again. The sense of humor and fun that goes into creating a magical working with a Lite Brite sigil or an action figure entity can bring back memories of more innocent times. When I see a G.I. Joe action figure I'm always reminded of the hours I'd spend setting up battle lines and creating a story around them. While I probably wouldn't do that now, working with the G.I. Joe character allows me to tap into those memories of the enjoyment I experienced when I did play with those toys.

We should never rule out the power of emotions, and in particular the initial reaction a person has to an experience. Reactions are automatic triggers, with a lot of built-in emotion to them. That emotion (energy in motion) can feed the magical working. I make substantial use of emotion, both my own and others', as well as attention and belief. The impact that these have on reality can never be underestimated. Emotions equal involvement on some level, because they are prompted by what the person is experiencing. Emotions play a significant role in magic in general and certainly with pop culture magic of any type because of how we identify with the characters that we love. Retro pop culture magic relies on the power of nostalgia, of people falling in love once again with some cherished pop culture from their past.

It's important to remember that retrobranding doesn't simply reboot a pop culture character or series. It also creates new value and markets for pre-existing content that had become static, but now is renewed through the rebranding that occurs (Jenkins, Ford, & Green 2013). This should matter to us as pop culture magicians, because when retro becomes popular once again, it drives new energy and attention toward the pop culture we love and allows us to further empower our pop culture magic workings as a result. What is old becomes new once again, and the power of nostalgia that is evoked in the rebranding nonetheless calls our attention to the beloved versions of pop culture characters we know, allowing us to rediscover why we loved them and how they can become magical allies in our ongoing spiritual work.

Exercises

1 Identify a form of retro magic and incorporate it into your magical practice. How effective, in your opinion, is nostalgia as a form of empowering this version of magic? What makes nostalgia effective or ineffective?

2 What other technology (besides Lite Brite) that is "old school" could you use for retro magic? For instance, could you an Atari or Nintendo game system (or whatever counts as old school for you—Pong, anyone?)? What advantages might these systems have over using contemporary technology for your pop culture magic?

3 These days you can sometimes find t-shirts and other items with retro pop culture characters on them, such as a *My Little Pony* or a *Care Bear*. How might you incorporate these symbols into a pop culture working? What advantages and/or disadvantages do you think would occur by using these retro images as opposed to more traditional symbolism?

4 Some retro pop culture, such as *My Little Pony*, has current incarnations as well. Which version would you work with? Is one version better than another, and if so why?

5. Create a hypersigil, with retro pop culture characters or actors. What version of character would you use? How will you empower the working via the characters you are using?

Chapter 5: Pop Culture Deities, Mythology and Older Cultures

Part of what makes pop culture so interesting is the interaction people have with pop culture characters. A character is never just a 2 dimensional being, but instead is brought to life through our interactions with it, if it doesn't already exist objectively. Add in the fact that older cultures, with their own distinctive beings, also tend to resurface in contemporary culture, and that international pop culture is continuing to become more available. What we end up having is a culturally diverse array of pop culture deities to work with.

In working with pop culture deities, I've found it useful to explore different models that can provide insight into how best to work with them. In this chapter we'll explore some of those models, both in respect to specific types of pop culture deities, and to pop culture magic in general. We'll also examine how to leverage it in our lives and spiritual practice. No model is absolutely correct. At best they are a description of what is being worked with and can point the way toward having experiences that shape your spiritual life. In some cases, as we'll see, work with a pop culture deity can possibly lead to working with more traditional deities.

What's Old is New Again

One of the most fascinating trends I've observed in pop culture magic is how traditional deities such as the Greek and Norse gods have infiltrated and become part of pop culture. These are the two obvious examples, but you can find other traditional deities as well. The stories told in pop culture about these deities aren't replicas of the traditional myths, so some people will feel those stories aren't authentic stories about the deities because they aren't rooted in the original traditional versions. I disagree and think that pop culture stories are part of the continuing interaction these deities have with us. They recognize that if they want to stay relevant, it's useful to show up in pop culture in order to attract more people to them.

When this occurs in pop culture it's known as iconotropism, which is where icons remain the same, but they are troped in the interpretation that one culture places over another. The gods may be kept, but the existing culture tropes them within the context of that culture (personal communication with R. J. Stewart). In other words, when a traditional deity shows up in pop culture, it shows up and adapts to the context of that cultural interaction. This isn't to say that the pop culture troped version is more valuable than the traditional deity, but if anything can be a gateway that leads to further interest in the traditional versions of the deity, because people will often end up researching characters they are interested in to find out about their origins:

> If you think Marvel's treatment of Thor, Loki, and the entire Norse pantheon doesn't have an impact on the way people approach those beings in religious practice, I think you're willfully ignoring reality. How could it not? The number of people who know of Thor through Chris Hemsworth dwarfs those who have read the myth of Thor and Loki's visit to Útgarð. Some of those people will come into Heathen religions because of that first contact. The conservative nature of Heathenry ensures that anyone who first discovers the Norse gods through pop culture will immediately learn the differences between modern media and ancient sources, but it can't help but have an impact. (Scott 2014).

Pop culture versions of traditional deities provide a gateway to older cultures and as a result shouldn't be dismissed. And at the same time, some people may find it easier to work with modern versions of traditional deities because of the context they are situated in. Nonetheless, I think that the Norse, Greek, and other gods who have infiltrated pop culture aren't so picky as to not work with someone who shows interest in them. More importantly, I think they recognize they can influence the interest of the readers, especially younger readers (Ward 2015).

The majority of pop culture material that comes out featuring older deities is typically geared toward kids and teenagers, who are more open to exploring alternate spiritualties by virtue of their age and desire to become their own people. Even in cases where material is created for older audiences such as the God of War video game series, you still nonetheless have interaction that is partially designed to foster additional interest in the featured Deities, using pop culture as a medium to accomplish that result.

Exercise

What classic deities have shown up in your pop culture of interest (if any) and how have your worked with them? Did that work lead to a deeper relationship with those deities and if so how did that manifest?

Myths and Pop Culture

I consider pop culture to be a form of mythology. True, it's a relatively recent form of mythology that has shown up in the last couple of centuries, a contemporary mythology, if you will, that is based on the experiences people have now, but nonetheless a mythology that seeks to simultaneously entertain and educate us about our world and why things are the way they are.

It could be argued that pop culture isn't mythology because there isn't a specific religious or spiritual aspect associated with it, but I'd argue that what makes something mythology is the choice the reader/viewer makes in terms of ascribing meaning to that mythology. Nonetheless it's also worth noting that mythology from older cultures was never sponsored by a corporation. Hills points out the following about celebrity, and I think it can be applied to pop culture in general: "Possibly the most significant difference between the icon and or celebrity and the cult icon relates to the distinction between commodity manufacture and contingency. The celebrity is often considered to be a synthetic creation, made for the purposes of audience appeal and subject to the transient and fleeting touch of 'fame' (Hills 2002 p. 138). Pop culture is also a synthetic creation of sorts, in the sense that it is sponsored by corporations.

Nonetheless, while corporations may sponsor pop culture, the actual content is created by a person or people who have a distinct vision of the story they want to tell.

The key word here is story. The pop culture characters are part of a story. That story is used to provide context, while entertaining and educating the people. However there is also something else significant about myths. Myths connect us to the imagination, specifically sacred imagination. The way imagination is treated in contemporary society is that it is for children. However that approach to imagination is inaccurate and causes us to lose touch with a fundamental part of our spiritual selves and overall identity. Imagination, when approached, as a sacred part of life, allows us to connect with mythology as not just stories, but as a way for us to work with our imagination and make it an active part of our magical work. The imagination opens us up to have encounters with the otherworld when we treat it as the sacred tool it is:

> The only concern of the Primary Imagination...is with sacred beings and events. They cannot be anticipated...they must be encountered. Our response to them is a passion of awe. It may be terror or panic, wonder or joy, but it must be awe-ful. Auden's sacred beings and events are our daimons, archetypal images which Imagination generates. They are chiefly personifications but Imagination can cast its spell over any object so that we see it ensouled, as a presence, as if it were a powerful living being...Imagination is independent and autonomous; it precedes and underpins mere perception; and it spontaneously produces those images - gods, daimons and heroes - who interact in the unauthored narratives we call myths. (Harpur 2002, p 36).

Imagination brings to life the characters we interact with, regardless of whether they star in the ancient myths of Greece or in the night time television shows of contemporary culture. The characters come to life, for those of us who choose to recognize that there is a mythical aspect to them. When we understand that pop culture is mythological in its own right, what it provides us is an understanding of the world. Myths explain why the world is the way it is, or at least the myths from older cultures do. It could be argued that pop culture mythology doesn't really perform that function. However, I think that pop culture mythology, in its own way, does seek to explain why the world is the way it is, as well as how we should respond to the world. Simultaneously, much like older mythology, pop culture mythology introduces the element of the fantastic and challenges us with that element, seeking to also introduce us to what the world could be.

What both the modern mythology of pop culture and the ancient mythology of various cultures have in common is two distinct aspects of mythology. The first aspect is the mythologizing of characters, heroes or villains, and this mythologizing sticks to specific themes:

> A hero does not survive in the collective memory unless he is to some extent mythologized - brought into line by the popular imagination with an archetypal pattern. Imagination always exerts a gravitational pull on historical events, bending them into confabulations, fictions, myths… Myths are naturally conservative, seeking out the archetypal pattern so that whatever elaboration we make on a myth will, if it is not from the mythopoetic imagination, be forgotten. (Harpur 2002, P. 82).

Themes can be specific types of characters, identified as heroes or villains, or they can be specific types of stories such as one where good always win, or where mischievous characters learn a lesson as a result of their mischief, or where a character goes through a cathartic journey that changes him/her. We see these themes show up in mythology and in multiple pop culture works because they are themes we can relate to. Part of the function of the myth, in terms of explaining why the world is the way it is, is also to model the kinds of experiences people need to have in order to change who they are. The myth isn't just explaining why the world is the way it is, but also why people need to go through the experiences they go through as well as how to handle the encounters with the Otherworld that occur as a result of having experiences that fall outside conventional reality.

Exercise

Do you feel that pop culture is a form of mythology? Why or why not?

How could you apply the model of mythology to a given form of pop culture in your work with pop culture Deities and Entities?

What are the potential problems with applying a mythological model to pop culture?

Pop Culture and Daimonic Beings

When I use the word Daimon, I'm not referring to the word demon, but rather to a specific meaning associated with Daimon, namely that Daimons are intermediaries that mediate the essence of the gods, elements, etc., into something we can interact with, and also interact with us in their capacity as intermediaries (Harpur 2002, Harpur 2003, Harpur 2011). Daimons provide a way for us to interact with the Otherworld, and do so in part by taking on the appearance of what we are familiar with (though not always what we are comfortable with). Harpur defines Daimons as:

> They [he's referring to Daimons] were held to inhabit the Soul of the World. They have some remarkable characteristics: firstly, they are always ambiguous, if not downright contradictory. They are both material and immaterial, for example, which is why anthropologists mislead us when they refer to daimons as 'spirits'. They are highly elusive, only caught in glimpses from the corner of the

> eye, if at all. They are shape-shifters. Fleeting, marginal creatures, they prefer to appear in the liminal zones such a bridges, crossroads, and shorelines in the landscape; or in time, at duck, midnight, the summer solstice, or Halloween; or in the mind, between consciousness and unconsciousness, waking and sleeping. In fact, there's no boundary that the daimons do not straddle, including the boundary between fact and fiction, literal and metaphorical (Harpur 2011, p. 29).

Why this is relevant to us is that it could be argued that the encounters we have with pop culture entities and deities are really encounters with Daimons, who've taken on those roles in order to interact with us in a manner that is relevant to us. They may recognize that the easiest way to interact with us is by taking on the form of pop culture because it's something we already identify with. More importantly, doing so allows the Daimons to continue performing their function as intermediaries between this world and the Other World.

Daimons have an integral connection to myths, as they are the representatives of sacred imagination and use myths to provide form to imagination and also to our lives. When we apply this principle to pop culture, we can see how much pop culture shapes our lives. The characters we care about take on a life of their own in our imagination, providing guidance and insights, as well as the occasional adventure. They connect us to the divine within us and around us by allowing us to experience our own lives within a mythical context, which is informed by magic, imagination, and the interaction we have with these characters. What we can take from this is that our interactions with spirituality, pop culture or otherwise, is contextually shaped by what is significant to us, what we connect to through the use of imagination. What we need to understand is that imagination, in this context, is a sacred part of our spiritual power that allows us to develop a deeper meaningful connection with the spirits we work with, but also with what they represent. Daimons, in whatever form they manifest, are representatives of powers that are more primal…they provide guidance to us in order to encounter those powers (Harpur 2011). And I would argue that one interpretation of pop culture magic and entities allows for the idea that a pop culture spirit or daimon could also represent those primal connections, because such beings aren't picky about what form they'll take. What they care about is making sure the connections happen.

Ironically, naysayers who critique the idea of applying the label of Daimon to pop culture entities and deities make a fundamental mistake in understanding the nature of Daimons. They fall into the trap of trying to make them a part of literal reality, defining them into something that is conveniently and safely categorized, instead of opening themselves up to experiencing a different version of reality, which is metaphoric and allows us to fully appreciate the role of imagination in spiritual work. When a literal perspective is applied to spirituality of any type, it attempts to reduce that spirituality and any manifestation of it into the unreal or fictional, but in the process denies a fundamental experience that the majority of people want, which is a connection to the imagination that allows us to experience reality as more than just a three dimensional space with nothing available beyond what is materially available:

> Our trouble is that we have been brought up with a literal-minded worldview. We demand that objects have only a single identity or meaning. We are educated to see with the eye only, in single vision. When the preternatural breaks in upon us, transforming the profane into something sacred, amazing, we are unequipped for it. Instead of seizing on the vision, reflecting on it - writing poetry, if necessary - we react with fright and panic. Instead of countering like with like - that is, assimilating through imagination the complexity of the image presented to us - we feebly telephone scientists for reassurance. We are told we are only 'seeing' things and so we miss the opportunity to grasp that different, daimonic order of reality which

> lies behind the merely literal. (Harpur 2003. P. 89).

I'd argue that pop culture magic provides many of us a way to re-engage our imagination into something sacred that allows us to move beyond the literal and back into the metaphorical experience of reality. We need such metaphorical experiences because they free us from the arid linearity of our modern times. And while there are more traditional avenues to have those experiences, ruling pop culture out ignores a fundamental part of our experiences. By accepting and integrating pop culture mythology as a form of metaphorical experience, we open ourselves to getting in touch with the deeper undercurrents of spiritual connection that underlie pop culture and are waiting to be discovered.

Exercise

What are the advantages and disadvantages of the Daimonic model of working with Pop Culture Entities? How might you apply this model to your work with pop culture magic?

Archetypes and Pop Culture Entities

Some people prefer a psychological approach to dealing with entities, arguing that that they are extensions of ourselves as opposed to objective beings. While I personally don't favor such an approach, I do think it's important to cover this perspective, because some of you will favor it and want to apply it to your pop culture work.

The psychological theory that is overwhelmingly used in magic is Jung's archetype theory. It's a convenient theory that explains deities and entities in general in psychological terms. Jung defines archetypes as, "The archetype is essentially an unconscious content that is altered by becoming conscious and being perceived, and it takes its colour from the individual consciousness in which it happens to appear" (Jung 1990, P. 5). You might note that this definition is somewhat similar to the concept of Daimons, in the sense that the Daimons appear in a form that is relevant to the person. The main difference is that

Daimons are external, objective beings taking on a form, while the archetype is unconscious content that becomes conscious through the use of something the person is familiar with. That distinction is important to note, because the psychological model will argue that any contact with "spirits" is essentially contact with unconscious content that is made conscious by becoming a construct we can interact with. Harpur offers his own interpretation of this distinction, "Daimons and gods are the divine images of archetypes, which come from outside us - that is, from an unconscious that is outside of our conscious lives and that, moreover, cannot even be located with any certainty inside us. It might be, as the Neoplatonists thought, a property of the world itself, like an underlying soul" (Harpur 2011, p. 56). What Harpur is referring to is the collective unconscious of the world. When people interact with archetypes they are living out the myth the archetype embodies in their lives in order to find meaning and make sense of their lives.

Archetypes come from the collective unconscious, which is not comprised of the personal experiences of a person, but rather are the unconscious collection of the overall experiences of humanity and their relationship with primal forces such as the elements, deities, etc., as embodied and manifested through archetypes which mediate these primal forces into forms that people can interact and relate to (Jung 1990). The archetypes can be understood to be images, which Jung explains as follows, "The term 'image' is intended to express not only the form of the activity taking place, but the typical situation in which the activity is released. These images are 'primordial' images in so far as they are peculiar to the whole species, and if they ever 'originated' their origin must have coincided at least with the beginning of the species" (1990, p. 78). Why all of this is relevant to us is because when we use terms such as archetype, collective unconscious or other related concepts to describe our magical workings, we should understand the origin of these words and what the context of use is in order to better to understand how it might affect our own understanding of what we are working with.

Pop culture entities, when framed in the context of archetypes, are the latest versions of archetypes, which nonetheless mediate the same primordial forces that older archetypes mediate. They come in a different form that we can relate to through the context of our modern culture, and use that modern form to help us interact with those primordial forces, or in some cases to bring those forces into our lives to shake us out of our complacency.

Applying a psychological approach to working with pop culture characters can be useful in the sense that it allows us to rationalize working with fictional characters. On the other hand, I also think it can keep us from deeply engaging with said characters because we are still treating them as fictional, instead of being open to the possibility that they may have an objective reality separate from our own.

Exercise

What are the advantages and disadvantages of the psychological -archetypal model of working with pop culture entities? If you've taken this approach to your own work, what have your results been?

My Theories about Pop Culture Spirits

In *Pop Culture Magick*, I developed several theories and practices based around those theories to explain how to work with pop culture spirits. The first theory argued that the characters we encounter in the various media of pop culture are channeled spirits that have reached out and connected to the writer, artist, etc., in order to make us aware of their existence. These pop culture beings have their own existence and universe and they are making the artist and writers a channel of transmission in order to connect with other people and introduce those people to their universe. This theory argues that the various pop culture media we see is depictions of alternate universes which already exist, and which we have access to through the media. While we can't necessarily physically visit those universes, we can interact with the "characters" through magic and vice versa.

Another theory I offered is that pop culture spirits and deities become spirits and deities because of the attention that fans put into them. When you have literally millions of people watching a show, reading a book or comic book or playing a video game, all of that attention and belief translates into energy for the characters that people are into, bringing those characters into a life of their own, similar in some ways to how traditional deities were worshipped. Pop culture magicians can work with that spirit or deity, as well as the energy that is directed to those beings from the fans. It does help if the magician is also a fan, especially because you are dealing with a distinct identity in the form of the pop spirit you are working with.

The attention and belief that people put toward characters can also be extended to actual people. Your actor, celebrity, or musician that is famous has a lot of attention and belief going into them, with all the energy that also creates. It's not a wonder then that sometimes such people go a bit stir crazy because of so much energy being directed toward them. They are their own embodiment of a pop culture entity, and yet I would argue that the musician/celebrity/actor is really a personification, as opposed to the actual person. What that means is that the attention and belief is directed toward the personification, as opposed to the actual person. As we'll explore in the next chapter, it's very important that you are careful in how you might work with an actual person who is a pop culture icon.

Exercise

Have you worked with either of these theories? If so, how have you used them in your work with pop culture spirits? Do you prefer one theory over the other and if so why?

Conclusion

Each of the theories we've explored in this chapter can be used to explain what pop culture spirits and deities are and how they can possibly be worked with. In the next chapter we're going to explore the practical aspects of working with pop culture spirits, and as you'll see any of these theories could be applied. I think it's good to know the theories because it can inform how you might work with a given pop culture character. For example, using the daimonic model will be very different from working with the model where pop culture characters are created from attention and belief. My advice is to examine all theories and consider how you can apply them to your magical work, and then give each one a try. From that you'll be able to discover which theory best applies, or better yet come up with your own!

Chapter 6: Practical Processes for Working with Pop Culture Spirits and Deities

In the previous chapter we covered the different theories that could be applied to working with pop culture deities and spirits. In this chapter, we're going to explore practical applications for working with pop culture spirits and deities, as well as what precautions should be taken. Some of this will cover information I've shared previously in *Pop Culture Magick*, but a lot of what is presented in here is updated to reflect where my own practice has taken me, as well as other people's perspectives on how to work with pop culture spirits and deities.

Precautions to be Taken when Working with Pop Culture Spirits and Deities

When working with pop culture spirits and deities, it's important to take certain precautions in order to get the most out of the work you are doing with these beings. Actually, the same applies to working with traditional Deities and spirits, but I do think that there are some precautions that are exclusive to pop culture magic due to the media and how some of the entities manifest.

Working with Celebrities

A celebrity is a living person who has some degree of fame/notoriety in their profession. A celebrity could be a musician, actor, author, politician, or some other type of person who is well-known in the public. In *Pop Culture Magick*, I explained that if you chose to work with a celebrity it's important to recognize that you are really working with the persona of the person as opposed to the actual person. What this means is that you're working with the public image or branding of the celebrity, which may or may not be the actual person. I also noted that one of the reasons some celebrities possibly go through seemingly radical changes in personality and habits is either because the celebrity is purposely changing their image to stay current, or the person is getting some not so healthy benefits from all the attention and belief that is put toward them (Ellwood 2004).

A person who is famous gets a lot of attention and belief directed toward them, which is its own form of energy, but most people aren't prepared for that kind of energy being sent to them day in and day out. Consequently, some of their actions may be a result of all that attention and belief going to their head and driving them a bit crazy. As a magician, you need to consider whether it's really worth it to expose yourself to what is happening to that celebrity, as well as a consider the ethics of how your magical work might have an effect on the celebrity. Emily Carlin shares the following advice, which I agree with: "Do not suck energy out of your idols; they have enough demands on them already and do not need you making things worse. Also be careful not to project your expectations onto a celebrity. Just because they created your favorite character does not mean they act like or have the values of that character. Celebrities are just people, often charismatic and brilliant people, but still just people." (2015b). If you do choose to work with a celebrity, be certain to build in appropriate safeguards for yourself and that person.

The way you build appropriate safeguards involves first recognizing you are working with the persona of the celebrity as opposed to the actual person. The persona is comprised of all the perceptions people have of that person, plus the marketing around the person, and so it is not quite the same and can be worked without necessarily affecting the actual person. I also recommend creating specific filters that purposely ensure that the working is limited to the persona. In other words, you would create a filter that only directs the magical work toward the persona as opposed to having any of it go toward the actual person of the celebrity. I've done this in the past with a few of my pop culture magic workings and it's allowed me to draw on the energy, attention, belief etc., of the celebrity without unduly affecting that person because the target is the persona.

The Bleed of Characters

The term bleed refers to the concept of identifying with a character, to the point that you immerse your own sense of identity into the character and become that character (what we magicians call invocation) (Gee 2007, Hook 2012, White, Harvianen, & Boss 2012, Gee 2013). If you are invoking a character, you made find yourself identifying with that character to the point that you become possessed or experience this state of bleed, where their identity, perspectives, etc., has an effect on your identity, perspectives, etc. Some might argue that's the point of doing invocation, and I would agree with caveat that it's important to nonetheless make sure that such an experience only lasts for the duration of the magical working and not beyond it.

If you find yourself in a situation where you are identifying with a character to the point of obsession, it might be wise to do a banishment. An alternate problem that can occur is where you invoke a character, but end up having some of their negative behaviors influence you. For example, in *Pop Culture Magick*, I shared the example of invoking Lu Bu from *Dynasty Warriors*. Lu Bu is a great warrior, but he is also arrogant and rash and when I invoked him some of those behaviors influenced my own. Eventually I realized what was happening and modified my working with Lu Bu so I only drew on his positive characteristics. It can be very easy to get caught up in working with a character you like, but you need to keep proper perspective.

Rules

Some characters (and worlds as we'll cover later) have specific rules for working with them. For example, Rumplestiltskin from *Once Upon a Time* is happy to work with you, but always has a price. Additionally, any magic he works has its own price (not a paradigm I recommend using for magical work by the way). If you're going to work with him you need to keep those rules in mind, as well as recognize that he'll always try to set up a situation to get an advantage over you.

Another example of specific rules involved with working with characters can be found in comic books. Heroes, anti-heroes, and villains have their own particular sets of rules that need to be considered when working with them. What works for a hero won't work with a villain and visa versa, because they have different moral codes, needs, energy, etc. (Ellwood 2004, Carlin 2014b). Carlin points out the following about working with villains:

> And then there's the true villains - The Joker, Darth Vader, Loki, Malificent. I adore villains and I tend to work with them a lot. Yes, I like to play with fire, but you should know that about me by now. Working with villains is just like working with anti-heroes, but much much hairier. Villains have baggage, lots and lots of baggage, and that carries over into the energy that's available surrounding them. Their energy is strong, often stronger than that of the heroes that fight them, but it's often tainted. It's the nature of a villain (in everything but horror movies) to ultimately lose the battle and that inevitable failure can, potentially, affect your working if you're not extremely careful. When I work with villains I tend to utilize just one or two qualities that the villain embodies. For example, utilizing Loki's ability to talk anyone into just about anything or the Joker's ability to disrupt established patterns (no matter what the cost or consequences). Villains also tend to have more of a mind of their own, so you must be extremely precise when outlining your intent in using them. Give the mind of a villain an inch and it will take ever so much more than a mile. I mean it, be careful! (Carlin 2014b)

The point is that it's important to know what the rules are for working with given characters. Not knowing the rules can create potential issues in your magical work and show up in your life in ways you don't want.

In the chapter on working with corporations I discussed how the culture and rules of the culture dictate how you work with the corporation. The same is true with characters and the worlds they live in. Know the rules and you know how to work the characters you want to work with, as well as what they expect from you. A given pop culture universe and the characters within it will have their particular rules which influence how they can be worked with while giving you an idea of the consequences if you break those rules.

Versions

Emily Carlin points out that pop culture characters can have multiple versions of the character and that what works with one version might not work with another because of how the character changes. She points out the following about living versus static characters and versions:

> You also need to decide if you want to work with a living character or a static one. When I say a living character I mean a character whose canon is still evolving - particularly characters in active series where new material is constantly being put out into the world. Living characters are still evolving and changing, so you have to keep potential changes to their natures in mind when you work with them. It's slightly easier to work with a static character, like one from a completed series or a standalone film or book. The character of Gandalf isn't going to be changing much, if at all, (even with new movies being produced) because the canon of his character is firmly etched in the works of Tolkien. You know exactly what you're getting with a static character, thus making it easier to know who they might behave magickally. Either way, know the version of the character you want to work with as thoroughly as possible so you know what you're getting yourself into. (Carlin 2014a).

I'd argue that even static characters can change…fan fiction is a great example of that, wherein fans write about characters and introduce their own versions of those characters. If that fan fiction gains some steam with other fans, that version of the character can become a viable version to work with.

Characters that are "live" do evolve. For example the character of Deadpool that was first introduced in the *New Mutants* series is quite different from the current version of Deadpool. When you want to work with a character it can be useful to do some research into what version you want to work with that is going to best fit your needs as well as match up with that version's characteristics and abilities.

An interesting perspective to consider is reflected in characters such as Harry Potter, wherein the version of each iteration is really depicting a person growing up as opposed to just presenting the latest version of a character which is just a different take on that character. The question that arises is whether it's really more advantageous to work with a "younger" version of the character when the character in later books is still essentially the same character. I suppose the same could be argued about different versions of comic book characters, but in the case of Harry Potter the same person is writing about the character over the 7 books that have been written about him, whereas with comic book characters part of what you get is different takes on the characters from different writers.

Offerings

Offerings can play an important role in your work with pop culture characters. The types of offering you make may differ quite a bit from what you'd offer a traditional deity or spirit. If you're working with the *Teenage Mutant Ninja Turtles,* for example, they may want pizza, but they may also want you to watch one of their shows, make an altar to them using action figures of them, or something else to that effect. Alternately, if you're working with characters that are part of a fictional narrative, they may want you to write fan fiction about them. In one case, part of my offering involved playing video games that had the characters in them, with the understanding that the act of playing the game was considered an activity where I was giving them energy through playing the game.

It's important not to judge how the offering is made, but also to be very clear that what you are doing is actually about the offering, as opposed to being done for your enjoyment. With that said, your enjoyment can actually be part of the offering. Just make sure it's what the pop culture character actually wants. It's very important that you honor your part of whatever agreement you make. If the requested payment is that you write fan fiction, then you need to write it and share it and not just expect the pop culture character to perform the requested work you've given it.

Exercise

What are some precautions (or rules) that you take when working with pop culture entities? What precautions that I've shared above do you work with and which ones do you disagree with?

What I've shared about are the precautions I take, or, if you will, the rules I follow. In some cases I learned them through experience, and in other cases I applied other magical systems to what I was doing with pop culture magic and brought the rules with me. However, it's important to experiment and test for yourself whether these precautions apply in your work with pop culture entities.

Purposes for Working with Pop Culture Deities and Spirits

Pop Deities and spirits are typically worked with in either invocation or evocation if you're doing practical magic. If you're developing a system of devotion around the deities, then what appears is usually a form of worship. In the chapter on building pop culture systems of spirituality we'll focus on that topic in further depth. For now though, let's focus on the practical aspects of working with pop culture deities and spirits.

When you choose to work with a deity or spirit, pop culture or otherwise, the usual reason is because that being can do things for you that you might not be able to do yourself, or at least not as efficiently. Additionally, such a being usually has an objective distance from the desired result, which may not be the case for the practitioner. Pop culture deities and spirits have the added benefit of understanding some of the problems a person encounters in a way that more traditional beings may lack because of the context involved. There is no classic deity for cars or other modern technology, but people have come up with the modern versions that are rooted in this culture and time.

How you work with pop culture deities and spirits dictates to some degree what purposes that work will be put toward. Invocation is excellent for the purposes of connecting with the deity or spirit in order to establish a relationship, commune with that being, or learn specific skills from it (taking on specific traits or abilities the pop culture deity or spirit has). Evocation, on the other hand, is focused on manifesting the pop culture deity or spirit externally in order to request that it accomplishes a task for you. That task could be as simple as finding a parking space in a city, or as elaborate as helping you climb the corporate ladder so you can advance your career. Pop culture deities and spirits can also be worked with in relationship to societal causes. Carlin points out that some villain characters are focused on "saving" society by tearing down the established order and prevailing societal mores (2015b). Other beings may reinforce the status quo or stand for certain values.

When you choose to do a working with a pop culture deity or spirit, you need to be very clear about what the desired result is. The more precise you are, the more focused the work and result will be, though you also need to keep in mind that this may go against the nature of a pop culture deity or spirit. For example, the Joker is a chaotic spirit (though he can get very focused when he needs to), and he delights in causing mischief and pain, amongst other things, so working with him is likely not advisable unless you can deal with the fallout. Batman, on the other hand, is very focused, but also very rigid. If your magical working doesn't fit into his code of behavior, then he won't be a good spirit to work with. As you define your desired result, define as well the type of pop culture deity you'll work with to help you accomplish that result. Let's consider in further detail some different types of workings you might do.

Searching for a parking space can be a real pain, especially if you live in a city. Additionally, if you want avoid speeding tickets or just be a safer driver, then it can be useful to work with a pop culture spirit of the roads. Asphaultia and Sped Limt are examples of created entities, designed for the purpose of helping you navigate the road and find parking spaces, but you could also work with Batman, who knows how travel around a city in style and find the right places to park, as well as keep you mindful of the speed limit and other potential hazards so that you don't break the law.

If you need to find hidden information, then working with a pop culture deity that specializes in finding information could be very useful, but make sure you are clear on the ethics of how you will use that information. Sweet, the demon from *Buffy the Vampire Slayer* that makes people sing their painful secrets, won't have an ethical issue if you choose to find secret information about someone you don't like or someone that you hope to manipulate (Carlin 2015b). Batman, on the other hand, would have a definite issue with how you use information he obtains for you. He's an excellent detective, but he also has a moral code and that informs how you would work with him versus Sweet. Nathan Drake from *Uncharted* falls in between both characters. He has a moral code, but he's willing to make certain compromises on finding information, whereas Batman won't.

If you want to get a promotion or raise at your career, working with the corporate spirit of the business could be helpful, but you might also find it useful to work with a pop culture spirit that doesn't have an allegiance to the corporation or the people working in it. In such a case, you also want to think about how you'll get that promotion or raise. Does it involve some trickery or manipulation of sorts or is it more straightforward? Your answer to that question will shape who/what you work with. You might work with a trickster pop culture deity of some type, such as Bugs Bunny, or you might work with a more straightforward by the book kind of pop culture deity, such as Superman. You could work with Frank Underwood from *House of Cards*, but you'll need to watch him carefully because he can be rather underhanded in his work.

If you're an entrepreneurial type then working with Kvothe, the character from Patrick Rothfuss's books could be useful, as could Lex Luthor. You could also work with Leonardo DiCaprio's version of Howard Hughes. In each case, its importance to recognize that the brilliance of the person in business is offset by their eccentricities, which may need to be factored in as you develop your own business and ideas for how to make that business succeed. Dr. Doom could be another pop culture spirit to work with because he's an inventor and he's ambitious and driven, which are good traits to have when owning a business.

Pop culture spirits can be excellent protectors. Superman, for example, can be an excellent protector, but remember he'll likely only come to save the day when you have an actual crisis. The majority of pop culture characters that could fall under the protection category are typically saving the day, and so are useful to work with in the capacity of anticipating possible events and having them arrive, ready to aid you in handling whatever comes your way.

Social causes are another example where you can draw on pop culture characters associated with social causes of their own to support yours. If you're looking to uproot the established order, then working with Ozymandias from the *Watchmen*, or V from *V for Vendetta* can be useful in terms of getting creative ideas and spiritual support for your endeavors. You may also want to think about specific social causes. For example if your social cause is supporting abortion, then Wonder Woman could be a useful ally. If you're focused on racism a character of color such as Fish Mooney from *Gotham*, or Falcon from *Captain America* might be useful allies to work with. Magneto or Charles Xavier (as mutants) could also be useful depending on what your goals are, in terms of how you are addressing racism. Look at a given social cause and think about who you might associate with that cause that could be an ally in your efforts.

Sometimes you may decide it's worth it to curse someone. If that's the case and you decide to enlist some pop culture help, then you might look to work with villains such as Voldemort or Dr. Doom who have no problem with cursing someone. Bear in mind that if you choose to take that route you may need to be able to handle whatever consequences come your way, which could include the villain turning on you. Of course if you make the right payment, the villain may stay loyal, but part of that is dependent on the moral code (or lack thereof) of the villain. Plan accordingly and use caution if you choose to curse someone.

If you need to do healing for yourself or other people, then working with a pop culture spirit such as Gregory House, from *House, M.D.* or a character from *Grey's Anatomy* could be useful. If it's a case of healing on an emotional level then Tohru Honda from *Fruits Basket* might be a useful character to work with because of her ability to help people communicate with each other and work through their various traumas. Remember that while you can work with these characters to help you in healing work, they shouldn't be substitutes for going in and seeing qualified professionals if you have medical or mental health needs.

Pop culture spirits, much like more traditional spirits, can also be teachers, revealing specific knowledge and information that pertains to their area of expertise. If there's something you want to learn, try working with a pop culture spirit that you'd associate with the information you are looking for. That spirit will be able to direct you toward resources and information you are looking for, or work with you directly to learn the information.

Exercise

I've shared some examples of pop cultures that could be worked with, but there are plenty of others you can work with. Think of the pop culture you like. Who would you work with as a pop culture spirit? What is the purpose you would associate with that spirit? What precautions would you need to take?

How to Invoke or Evoke a Pop Culture Spirit

The invocation and evocation of pop culture spirits isn't substantially different from how you would invoke or evoke a traditional spirit, but there are certain details that need to be considered when doing either type of magical operation. When you invoke or evoke a traditional spirit, you typically use a symbol associated with the spirit as a way of making contact. You might provide an offering that the spirit would like, and you may use specific tools and equipment as part of the process of invoking or evoking the spirit. The same applies to pop culture spirits, but you need to use what is relevant to that spirit, which may differ from what would be used to work with a traditional spirit.

Pop culture characters may or may not have symbols associated with them. In the case of Batman or Superman you have specific symbols, and for that matter specific colors associated with each character. The colors and symbols make it easy to invoke those characters, but if you're working with a pop culture character that doesn't overtly have a symbol associated with it, you might need to get creative. Dr. Who doesn't have an overt symbol that a person might work with, but there are thematic elements such as the Tardis, Sonic Screwdriver, and clothing that a given version of Dr. Who wears that can be used. The key to figuring out how to invoke or evoke a pop culture character is to look at the thematic elements of the character.

If you can use a symbol to invoke or evoke a pop culture spirit, then by all means go ahead and use that symbol. If you don't have a symbol then work with the thematic aspects of the pop culture. If I were to invoke one of the Doctors, I would dress up like the doctor and use the costume as part of the process of invoking that version. If I were going to evoke the Doctor then I would get one of the sonic screwdriver toys and use it as part of the magical working to evoke the doctor. By using thematic aspects of the pop culture I create the necessary rapport needed for doing an invocation or evocation.

Part of what drives invocation and evocation is your ability to identify with the pop culture, to make it part of your identity and your universe so that it can have a presence to work through. Using the thematic aspects of the pop culture is part of how you identify with it, but part of it is also your choice to believe in that pop culture universe and see it as a viable otherworld through which you can connect with the pop culture spirits you want to work with. If you want to work with Dr. Who, you need to identify with the Doctor enough to enable him to have a presence in your life.

Another way to build rapport with the pop culture spirits you wish to invoke or evoke is create specific altars or shrines for them in your house. A Dr. Who altar might have a sonic screwdriver on it, a replica of the Tardis, and posters of Dr. Who around it. Additionally, you might make offerings to Dr. Who based on what is communicated to be appropriate, when you first connect with whichever version (or all of them) you work with.

As you can see, what I'm describing here isn't different from how you would work with a traditional deity or spirit. The main difference is the context, which is based on the theme or brand of the pop culture. Keeping that information in mind when doing your invocation or evocation will make the working more effective, as well as any other magical work you do around that pop culture.

Exercise

Think of a pop culture spirit you would like to invoke or evoke. What would you need to draw on in order to invoke or evoke that spirit? What brand or thematic information do you need to include in your magical working? What type of pop culture altar would you create and what would you put on the altar?

Conclusion

Working with pop culture spirits is easier in some ways then working with more traditional spirits and deities, mainly because we have easier access to whatever we need to work with those spirits. Additionally, there is a context with pop culture spirits that can make them more relevant. At the same time, not all pop culture spirits have the staying power of more traditional spirits and deities. Pop culture comes and goes, and unless the pop culture in question is continually being added to, at some point it can fade to obscurity, especially if there isn't much of a fan base to support it. Part of what sustains a given pop culture isn't just the official creators of that pop culture, but also the fans. While J. K. Rowling may or may not write another book about Harry Potter, there is plenty of fan fiction being created that helps to sustain interest in Harry Potter. Some might argue that fan fiction isn't the same as the work developed by the person who is officially the creator or inheritor of a particular pop culture, but I'd argue that fan fiction is in some ways a devotional act of worship, driven by the love of the characters. If that's not a viable means of continuing to keep pop culture spirits relevant, I don't know what is.

Pop culture magic is shaped by how relevant a given pop culture is. *Buffy the Vampire Slayer* was much more relevant a decade ago when the show was still being produced, as well as several spin off shows. There were also books, comics, and video games being produced at that time. Now the series is still relevant, but not to the same extent because nothing new is being produced to feed that pop culture universe. Instead what sustains it is the fans, and their continued interest in watching the shows, reading the books, and producing their own content. If you're not a fan of the show, you won't relate to that universe.

Buffy could become more relevant again if the show is ever remade. For example, in the 1990's *Star Trek The Next Generation* revitalized the Star Trek industry and created new fans, increasing interest in both the original series and the new ones. Currently Star Trek is on a hiatus (other than the occasional movie), but when something new is produced that relevance will surge and get new fans. You can see this upswing starting to occur for Star Wars with the new movie coming out in December 2015 (at the time of this writing). My point is that pop culture spirits are partially made more or less relevant based on what is being produced or not produced around those characters. This aspect of pop culture shouldn't stop us from working with a pop culture character that we like, which may not be that relevant to most people, but it does inform how people overall become fans of pop culture and how a given pop culture universe and characters become relevant to more people or stay relevant to the diehard fans.

Chapter 7: Role Playing Games, Identity, and Magic

Role playing games occupy an interesting intersection in pop culture magic. In a role playing game (RPG) you have a created universe with specific rules in place that dictate what can and can't be done by players, as well as by the omnipotent game master who can make changes. Additionally, players create their own characters, or in some cases work with pre-created characters, that nonetheless can become extensions of the player and, as such, have a hybrid status of being an aspect of the player and a pop culture entity. Finally, everyone involved needs to invest enough of themselves into the story in order to make it and the characters come alive.

Magically, role playing games provide opportunities to experiment with rules and principles of how things ought to work, while also allowing the people involved to work with their identities in novel ways that can change how they show up in life when not involved in the game. I also think you can set magical workings up in such a game and have those workings extend outward into the rest of your life through the flexibility of identity. A significant part of the magic of role playing games is found in the act of creating and telling the story:

> The desire to construct narratives is also inherent to the human experience. We formulate stories in order to make sense of our reality, designing narrative arcs in a linear fashion…what we define as the conscious Self is produced through a complex method of filtration and narratization. We highlight key moments of significance and attempt to string them together in terms of some sense of causal logic. These narratives teach us where we have been and indicate where we might be headed. We can also learn about ourselves by vicariously experiencing the narratives of others, both fictional and non-fictional…We enact these stories in an attempt to understand the

> intricacies of human experience through the examinations of constructed sequences of events and emotional interactions. These narratives aid us in making meaning of our own lives and instruct us on the complexities and potentialities of life. They also provide models for us to either embody or avoid, depending on our reaction to the personalities and events presented by the story line. (Bowman 2010, P. 13).

The narrative aspect of role playing games plays a significant role in the magical work a person can do with the game, because the story is a place where a person can experiment with reality in a manner that puts disbelief aside in favor of belief and consequently opens the door to possibilities turning into realities. While a framework is provided for the story to occur in, the story is nonetheless a creation of the people involved in playing the game, and as such is unique to that group of people. The act of creating and playing in the story becomes a ritual, and ultimately a form of mythology for the people involved (Bowman 2010, Torner and White 2012).

Each role playing world comes with its own mythology. For example, if you are playing Star Wars role playing game, then you are interacting with the mythology of Star Wars. If you are playing Vampire the Masquerade, then you are dealing with that RPG's mythology. The story that your group creates becomes part of that mythology, though only to the extent of the group itself and anyone else you share it with. However, that created mythology can be useful for pop culture magic workings that you do, because it brings the group together and creates rapport, which is always useful for magical work.

Part of how that magical work may occur is through the actual characters that are created. You can think of RPG characters in one of two ways. The first way is to think of a character as a thoughtform you've created. You've written about the character, created a history and life for it, and even given it specific attributes. This is similar to creating a magical entity. You can even set it up so that the character performs specific roles for you in a magical context, such as being a healer or protector (Carlin 2014a). As we've already covered how to work with pop culture spirits in previous chapters, I'm going to focus on the second approach to doing magical work with RPG characters.

The second way you could approach a character is as an aspect of your identity that you take on whenever you play the game. I'll admit that I find this model to be intriguing, not the least because of the potential it can offer for identity alteration. This approach to role-playing is enabled through a person's ability to immerse their own identity into that of the character, allowing the character's identity to influence their own (similar to invocation). Identity alteration, in RPGs, helps players empathize with other people, because they essentially become another person, and thus better understand the motivations and choices other people make (Bowman 2010, Fuist 2012). The act of creating the character can involve the player doing research on history and culture, as well getting the right costuming effects to be used in order to take on the persona of the character (more so in LARPs than in other types of role play). That work isn't the creation of a magical entity, so much as it's the immersion of a person's identity into the identity of the character:

> Immersion into alternate worlds is an alteration of consciousness; the individual begins to view his or her self differently when projecting different or exaggerated personality traits. Even when portraying an identity exceptionally different from the Actual self-concept, the player must find a point of identification with the 'alter' and manifest his/her behaviors accordingly. Repeated immersion further solidifies these personas into more tangible mental forms. (Bowman 2010, P. 139).

The adoption of a different identity provides the player a chance to be someone else, to act differently, even to access skills s/he would otherwise not have. And this can carry over into the regular life of the person so that s/he can call on the identity of the character to help them be more confident or approach a situation differently than they normally would (Bowman 2010, Fuist 2012). What we have with role playing game characters is more than just another pop culture spirit. We have a way to use identity to access aspects of ourselves that are otherwise ignored or not worked with, unless an environment is provided that is separate from the realities of everyday life.

Role players who immerse themselves into the identity of the character might argue that they aren't really accessing a part of themselves, but becoming an entirely new person. In my opinion, either approach can be used if you decide to utilize role playing for the purposes of magical work. An essential aspect of immersion is the ability of the player to empathize with the inner experiences of the character and the world the character is part of (Lukka 2014). The process for immersion is described in the following passage:

> In role-playing games, the first contact to immersion often comes from reading the game materials or the character. The player creates an internal model of the character, the goal to be pursued. Then, the player imagines the diegesis through the eyes of the character. Using the theory of mind, the player pictures the reactions of the character to fictional events: how do they feel and think about the state of the world, and how do they relate to others. This self-suggestive interplay, interaction, between the player, character and the diegesis sets the stage for immersion. The player guides their attention to the internal and external elements reinforcing the changed perspective such as the game environment, other players pursuing immersion, and alternative patterns of thinking. The less external factors there are reinforcing immersion, the more important are the inner factors. As immersion grows deeper, the player is required to use less and less effort and energy trying to consciously guide their attention: when immersion is sufficient it will uphold itself and the player is only required to correct this process when they become aware that immersion has decreased. When the player is immersed, they

> lock their perspective to that of the character and attempt to uphold the diegetic reality. (Lukka 2014)

The immersed player becomes the character for the duration of the role playing experience. Ideally the person doesn't go out of character in any way that can be avoided. The character's identity encompasses the identity of the person and opens up some intriguing possibilities for magical work.

How Immersion and Magic Can Work Together

Role playing games call on the player to suspend disbelief and enter into a world where they then take part in adventures of some type or another. Whether you are LARPing (Live Action Role Playing), playing a tabletop game, or using figurines on a board, what you need to bring to the game is your willingness to become the character. I'd argue that if you are intent on using role-playing as a way to do a magical working, then the very first magical act is the invocation of the character.

How you invoke yourself into the character may be somewhat dependent on the type of role playing game. If you're playing a LARP, then your process of invocation will likely involve a costume that you'll use to get into character, but it could also involve a change in accent and even how you hold your body. You might even create a specific anchor[6] that you use to change your identity into that of the character.

If you're playing with figurines, then you might use the figurine for your character as a house for the identity. When you touch that figurine, you'd invoke the identity into yourself in order to become the character. As mentioned above you might also use a change in accent or other aspects of yourself to help you with the process of taking on the identity of the character.

If you're playing a tabletop game without figurines, but with a character sheet, then you might invest the identity in the character sheet. When you start to play and you pick up the character sheet, that's the moment the invocation starts. And again, an anchor or props can also be useful. Most important

[6] An anchor is a neuro-linguistic programming technique where you use a gesture to call up a state of consciousness.

with all of the above types of RPGs and invocations is the name of the character. The name is the power behind the identity and the true means of assuming the identity. So when you get ready to play the character, to become the character, then using the name is a way for you to invoke that identity, used in tandem with an anchor and whatever other tools you have on hand that help you become the character.

Once you've invoked the character and become that character, it's time to evoke the RPG world. The RPG world is evoked in order to help with the process of immersion into the character, and for that matter into the magical work that will be done in the RPG world. The evocation of the RPG world is created by moving participants into a different relationship with the space and time they are in, much like what happens when you do magical workings. This different space and time could be considered a Temporary Autonomous Zone (T.A.Z.) or a Chronotope. Either term works, as long as you understand that what you are creating is a specific experience that can only happen with a unique time and space because your regular sense of reality is suspended in favor an experience with reality that is magical because it brings with it a connection to the other world. This occurs in magic, in RPGs, and even in theme parks such as Disneyland:

> The spatial immersion experience Disneyland offers is marked by the connection between desire and fictional world. This connection supports both spatial and temporal dimensions and projects a unique chronotope - a unique space/time construct of immersion experience. Theorist Mikhail Bakhtin defines chronotope as the intrinsic connectedness of temporal and spatial relationships that are artistically expressed in literature. The chronotope of immersion hinges on spatiality, on the physical aspect of interaction with the narratives Disney's parks encompass. The temporal aspect of the chronotope of immersion is connected to nostalgia; participants in the Disney park immersion model desire the simplicity of the

> past that the park's architecture projects and look forward to a future of family unity which the immersion experience promises. Thus, immersion and narrative desire go hand-in-hand within the Disney consumer/fandom model and understanding the connection between desire and narrative is therefore useful. (Koren-Kuik 2014, p. 150).

While Disneyland isn't an RPG per se, it is a useful example that demonstrates how people can suspend their disbelief and encounter a world of "fantasy" and imagination, where they interact with their favorite characters to create an experience that is magical (and which can be taken back to the mundane world). What Disneyland creates is a spatial narrative, which serves to anchor the temporal experience people have in that narrative in such a way that their experience of reality and what can occur in reality is changed so long as they are part of the spatial narrative. A magical ritual and RPG session ideally accomplishes a similar feat and this is usually done by creating a spatial narrative that immerses the people into the desired reality they wish to experience.

The spatial narrative is essential because what it enables participants to do is engage all of their senses in the experience, as well as the perspective of the participants and their desire to be in the spatial narrative they are in. The spatial narrative is created partially through whatever physical objects are incorporated into it, and partially through how people interact with those objects to create the experience they wish to have (Koren-Kuik 2014). In a magical ritual, people might wear specific ritual clothing, both to aid in the invocation of whatever they are working with and to set-up the evocation of the environment. They might also use various magical tools including candles, athames, chalk, or whatever else is deemed appropriate to create the space they are going to work in. In an RPG, a person playing a character might dress up as that character, as well as use specific props associated with that character. Additionally, the environment might be changed to create a sense of otherness. For example, you might get plastic castle wall sheets at Party City in order to put them on your wall and provide a sense that you and other players are in a castle. Some types of RPGs are more immersive (such as LARPing), but I think you could actually take this idea of evoking the environment and apply it to any RPG, provided the people involved are willing to suspend their disbelief. That suspension of disbelief is essential for evoking the reality you want to create (whether in magic or RPGs).

Part of the evocation of the reality occurs through the props that the players use. A prop is any object or artifact considered to be part of the desired reality. So for example, if you play a character who wields a sword, and you bring a play sword with you when you play the game, then that play sword is used to evoke the reality of that RPG world (Sandvoss 2007, Bowman 2010).

Another part of the evocation can actually involve creating specific geographic aspects of the RPG (such as the castle wall I mentioned above). Fans of T.V. shows sometimes visit specific geographic sites that are pertinent to the show to experience the spatial narrative of the show. They may even role play characters from the show in those settings in order to feel like they were part of the experience of the show (Hills 2002, Couldry 2007, Brooker 2007). The familiar geography gives them a sense of immersion that allows them shift from observer to participant and through that process experience an altered reality, namely that of the show. The same principle applies to evoking the reality of the RPG world, because what occurs is you invest yourself in creating the environment in which the players will become part of a different reality. Whether this is done by picking a physical location by creating the location in your home, or even by simply putting a model set that nonetheless allows you as the character to interact with an environment, what happens is that this process creates the RPG world for you to play in, and by extension practice magic as well.

Exercise

How would you immerse yourself in the identity of your character? How would you evoke the game environment and make it an actual environment you can work in?

Magical Workings and RPGs

You might, at this point, ask the sensible question as to why someone would even go about doing magic in an RPG game when they can just do it without the RPG. It's a good question to ask. The answer comes down to two factors in my opinion.

The first factor is the suspension of disbelief. RPGs are about the suspension of disbelief, in order to experience a different world. That, in and of itself, is very magical. Additionally, the rules of an RPG world may differ in such a way that a person feels that they can apply those rules to their magical work in a manner that enhances the working. These are valid reasons for deciding to integrate magical work into an RPG.

The second factor is the assumption of an identity not your own. By becoming the character you may find that the character can do things you wouldn't normally consider doing. For example, if you aren't comfortable doing curses, then becoming a character who is comfortable with that might be helpful in a case where you feel need to do a working for that purpose. Alternately, if you don't feel confident in certain magical skills, working with a character who does feel confident in those skills could be helpful in doing magic work of a specific type. If you don't feel confident in doing enchantments, then creating a character who has some skill at enchantment allows you the opportunity to become that character and work that type of magic.

Potential issues that can arise when doing magic via an RPG is whether everyone is really consensually invested in the magical work, and whether the magic done in the RPG world will really have an effect in your everyday life. In the case of the former it could be argued that because everyone is becoming a character and playing in the game, and if the characters are ok with the magical work, then that should suffice, but I think that's a bit of a grey argument to make. If you're going to work actual magic in the RPG I would suggest making sure people know it ahead of time, so that you know they are okay with it, and can coordinate their own activities as part of the magical working.

In the case of the latter, magic done in an RPG should still carry over to your everyday life. The character is an identity you've become, but when you step back into your usual identity you bring those experiences with you and embody them in your life. This includes any magical work you do, and consequently you embody the magical work you've done in the RPG, carrying it over to your everyday life. Actually, it really isn't any different than when you do a magic ritual, beyond the fact that playing the RPG is a social action, while a magical ritual is an asocial action. An asocial action may happen with other people, but the primary purpose isn't for socialization, while a social action is primarily focused on socialization. The real challenge with doing magic in an RPG is being able to go into a space where you can do that magic work without making it be about the social connection.

To do a magical working in an RPG involves first getting clear about what you're actually doing and getting everyone who is playing to participate in the working. Participants need to recognize that it is simultaneously part of the playing of the RPG and something with its own space, which happens to be using the RPG to create that space. You also need to be clear on what tools you'll be using to accomplish this working. For example, if it's a LARP, will people need to bring specific props that their characters would use regularly, which can also be used for the magical working. How will those props be used in the magical working in a manner that is consistent with the RPG and your character, and yet relevant for the magical working? Finally, are there specific actions you want the characters to take in order to accomplish the working? These are somewhat technical questions that nonetheless are important to answer in the context of doing a magical working within the RPG.

Here's a possible example that could be used as a magical working in the context of an RPG. The props include candles, matches, a lighter (if it's appropriate), and a knife. The characters are meeting in order to do a ritual to stop a particular monster or alternate character they are facing. The game master sets the scene. Each player takes the knife and carves a sigil in their respective candles. The sigil is used in game as a binding for the monster, and as it applies to the everyday life of the actual people it is used to address situation in those people's lives. The candles are burned while the players do a chant that activates the magic in game and out of game at the same time. The characters then move onto the next scenario, but play it with the recognition that the spell has worked in game and out of game. When they finish playing and become their usual selves, they bring with them the character's awareness that the magic has been performed, and their own awareness that the magic has been applied to their lives. This is a simple example, but I'm sure more complex scenarios could be devised, depending on what players want to do.

Alternately, one of the ways that I like to approach doing magic in an RPG has more to do with tying a magical working to the accomplishments of the players, with the understanding being that any and all actions serve to charge the magical working, The completion of the scenario fires the working. So if you're playing a tabletop game with miniatures or your character sheets, you might put together a sigil or an equivalent that is charged by playing the game. No matter who wins or loses, the magical working is accomplished because you're using all the efforts of the players and their characters to power the magical working. Every choice that is made, everything that is said, even how the miniatures are moved and what they do, is used to empower the magical working, and only when the game is done is the magical working finished.

Exercise

Come up with a magical working you could do in an RPG. What type of RPG would you use? What factors would need to be considered in order to make the magical working occur? What would you do to make the magical working seamlessly blend into the game, but still be a working?

Conclusion

Role playing games aren't the only pop culture where you can take on the identity of a character. However, out of all the pop culture available, what they offer you is a relatively blank slate in which to experiment with the creation of a new identity. In my opinion, that is one of the most intriguing aspects of RPGs as it applies to magical work and what you could do with it. The only other medium that has a similar potential is found in virtual environments such as video games or virtual worlds.

Chapter 8: Videogame Pop Culture Magic

Video games are the other pop culture medium (other than RPGs) where a person can take on the identity of a character. Not all video games are set up to enable you to create your own character. Most games come with pre-scripted characters, but even those characters can be modified to some degree, which is the point of a video game. You become the character in the game, and in doing so take on the identity of that character. In some games you do get to create your own characters and modify them within the parameters of the game.

The main difference between RPGs and video games is that video games come with the stories already developed. You just have to play the game in order to activate the stories. RPGs also come with stories, but aspects of the story can be changed more readily by the players because the environment isn't fully developed already. With that said, video games have continued to evolve and recent iterations provide players with more options. Additionally, with some games, players can create their own levels and stories, which brings with it opportunities for magical experimentation through the virtual environment of the game. James Gee points out the following about video games: "The content of video games, when they are played actively and critically, is something like this: They situate meaning in a multimodal space through embodied experiences to solve problems and reflect on the intricacies of the design of the imagined worlds and the design of both real and imagined social relationships and identities in the modern world" (Gee 2007, p. 41). In other words, as a person plays a game, that person is given the opportunity to construct an identity, not merely through the character, but through the entirety of the video game. Most importantly this allows s/he be able to bring that identity back into his/her interactions with everyday life. The significance, as it relates to pop culture magic, is that video games provide the practitioner a way to change their own identity in a virtual environment and bring that identity back into themselves and change who they are, as well as their relationships to other people and the environment. Essentially, the magician reprograms themselves on an ontological level, and by changing their state of being they also change the possibilities available to them.

Video games get players invested in the story of the game by creating a stated of embodied awareness via the character. The player has to learn skills and repeatedly work at those skills in order to progress in the game. The player can get so caught up in the game that s/he "feels" what the character feels and loses their own sense of primary identity in the process. From a magical perspective that kind of state can be quite useful for doing magical work, because your mind is open and receptive. Consequently, if you can prepare a game ahead of time as part of a magical working, you can use the playing of it to execute magical workings, because your state of mind and being is receptive to change. Gee points out, "Human understanding is not primarily a matter of storing general concepts in the head or applying abstract rules to experience. Rather, humans think and understand best when they can imagine (simulate) an experience in such a way that the simulation prepares them for actions they need and want to take in order to accomplish their goals" (Gee 2013 P. 16). The embodiment of identity allows the practitioner to turn goals into reality by making them something achievable, and games, video or otherwise, are designed to make you work to achieve some goal. The player needs to factor in the challenges of the environment in the game, as well as what the character can or can't do in order to achieve those goals. The process of doing that subsumes the everyday identity of the player into that of the game, in order for the player to beat the game:

> For humans, effective thinking is more like running a simulation than it is about forming abstract generalizations cut off from experiential realities. Effective thinking is about perceiving the world such that the human actor sees how the world, at a specific time and place (as it is given, but also modifiable), can afford the opportunity for actions that will lead to a successful accomplishment of the actor's goals. Generalizations are formed, when they are,

> bottom up from experience and imagination of experience. Video games externalize the search for affordances, for a match between character (actor) and world, but this is just the heart and soul of effective human thinking and learning in any situation (Gee 2013 p. 18).

By prioritizing experiential thinking, games engage players in a way that is often missing in more abstract and generalized learning. Magic, in a similar way, engages the practitioner in experiential learning and work. One of the reasons video games (and games in general) lend themselves so well to magical work is because like magic, they are based on situation and experience, as well as on rules and principles which inform what possibilities are available and what can be done to realize those possibilities. What we are taught in experiential learning is how to become the possibility we need to achieve. We are taught to look at each situation from a variety of perspectives in order to achieve our goals, and also taught on how to take on the right identity in order to succeed:

> First, we look at the real world, at a given time and place, and see it in terms of features or properties that would allow and enhance certain patterns of actions in word or deed. Second, we see that these actions would, in turn, realize the desires, intentions, and goals of a human actor who took on a certain sort of identity or played a certain sort of role (and not others). These two steps amount to seeing, imagining, or construing a fit or mesh among the world (construed in a certain way), a particular type of actor, and specific goals that actor wants to carry out. Third, we then try to become that actor-become that sort of person, but also attempt, within that framework, simultaneously to realize goals and values that are part of the core self (our own personal history) we bring to any social identity we enact. We act in word or deed in terms of that identity (Gee 2013 P. 41).

Identity is central to the practice of magic. In choosing an identity a person provides him or herself a foundation. The identity may change as a result of the magic, but it gives magic something to act on and from. It is the basis by which a person forms an agreement with the universe as to his/her place within it, as well as how that agreement is changed. Magic is used to not merely to change circumstances, but also the actual identity of the person. For example, when a person focuses on spirituality above anything else, and has a belief that the body is not part of spirituality, the identity that s/he takes on is not merely that of a spiritually focused person, but likely also someone in poor physical health because that is the identity s/he has manifested with the universe. It anchors a person's connection to other places, people, events, etc.; and yet identity is fluid. What we cling to with identity is not so much who we think we are, but rather the behaviors and patterns that are reactions to situations and experiences (Epstein 1995). Video games (and other games) allow us to construct alternate identities. We can bring those alternate identities into our own identity and change that identity, as well as the possibilities available to it.

Design and Identity in Video Games

In *Pop Culture Magick*, one of the video games I referred to was *.hack*. In this console game I played a character who was trying to solve the mystery behind why his friends had become comatose while playing a Multi-Player Online Reality Game (MPORG). This was a simulated world that the character played in, but which (for the player in this reality) didn't have the online capacity of a real MPORG. Still, I saw in this game real potential beyond just entertainment. The entire purpose of the MPORG in the story that *.hack* was centered around was to basically act as a host for an online A.I. that would eventually be born. Different information from players was used to help in the birthing of the A.I. Your character eventually helps with this matter as well, because the MPORG itself also obtains a level of sentience and doesn't want the A.I. to be born. Your character helps defeat the MPORG to allow the birth to happen.

What's so exciting about *.hack* is that the actual purpose of the game isn't really about the playing of it, but is about helping in the creation of this A.I. With the creation of Xaturing[7], the pop culture entity Lain[8] and even the computer Deep Blue[9], it could be argued that an A.I. has already been created (though not necessarily in the concrete form science requires). But an intriguing challenge for the magician is to create a virtual world with objectives that are different from just playing a game. Play is only one of the obvious methods for how these virtual worlds can be used. There's a lot of potential such as ritual work, sigil casting, creation of online personae that virtually house you, and the design of certain virtual conditions that when met, prompt a real world magical change.

It's already possible to create synthetic worlds like this through games where you can devise your own RPG. This includes creating virtual systems of magic, defining how that magic works, and what the effects of it are. These games teach you the importance of detail, and show you how to devise a game for more than just entertainment. They can be teaching games, or can serve a specific function of creating conditions that the player fulfills. The accomplishment of those objectives and the energy put into achieving them goes into triggering the events in the real world that lead to the manifestation of the goals. While the game is being played, the gamer is also programming his/her subconscious to work toward manifesting the real world goals into reality. The player directs his/her energy to the game, but is also exchanging energy. The exchanged energies carry the goals into the subconscious and from there into the real world actions of the player.

In *Starcraft, Command & Conquer*, and other strategy games, there is always the possibility of building your own maps. I've built sigil maps for *Starcraft* with the sole purpose being to charge a specific sigil up and fire it. This is done by beating that board. I try to make these boards as difficult as possible so that I have a real challenge, investing a lot of effort in order to fire the sigil. Every time I don't beat the board that energy is still stored

---

7 Xaturing is an online entity created by the Temple of Set. Visit http://www.waningmoon.com/xaturing/ for more information.

8 Lain is an anime series about a goddess of the internet.

9 See http://en.wikipedia.org/wiki/IBM_Deep_Blue for more information.

in the map, charging the sigil until it is beaten. I personally prefer to win every time, but I also figure if you lose, at least you aren't wasting that energy. That said, I wouldn't lose on purpose, as it defeats the entire point of the magic you're attempting to work, because you're focused on losing instead of actually charging and firing the sigil. Alternatively, you can make a map of resources arranged in specific sigil patterns with the goal being to gather up those resources, firing the sigil off by destroying the patterns and incorporating the resources into your base. You can even use the construction of the base as a correlation of building a particular reality you want to manifest. The base represents the goal you seek to achieve, and when that goal is achieved in the online world you then target the result into the real world by successfully ending the level.

You also have games such as *MineCraft, Disney Infinity,* and *Little Big Planet,* where there is no overt strategy involved. You can simply explore the world you are provided or play games in it, or you can design your own levels. The act of designing can become a magical working in itself, with your identity invested into the level while you program that level and your identity to become something different. With the right understanding of virtual tools you can set up a board where when certain activities are done, changes occur to the environment, and those changes are reflected in your identity. The magical work is done through the creation of the level and set up so that when conditions are met, changes are activated that are embodied in that level and in your life. If you don't think that's magic, remember that it's not the tools that make magic happen, it's your understanding of how magic works that makes magic happen, and as such any activity can be a magical working if approached with the right understanding and the ability to make connections occur between the activity and the desired possibility you are manifesting.

Consider interactive MPORGs such as *Everquest, World of Warcraft, Second Life,* and even shooter games like *Halo, Fallout,* or *Mass Effect*. One of the reasons these games have been so popular is because of the ability to customize identity. In such worlds, a player can actually be who they wish they were in real life. They offer escapism and a different life to the player who wants more than real life is offering. It's fairly easy to create an online persona that's an archetype of yourself. This persona can be customized in appearance with colors, clothing, facial features, and even species. In at least one game, *Second Life*, the users can actually exchange online currency for real currency, and hold virtual jobs. Some real world companies have even opened up virtual stores in that game that sell virtual items for real world profit. Universities (and at least a few magicians) have also started teaching classes in *Second Life*. Perhaps the best feature of *Second Life* is that you can buy virtual land and design it in whatever way you see fit. The ability to build different tools and other objects is also useful. *Second Life* has a lot of potential to offer those who'd prefer to meet up with other magicians online to do magic. At the same time, it lives up to its name, offering players a chance at a different life than the one in the real world. In games, where there are multiple players you can set up workings with others players, using the virtual space as a place to meet and do your workings. This can simultaneously involve players performing a virtual quest, while also sharing what they are doing in their real time spaces to take part in the working.

In other games, such as *Everquest*, users can control guilds of players who go out and accomplish missions. These leaders become virtual CEOs and have the respect of the other players. It's no surprise that some people get so obsessed with these games they lose touch with their family and friends in real life. Those people remind them of what they don't have in the real world, which the online reality offers them if they stay in it. However, this can also be applied to people who obsessively play console games, or even traditional pen and paper or live action roleplaying games. There is an element of escapism in becoming another identity within all such games. When it's extreme, this can be a problem, but if moderated it can be a useful exercise in identity work.

The reason such escapism can be useful is that it teaches the player to be fluid with his/her sense of identity. S/he can even take on personality aspects from the identity s/he assumes. This is again related to that exchange of energy mentioned above. In the process of playing the game and assuming the identity of the character, the player studies the character and incorporates some of his/her personality and abilities into his/her own sense of identity. Think of a game which you've really enjoyed. Chances are that part of what you enjoyed was the character. Maybe the character could do things you couldn't do, or acted in a way that you normally wouldn't act, but wish you could. When you play that game you give yourself permission to temporarily become that character and do things s/he does. Because of the psychological and energetic link established by the playing of the game, some of the personality of that character is imprinted into your personality. Don't be surprised if you find yourself mimicking how s/he moves or acts outside of gameplay. Partially this is a result of the playing of the game, which teaches your body, to some degree, how to move and act like the character. I've done this with stealth games, finding myself mimicking the walk and movement of the character, usually right after I've played the game. I gravitate toward the stealth characters partially because I find the focus on movement to be intriguing, and this form of low-level invocation gives me a chance to explore that. On another level, games in general can have an impact on the kinesthetic awareness, or body image, of the person playing the game. The human body is capable of interfacing with what's observed and then implementing that into how it moves. Your body's kinesthetic awareness is what allows you take what you observe and mimic it. Kinesthetic awareness is the awareness of the motion of the body, but also the conceptual image you maintain of how your body appears and how it moves. When you play a game, you are imprinting into your kinesthetic awareness the movements of the character in the game. You might identify with the character enough that you unconsciously take the stance of that character, or move the way the character moves. Actors consciously employ similar techniques for helping them get in different roles they play.

The use of skill sets for virtual characters is one way that identity is shaped. Depending on the skills a person chooses s/he will thrive in certain situations and in others won't do as well. The act of playing the character involves learning conventions and social roles that occur while interacting with other people in the virtual world (Gee 2007). The skills give each virtual character abilities, but also a back story of how that character got those skills and why. Sometimes that story is told in the course of a game, but sometimes it's left up to the player's imagination. S/he can come up with a history about the character that explains the motivations of the character and even the player's motivation for being the character. As a result, the imagination shapes not only the person's concept of the character's identity, but also his/her identity, because it blends the character's story into the life of the player. Gee argues that video games encourage reflection on what identity is and presents a model for a tripartite identity, which is a formation of the identity of the player, the identity of the character, and the projective identity, which involves both the projection of one's own sense of values onto a character, and also the sense of the character being an ongoing projection or creation of the player (2007).

The projective identity is of particular interest here, as Gee illustrates in the following passage, "In my projective identity I worry about the sort of 'person' I want her to be, what type of history I want her to have had by the time I am done playing the game. I want this person and history to reflect my values, though I have to think reflectively and critically about them...but this person and history also reflect what I have learned from playing the game and being Bead Bead in the land of Arcanum" (Gee 2007, p. 56). On one end there's the projection of the values of the player and how those values shape and are shaped by the virtual identity of the character. But on the other end, there's also the effect that playing a virtual character has on the identity of the player. It isn't just the virtual character who learns skills, but also the player, and indeed the player is able to "safely" explore behaviors that s/he might never indulge in, in real life--at least until after the player has played the game and allowed the play to imprint on his/her psyche. (On the other hand, this substitute learning only goes so far--it's probably not a good idea to try and learn CPR through a *Second Life* seminar.)

Whether a player realizes it or not, his/her identity is impacted by playing the virtual character. A person feeds energy into the creation of the virtual identity and also the various activities the virtual character engages in. This opens a two way link between the player and the character. Invocation of a video game god form is an obvious example of this two way interaction, as is the video game sigil magic I discussed in *Pop*

Culture Magick. The advantage of video games, when it comes to working with identity, is that the virtual settings are active worlds that have their own rules and demand interaction between the character and the player. Once the character parameters are created, they impact the potential actions of the player (Gee 2007), and not just in the virtual world. They can easily extend into the real world, in terms of how a person applies the experiences gained from video games to real life (for example, problem solving skills learned from games can be very useful in real life interactions).

The impact of playing the character can be thought of as a form of shape-shifting. The video game character not only allows a player to act in a different manner than s/he normally would, but also dissolves the ego identity of the player, allowing him/her to adopt a metaphorical identity instead, "For us to recapture this sort of identity requires an act of imagination as…when we put ourselves in another's place (the essential movement of compassion). Daimonic shape-shifting is precisely a metaphor for the transformation of self that begins with such acts" (Harpur 2002, p. 84). A video game serves a similar purpose of putting a person into another's place, albeit in a virtual world. The game breaks down barriers that the player's ego normally erects to monitor the everyday behavior. The breaking down of these barriers enables the changing of identity temporarily or permanently (Gray 1970).

To fully understand why this is, I turn to Lisiewski's concept of the subjective synthesis[10], which can be applied to more than magic, and indeed plays a role in identity. Yet while it has much potential to offer, the subjective synthesis is incredibly limiting as well in the sense that it *is* subjective. Buying too much into an established set of rules on how to do magic can negate potential creativity and innovation. Lisiewski notes that the first requirement of a successful subjective synthesis is the conscious realization and acceptance of the beliefs a person has. It also provides a conscious understanding of the fundamental rules or dynamics that make a ritual work for the practitioner, based on those beliefs. If a practitioner knows what him/her beliefs are,

[10] The Subjective Synthesis is the conscious understanding, comprehension and acceptance of the principles of a given magical act.

s/he can purposely alter them to make the subjective synthesis always work for him/her, as opposed to against him/her (Lisiewski 2004). Of course, we needn't limit this to rituals. The subjective synthesis can also be a conscious understanding and integration of desired identities and the tools used to assume those identities. The virtual world is one such tool and involves a conscious integration and understanding of how to play a character and assume his/her identity. But as the game is continually played and choices are made, the identities of the character and player are molded and shaped. The subjective synthesis of identity comes into play, so that subconsciously the virtual identity inserts itself into the player's identity and merges with it, creating multiple avenues of potential aspects or new identities. In other words, a person is changed constantly by his/her interactions, and a conscious awareness of this change can allow for an integration of a subjective synthesis that is helpful to the process of working magic, as opposed to sabotaging the working. Note the word *conscious*. In order to really use the subjective synthesis, the magician must be conscious about how s/he approaches situations and/or sabotages them.

As a practical demonstration of what I'm writing about, consider this example from my own life. One meme I've had to work with is a fear of success. When I was a child I was taught that even if I was successful promises wouldn't be followed through on, or if they were, shortly thereafter what had been given as a reward was taken away from me. This early negative behavior led me to believe that even if I was successful, the success would just be taken away. Later imprinting led me to also believe that any success I gained would only be gained through lots of struggle and obstacles. As a result, I had a deep fear of success ingrained into me until I decided to consciously transform those behavior patterns into healthier behaviors.

One of my methods for changing this behavior involved using video games. By adopting the identity of the video game character temporarily, I left myself open to whatever I charged that identity with. Playing video games, for me, involves a state of no-mind, of receptiveness. By playing a game and winning, my character embodies success. I used that principle to reprogram my identity and subjective synthesis. I mentally chanted a mantra in my mind while playing, stating that "I am successful". By using that approach in conjunction with some meditative approaches, I was able to deprogram my old pattern of thinking and put in a new pattern that allowed me to not only feel more comfortable with success, but also find more opportunities for it in my life.

The best way to illustrate this is to think upon your own life and specifically the actions you have done that have sabotaged situations for you. Inevitably, a person will sabotage themselves when s/he isn't fully aware of how s/he has integrated certain aspects or attributes from prior experiences. The reactions a person has are usually due to a past situation, as opposed to the present. Something happening now reminds a person on a subconscious level of how s/he acted in a similar, previous instance and s/he draws on that behavior to deal with the situation, even when it is no longer warranted or appropriate. It could be argued that these reactions are part of the person's subjective synthesis, but even if that's the case there are ways to change that. Personality aspecting and invocation offer several ways to become consciously aware of how your identity is shaped by other influences. In turn you can consciously change those patterns so that you don't sabotage yourself further.

Exercise

How would you design a level of a game to fit into a magical working of your own? What triggers would you need to set up in order to activate the working? What other ways can you think of to use video games for magical work?

Uploading the Self

Uploading the self is a variation of my technique of invoking yourself into another person or a godform. Invocation shapes the identity through assumption of another presence, and can be used consciously to work with and shape your identity in particular directions.

In *The Matrix*, for people to enter the computer world, they had to upload themselves into the computer world. At that point, they could download information and skills into their virtual persona. They could also die there and the bodies would die if the persona did, because so much of their personalities were invested in the archetype. Your personality isn't nearly as nebulous as it may seem. It's this fact that's essential to really understanding the full potential of invocation or uploading the self into cyberspace. Your conscious sense of identity is limited, and that limitation often causes you to miss out on the potential that an aspect of your identity can offer you. An example of a personality aspect that many people take for granted is the body. We all have one, but we don't necessarily pay as much attention to it and how it shapes our perceptions of the world.

The body you inhabit is a reality in and of itself, but it's also a reality you've constructed through your perceptions of it. In other words, your perception of your body creates a residual self-image that you use when visualizing yourself. This self-image may not be accurate to the actual reality of your body. However, a person's perception can shape reality, and this includes the body consciousness. In fact, how you feel about your body, or how you imagine it appears, will affect how you present yourself to other people. If you think you are beautiful then you will act beautiful. The body consciousness has its own input and personality aspect that interfaces with the ego. The survival instincts that most people have are an example of the body consciousness taking an active role. We don't think about it when the body consciousness takes over, but it's a part of our personality wired to protect the mortal existence of the body. Unfortunately, many people aren't consciously aware of the body consciousness.

The residual self-image is an identity point, a way of anchoring your personality to something familiar to you, such as your body. The self-image is the ego of the person, and it filters out whatever doesn't fit it. At the same time this self-image, and indeed all aspects of your personality, rely on the physical body to establish a sense of reality. One of the functions that the five senses of sight, hearing, touch, smell, and taste have is the ability to help the person construct a sense of reality and self:

> Touch is every bit the creative process that vision is. When you run your hand over marble and feel its cool

> hard smoothness, you construct that feel. When you put your hand in your pocket or purse, fumble for your keys, and finally find them, you carve your world of touch into distinct tangible objects such as keys, through a process no less active than when you carve your visual field into distinct visible objects. (Hoffman 1998, p. 176)

Touch is used as the example in the quote above, but this concept is applicable to all the senses. We rely on our senses to provide us perceptions, but they also create our ability to sense, and make sense of, reality. Sight, as another example, allows a person to construct an object, its depth or dimensions, its surface appearance and texture, and even the movement, or lack thereof, of the object (Hoffman 1998). At the same time, our senses also help in the construction of identity a person has. They are the medium through which we experience the self and the personalities of other people. In fact, I think that the reason people personify objects is because of the need to find identity in what is around them, as a way of constructing and grounding the self.

What this means is that some people will have a self-image that may only partially use the body as an anchor for the reality of the personality. Other residual self-images may be used that don't draw on the body you live in, but may draw on archetypes you identify with. These archetypes could include an animal, ancient god forms, or modern pop icons. The body is only one facet of the self-image, but regardless of what your self-image is based on, your body will influence how you conceive of yourself when you invoke yourself into another person, upload yourself into cyberspace, play video games, or any other interactive activity. The body plays an integral role in allowing you to identify as something because of the kinesthetic sense. This sense is your awareness of your body, and yet it also seems to extend outward toward whatever you connect with. In the process of playing a game, our senses extend to the character we play, to some degree, enough that a person can feel like s/he becomes that character. When I play games, I feel connected to the character to the point that I can feel the movement the character is engaging in. It's a subtle sensation, but identification with the character is imparted by it. Consequently, the kinesthetic sense is not just responsible for our awareness of our body, but also anything else we happen to identify with and can be helpful for invoking yourself into another person.

The variety of media that many people have access to allows us to radically change the self-image. For instance, with social media you can use any image as your icon, and for many of the online games it's entirely possible to create your own avatar that represents how you perceive yourself and/or your body. Nor are your options limited to online games. Zac Walters has used a console wrestling game to actually modify his body image. He's created characters that represent the ideal body image he's going for and invoked himself into those characters, and along with exercise and other mundane efforts, used the game to modify his own body so that he eventually creates the body image he wants for his physical body. The game character acts as a mirror, storing up the energy of his intent and slowly molding his body into the shape that he wants it to be in (Walters 2007).

There are dangers with uploading (invoking) yourself online or into a game. It's entirely possible to get so caught up in the "reality" of such games that it ends up taking over your life. A good example of this is the people who obsessively play MPORGs such as *Everquest* or *World of Warcraft*. Not only are some of these people willing to sell their very families to someone else just to get a precious object in the game, but in *Everquest 2*, Pizza Hut actually made a deal where people could order pizza while playing the game and were reminded of this every so often in the game itself. In other words, people get their identities so enmeshed in the reality of the game that they forget the needs of the physical body. Obviously if you neglect your body long enough, it will get sick and/or die, and so will you. The recent deaths by several gamers are illustrative that, as with anything else, the online realities and identities that go with them should be dealt with in moderation and with recognition of your body's physical needs.

It's not too surprising that some players immerse their own identities into the virtual world to the point that eventually the virtual character is the real person, and the person in the real world is just a game being played to get by so that the person can once again return to the virtual reality s/he would rather live in. When this occurs the self-image of the person is so distorted by the online reality that s/he has lost touch with the grounding anchor of the body. The body signals get lost in the midst of the signals of media that are dealt with on a daily basis. The one point I wish to make is that while psychologically the virtual world can be as real as the real world, it's important to keep yourself grounded and realize that however much you shape and change your identity as a result of the virtual interactions you involve yourself in, there's still the need to live life in the physical world around you. Escaping the real world isn't a solution, and any identity work done through the virtual world should be done for the improvement of the overall person.

With that being said, it's time to consider how to actually upload yourself into cyberspace. The most obvious way is to create an archetypal figure that embodies, at least partially, how you conceptualize yourself. Whether you do this through icons on social media, or create a game avatar, you can use what you create to house your personality. In the case of social media, Photoshop or another image editing program is useful for creating an icon, but you can also use your own artistic skills with traditional media, scan whatever you make into an image, and then upload it (and yourself) into the blog's server.

With the game archetype, you'll usually be given some options on how you want the character to appear. Customize the character as much as possible and either use your name or one you come up with which represents your identity. The name is particularly important because you'll use it as a signal, or, if you will, a specific resonance of your energy, that guides you to your character. The *Final Fantasy* series is excellent to study in terms of archetypes. Although the individual games differ from each other to some degree in terms of design and character archetypes there's still a lot of crossover. The job system, for instance, is used in multiple *Final Fantasy* games. Characters take on different jobs with specific skill sets. These jobs represent archetypes; for example the knight job represents the archetype of the knight. The skill sets are specific attributes associated with the archetypal position; some of the skills of the knight, for instance, are the ability to protect other characters by taking the wound intended for them or the ability to hold a weapon in two hands (remember this is a video game so the abilities are action specific to that class of character). When the character chooses a job class the job is integrated into his/her personality and allows him/her to use specific skills that wouldn't be available in other jobs. In *Final Fantasy XII* this is expanded upon further. The characters purchase licenses that allow them to unlock skills and equipment they can use. The customization is limited in some ways, but it does mean that you can change not only what the characters can do, but also to some degree the identity of the characters. In a sense, what we do does define who we are and the *FF* series plays with that concept quite a lot.

Second Life is another game that has become increasingly popular not only as a medium to interact with, but also as a way of changing the character archetype that a player uses for interaction. Most people who use this program prefer to create a character who is similar to them, or a character who looks the way they'd like to look. Some players will choose a character who represents the desired gender they might wish to be. Others create a non-humanoid character by experimenting with its appearance. This could involve creating extra limbs or changing the appearance by adding scales, etc. If you have the programming skills you can become a bunch of floating orbs that aren't even attached to each other or something else entirely different.

My own experiments with my character were fairly tame. I chose a cyberpunk character and lengthened the arms until they were very thin. The legs were thick, while the body and neck were elongated. I chose these changes to see what they'd look like and I mostly wandered around and explored the virtual worlds. I didn't find *Second Life* to be as useful as some people have. While the ability to fly or create different tools and land modification was fun, it just wasn't something that appealed to me. But I could see that the creation of homes and different tools would be very useful for a technomage and that the ability to change the appearance of the character could be a useful invocation/identity exercise for someone who wanted to externalize a personality aspect of him/herself.

Both the *FF* job aspects and some of the features in *Second Life* would be very useful in entity creation. The job aspects give the entity specific skills and parameters to perform the task, while the modification of the appearance allows for a unique method of housing the entity in a cyber-reality. In invocation, the attributes, parameters, and job provide structure to the act of invocation, setting up boundaries, as needed, for working with the entities, when they possess you or you possess them.

Generally the different godforms a person can work with are situated in domains of specific activity. Aphrodite is a goddess of love and beauty, and concerned mainly with that task. If she were to go to war she'd probably get hurt, because that's not in her skill set. In fact, the *Illiad* tells the story of just such an occurrence during the Trojan War. Ares, on the other hand, is a god of war and can handle the tasks associated with war easily, but would probably have a rough time performing the task of spreading love in the world. Job tasks in games are similar; they provide set domains to work in. This can be useful in understanding the kinds of entities you invoke. What kind of skills does the entity have? How are those skills relevant to the situation you're dealing with? Learning to recognize the "job" of the entity can help you determine how to customize your character to fit specific needs you have. To upload yourself into your character, use the monitor/television as your astral tunnel leading you to the construct you've created. The keyboard and mouse/console controller are terminals for your energy to flow into, and ritual tools to direct the action of your character. Each push of any button is an act interfacing with the identity you are creating. You can also vibrate/vocalize the name of your character, using it as a mantra to focus your attention on the invocation and draw you into the virtual reality.

First and foremost you should feel as if you exist in that virtual world, as if it's the only reality you're in. At this point your body is (temporarily) just a shell continuing to supply the actions needed to keep your presence online. In accepting the reality of the virtual world you will have successfully uploaded yourself into your character or blog. There's no reason then not to use those virtual worlds for a variety of different purposes. Your virtual environment conveys advantages a real environment doesn't have. For example, you could kill a monster as a sacrifice of pixels to the gods. In the real world sacrificing an animal could bring very real legal (and ethical) problems into your life, but in the virtual world, where the violence is only simulated, the legalities aren't an issue. You'll still be sacrificing a being that is alive in a certain manner. You can direct the energy toward a specific purpose, such as offering it to the gods.

You're not just limited to acts of violence, though, depending on your choice of games. Build a house, or create a city. Design a game within a game. Take a class. In the process of doing that, construct the real world objectives you want to manifest in your life. When you stop the invocation and come back to your body, bring the energy you drew on to create the virtual world and project it into the real world to fulfill your goals. The advantage a virtual environment offers is ready access to the energy that people put toward a given virtual world. The belief that people put into such worlds makes those worlds into reality and gives them the means to be more than just a collection of pixels. Other advantages include an environment where you can interact with other people that you might never meet in person. In this way you can still work magic with them and form a close-knit community, while establishing connections all over the world.

Exercise

What are some games that you've played where you've felt a strong connection to the identity of the character? Have you integrated that identity into your personality and if so how? In what ways could you use invoking yourself into a character for magical work?

Practical Video Game Magic

In *Pop Culture Magick*, I shared a technique I've used with video games where I visualize a sigil on the back of a character and then play a game, using each push of the buttons to empower the sigil until the game is won, at which point the sigil is released. In the last decade, I haven't seen a significant change in video games that would change the practicality of this approach. If anything, touch is becoming relevant in games, and games are changing so that you can play on anything, including your phone. This makes practical video game magic into something which can easily be implemented anywhere.

An additional factor is your ability to share screenshots of what you are doing or even videos of your game play, which can be useful in the sense of not only using your own efforts to program a working, but also the attention other people give to the playing of a video game. This is aptly demonstrated by the numerous Youtube channels where people play games and comment on them, for the entertainment of whoever wants to watch the videos.

The one possible change to this model is virtual reality. Currently virtual reality goggles and headsets are being developed for people to use in order to play games. However, I think virtual reality will actually fit into the practical model I've previously describing, with the only thing changed being the interface. The participation of the player won't change. Additionally I suspect that touch oriented approaches to games aren't going anywhere anytime soon, as regardless of what medium you use, people still enjoy the visceral feel of touching something in order to cause actions to occur. Touch provides a needed kinesthetic feeling that connects the player to character and to the game world itself. Add in sight and sound and you have a mostly immersive environment that people are willing to invest themselves into. That investment can become a form of magical work in and of itself.

Each push of a button or a touch screen is an investment of attention, belief, energy, or whatever else you want to label what you and other people are putting into a game. Add some intention and a way to activate that intention and you have a magical working. You can optionally include other people watching your game and use their attention to further empower your intention, but it's not an absolute necessity. The simple fact is that your average gamer puts enough of their own effort in to easily empower whatever working they want to do that is linked to the game.

How you link a working to a game is up to you, but I stick with sigils because they are simple and effective. The sigil is a symbol that represents your intention, and each push of the button charges that sigil, getting it ready for when you want it to launch. The more effort you put into the game, the more you'll charge that sigil up. You can even make the game harder in order to get more effort from yourself. All that effort goes into the sigil, and when you beat the game or just finish playing it for that day or night, you can fire the sigil by visualizing it being activated as a result of you reaching whatever checkpoint you need to reach in order to allow it to be activated. My approach is to actually simultaneously charge and fire the sigil. Each button push charges the sigil, but also fires it so that it can perform the working and accomplish the desired goal.

Your emotions can also be another source of fuel for your workings. When you are playing a game, you will invest a lot into it emotionally. Whether you feel frustration over failing a challenge, or feel triumph because you succeeded, or feel happy or sad for your characters, those emotions represent an investment in the game that can be converted into energy that empowers your magical working.

Game designers can also set their own games up to be magical workings for them, utilizing all the attention and intention that players put toward the game to power up the magical working, which can be imbedded in the game. While I don't know of specific cases where this has been done, a game designer could set up code in the game to be a magical working that is launched by the various activities the players perform.

Exercise

How would you integrate video games into your practical magic workings? What would you do differently from what I've described above?

Conclusion

Videogames present some intriguing possibilities for pop culture magicians to explore. As they change, we may find that they provide opportunities to change how we practice magic. Even if that doesn't occur, they do provide another medium for the magician to work in, and another way to connect with other people who might be interested in doing magical work with you.

Chapter 9: Social Media Magic

Social media is another medium that the pop culture magician can work with. While the term social media has only shown up in the last ten years, it's fair to say that social media has been around since there were bulletin boards and news chat groups. Social media has become increasingly sophisticated and brings with it a variety of tools that the magician can work with. There are various types of social media the magician can utilize. What's most notable about social media, however, is how it can all be interconnected so that what you do on one platform is shared on others, expanding your magical reach and audience, which naturally plays a role in whatever social media magic you do.

To use social media magic effectively, I think it's useful to have a presence across multiple platforms and have those platforms set up so that you can across them. For example, if you have an Instagram account and like to take lots of photos, linking that account allows you to share those photos to all of your other social media accounts, and increases your audience as a result. The magical aspect of social media is that it enables you to get the attention of your audience and harness it toward your magical work. However, there are several models that describe social media behavior that can also apply to magical work. Let's explore those models and then tie them into magical work.

The Viral Model of Social Media

The viral model of social media is one used by marketers to describe how information and marketing is ideally interacted with by the audience. This particular model originates in part from William S. Burroughs' notion of the word as a virus, but also from marketing and advertising. The viral model argues that information is spread virally from one person to another, where each person's consciousness and subconsciousness is infected by the information and then that person is compelled to pass that information to other people. For example, the catchy song of an advertisement is developed with the idea that if a person sings that song, other people will hear the words and tune and think of the product. Memes are another example of the viral model, wherein someone creates a specific image and words and then shares that with other people, in the hopes that those people will pass it on. The viral model treats people as passive recipients of information, who pass it on to other people. Marketing agencies and companies like this particular model, because it allows them to feel like they are in control of what is being shared (Jenkins, Ford, & Green 2013). Not too surprisingly a lot of occultists also apply this model to their social media magical efforts, ultimately for similar reasons as the marketing agencies and corporations.

One of the problems with the viral metaphor is that it assumes that information is spread without the consent of the people involved…that people can't help but pass it along. The problem with that assumption is that people aren't simply passive receivers nor do they just pass information on:

> The viral metaphor does little to describe situations in which people actively assess a media text, deciding who to share it with and how to pass it along. People make many active decisions when spreading media, whether simply passing content to their social network, making a word-of-mouth recommendation, or posting a mash-up video to YouTube. Meanwhile, active audiences have shown a remarkable ability to circulate advertising slogans and jingles against their originating companies or to hijack popular stories to express profoundly different interpretations from those of their authors. 'Viral marketing,' stretched well beyond its original meanings, has been expected to describe all these phenomena in the language of passive and involuntary transmission. Its precise meaning no longer clear, 'viral media' gets invoked in discussions about buzz marketing and building brand recognition while also popping up in discussions about guerilla marketing, exploiting social network sites, and mobilizing audience

> and distributors (Jenkins, Ford, & Green 2013, p. 20).

Viral marketing, as a concept, is overused. I agree with Jenkins, Ford, and Green's assessment of the viral model which is that it is used as a label to describe activities that are anything but viral. Those activities are better described under the spreadability model.

The Spreadability Model of Social Media

The spreadability model of social media acknowledges the agency of people in passing on information and interacting with it in general. It acknowledges, for example, that a person chooses to like something as opposed to just liking it reflexively. The audience plays an active role in passing on information, as well as modifying it for their own usage (Jenkins, Ford & Green 2013). What social media does is create a participatory environment where people can actively engage in whatever interests them, up to and including pop culture. For example, in 2008, a number of fans of the show *Mad Men* took to Twitter and created accounts for their characters. They then pretended to be those characters while sharing insights about marketing and advertising. The creators and producers of the show were initially antagonistic toward these people, until it became clear that their antagonism was actually hurting the show, at which point the continued activities of the fans were accepted and recognized as helping both the show and those fans (Jenkins, Ford, & Green 2013). The spreadability aspect of this situation was something that the company behind *Mad Men* had trouble working with, precisely because it demonstrated how much power the fans have when it comes to pop culture. Fan participation and creation of content in relationship to a given form of pop culture increasingly raises awareness and drives the success of the pop culture, but brings with it less control for companies, who must decide how much control they are willing to give away.

Part of what defines the spreadability model is how people approach the spreading of information. Whether it's a company or a fan who is creating content, part of what needs to be factored in is how to make that content into something which will be spread. Social media, by how it is set up, encourages sharing of information, which enhances both the spreadability and viral models. But social media in and of itself isn't enough to guarantee that content will be shared: "Success in creating material people want to spread requires some attention to the patterns and motivations of media circulation, both of which are driven by the meanings people can draw from content. After all, humans rarely engage in meaningless activities. Sometimes, it may not be readily apparent why people are doing what they are doing, but striving to understand a person's or community's motivating and interest is key for creating texts more likely to spread" (Jenkins, Ford, & Green 2013, p 198). In other words, for the spreadability or viral models to work you need to understand why people will spread and/or modify information. In the spreadability, you also ideally want to encourage people to modify information, as well as create their own content around the information, if it'll get them to also share it. Part of this understanding involves recognizing that people share content according to their personal standards and the perceived value the content has in their social circles. A person won't necessarily share something they find personally meaningful, but may share something they perceive as socially meaningful (Jenkins, Ford, & Green 2013). The distinction is important and explains why some content on social media does better than other content. For both the marketer and magician, this variable influences what can be successfully placed onto social media in order to accomplish to the goals of the creators of the content.

Exercise

Which model of information sharing (viral or spreadable) do you agree with? Which model would you in your social media magic efforts? If you used either model, what made that given model effective for you?

In my opinion, most of the activity that I'd characterize as social media magic appears to use the viral model. In particular chaos magicians, influenced by Burroughs, take such an approach in their social media magic work. However, I also see more of the spreadable model showing up in content that people share and significantly in how that content is sometimes modified via various social media channels.

Practical Social Media Magic

Part of what defines social media magic is the technology itself, which is somewhat changeable and yet also somewhat static. For example, icons are a static example of social media magic. Icons or user pictures are pictorial representations of a person (or something they want to show) that helps to identify that person to other users on a social media platform. Every social media platform integrates icons into their technology so that people can identify each other. It's unlikely that this particular feature will change drastically, and as such it makes it easier to use social media magic. On the other hand, features specific to a social media platform can and will change. A while back Facebook introduced the timeline feature and since that introduction it's been changed several times, so that how you access it and use it also changes. That consequently can change how you might use the social media platform for magical purposes. In order to use social media for magical purposes it's a good idea to understand what the static features are, as well as what the changeable features are.

Static Features of Social Media

As I mentioned above, the icon or user picture is a static feature of social media that is unlikely to change. For that matter, on several sites you also have banner pictures for your profile, which, similar to the icon, are unlikely to change. You can utilize the user picture and banner picture for magical purposes. For example, one practitioner I know will actually create specific sigil pictures which she uses as her user picture. The sigil pictures are usually magical workings used either for her benefit or a working for or against another person. She utilizes the attention that people give to the pictures to charge them. Every like, comment, or view a picture gets becomes part of the magical working. If the working is targeted toward a specific person, then she'll make sure that person sees it by tagging the picture with the person's name.

A variant of this kind of magical working involves using memes. Memes on social media are usually pictures with specific messages on them. Some are silly such as lolcats and some have specific meanings related to social events, such as the 99% pictures. With Photoshop, you can add sigils to the memes or to your own pictures and then put the image on your banner user picture, or on whatever social media platforms you are using. On sites that are picture or video heavy such as Instagram or Tumblr, you can actually create stories with the images, and in the process use reader engagement to activate the sigils in each of the pictures.

Three other static features of social media are comments, likes, and shares. These features are used in tandem with each other, and can be included in the magical working. These features represent engagement. Even when a person just likes something that a person has posted, that like represents the engagement of attention and the person putting something toward what they liked. When the person comments on the post, then there is further engagement. Likewise, if the person is moved to share something you've written, then they are spreading your information to other people. All of these actions involve some level of attention and effort on the part of the people doing them. Ironically, in the case of the like action it's a somewhat automatic action, but it shows that you've engaged the subconscious of the person, and gotten past whatever filters they have in place.

Some sites allow you to share a post to other social media platforms you are on. For the magician, sharing something they've posted to multiple platforms is useful for engaging multiple audiences, but it's even better when other people share what you've created with their audiences because it means they found it important to them. One of the challenges with this type of social media magic is coming up with content that is engaging enough for people to like, comment on, and share. If you are using social media for a magical purpose and using the engagement as part of how you power the magical working it's essential you create content that invites people to want to share it. A like, while useful, isn't going to be as potent as a comment or as a share.

Tagging is another feature that most social media sites have and is used to include and notify a person that a post has been made mentioning them. In terms of social media magic, what makes tagging most useful is that it can provide a specific target for people to focus on, whether for good or ill purposes. Typically you can't tag someone you aren't friends with unless you are in a shared group and then only in that particular group. I think that tagging has limited uses for social media magic, but if you think it might be useful, include it in your workings.

To one degree or another all social media sites have these static features. Tumblr, for instance, has a heart icon for liking a post, as well as a comment function, which doubles up as a share function. Twitter allows you to retweet as well as comment on posts. If you can get people to engage in using the static features of social media, then it makes your social media magic viable.

Changeable Features of Social Media

Changeable features on social media sites tend to be features that are specific to a given site. In other words you typically won't find these features replicated ad-nauseum across other social media sites. The problem this presents for the social media magician is that such features get changed, and often you may not discover the change until you need to use them again. The benefit of such features is that you can do some interesting magical work with them, dependent on what those features actually do.

A couple of years ago, Facebook rolled out the timeline feature, which allowed users to post events to their status update but date the actual post to any time since their actual birthdate. Initially this feature was integrated into the status update, but most recently you can only use this feature if you go to your profile page, and at some point it may be accessible another way or just disappear altogether.

When it was initially rolled out people used the timeline feature to share events, both factual and fictional. One of the ways I experimented with it was writing about and pictorially representing past events in my life, but changing what had happened in the post, so as to re-write the actual event. I figured that by putting it onto a medium such as Facebook I could retroactively manifest it and use the attention and interest generated to help manifest the desired change into reality. When timeline was first rolled out you could also create future events, but as of now you can only create past or present events and the feature is fairly well hidden.

Changeable features come and go in social media. For purposes of social media magic a changeable future will typically have a limited use. Such a feature is often novel when it's first rolled out, but once it's changed it becomes something else you need to learn again. The majority of people only want to learn the technology they need to learn.

Exercise

What features of social media would you use for your magical workings? How would you integrate those features into your workings, and what do people need to do with those features in order to make them viable for your magical work?

Videos and Social Media Magic

Video is another medium which has been transformed by social media. Early fan videos were created painstakingly by splicing video with music to create narratives that weren't originally in the video. Now people can make their own videos using webcams or mobile phones and share them on Youtube and other social media platforms. Additionally, because video recording technology is easier to access, fans have come up with their own movies featuring their favorite pop culture universes. You can find Star Wars, Star Trek, Harry Potter and other related fan movies, sometimes focused on new adventures in the universe and sometimes set in the mundane world. What all of them have in common is the desire of the fan to create their own narratives with the pop culture that means a lot to them.

The pop culture magician has a variety of possible avenues for using videos. For example, you can create your own fan video narrative, complete with costumes and props and set in the pop culture universe of your choice. You could do a pop culture magic ritual in the video and then upload and share it. Alternately, you could create your own video channel and do monologues on specific topics you want to share with people. Finally, you can always splice some video together and pop in a sigil or two for good measure. If you're going to use videos as part of your magical work, the name of the game is making the content interesting enough that people want to watch all of it and share it with other people. Then you need to determine what magical workings you'll do that will be linked to the video.

While you can certainly take a similar approach to what you might do with social media, i.e. putting sigils into video and letting your audience charge and fire them, video offers more versatility because it allows you to capture an activity you are doing and share it with people. It's still static in the sense that a specific moment in time is captured, but because you are actually doing something in that moment it gives you more to work with. On the Magical Experiments Youtube channel, I have videos where I just talk about magic, but I also have videos where I'm doing magic and inviting the viewers to be part of that magical work. I might do a chant and invite people to chant with me, or I could do a magical spell and invite people to add their own effort to that working. The risk you take with doing magic on video is that you are sharing it with people and some might be inclined to try and sabotage the working, but I think it can be worth it to actually video what you are doing as a way of inviting audience participation.

If you want to do pop culture specific magic in video you might cosplay as a character and have that character do a magical working, or get a group of people into the pop culture and have them do a ritual as the characters. Or you might explain your particular version of pop culture magic in the hopes of sharing it with people who would take up the practice. I remember watching a video where people cosplayed as Jedi Knights and Sith and fought each other with lightsabers. The amount of effort they put into the fighting really demonstrated how people can immerse themselves into a character to the point where they aren't self-conscious in front of a video and are able to share what they are doing in a meaningful manner for an audience they may not see.

The magical aspect of this can certainly harness views, likes, comments and shares as one of the ways people contribute attention and energy to the magical working. However, I think inviting people to take part in the working can also be useful. The video, after all, can be paused, so that the people watching it can get whatever they need. You can explain what they need to do and how to do it, and then do the actual ritual. Those people can do the working alongside the video and add their own effort to it, or can do it on their own, but if they choose to do the working they are adding their own effort to yours and while they may have their own specific goals in mind, they are also contributing to the achievement of your desired results.

If you are already using video, give some of these ideas a try. There is a lot of potential for experimentation with videos and magic and I think if done right the magician can use them to empower his/her own workings while also helping other people become either interested in magic or better magicians.

Vanity and Social Media

Another aspect of social media that pop culture magician can use is vanity. Social media appeals to the vanity of people because you are sharing the minutiae of your life with people you may have never even met in person. I've noticed that people will often share the food they are eating or bland details of their lives, or frequently change the pictures of themselves usually to get attention from people. While I personally don't find vanity all that useful, if you're someone who likes to get a lot of attention, you can use the vanity aspect of social media to fuel your magical workings. Every time a person likes your status or comments or shares it, you can apply that attention toward your magical workings by linking the activity to whatever working you are doing. The link doesn't even need to be on your pictures or in your status. It just needs to be an energetic or psychological link that you know is in place to capitalize on the attention directed your way.

Conclusion

As technology continues to progress and change, the magician must be willing to explore how that technology can be integrated into magical work. While it could be argued that social media magic isn't really pop culture magic, I think social media has become such a pervasive part of pop culture that the pop culture magician and indeed magicians in general are missing out if they don't think of how to integrate social media or other changes in technology into magical work.

Chapter 10: Practical Pop Culture Magic

While a lot of pop culture magic is based on working with pop culture deities and spirits, limiting yourself to working just with those beings can leave you missing out on a lot of pop culture magic. In the previous chapter we explored how you could integrate social media and other technology into your pop culture magic workings, but I think it can also be worthwhile to look for other sources of inspiration from pop culture that you can integrate into practical pop culture magic.

Practical pop culture magic is magic that either uses pop culture resources or is inspired by pop culture, but doesn't involving working with a pop culture deity or spirit. For example, in *Pop Culture Magick* I shared a technique I developed that involved using comic book panels and sigils. The technique was inspired by Scott McCloud's *Understanding Comics*, where he discusses how comic books are designed both artistically and narratively. His explanations helped me look at comics in a different way and allowed me to develop a technique where I'd use both the artistic, and narrative design features as part of the magical working. You can design your practical pop culture magic workings in a similar manner. All it requires is a solid understanding of the principles of magic and a willingness to explore pop culture to find what you can use to apply those principles successfully.

In the case of the aforementioned technique, after I read *Understanding Comics* I began by asking myself how I could take what McCloud shared and turn it into a magical technique. I also asked myself what magical techniques could actually be applied to the format of a comic book, coming to the conclusion that sigils would probably be the best technique to apply to comic books. Sigils, the chaos magic version, are statements of desire that have been turned into symbols in order to imprint those symbols on the subconscious of the magician. Typically, sigils are one off affairs, with a person making one sigil for one situation, but in the case of using the principles of comics, one sigil wasn't going to do. So I decided to create multiple sigils for different situations, but what I also did was put those sigils into a story format of sorts using the design of comic books. Each sigil went into its own panel. Each panel represented the idealized manifestation of the sigil, in its own time and space. The panels were placed beside each other, and lines were drawn between the panels to show that there was a narrative connection. This entire process charged each sigil, and all of them were then fired off with the understanding that they were all linked together by the common element of the person casting the sigils, and that when one manifested, it would set it up so the others would manifest as well. The principles of magic that were employed were Identity and connection. The identity aspect was the identification of the sigils with the practitioner, and the connection aspect was the panels and the narrative "reading" of the sigils as related to each other.

As you can see, it's not hard to develop a practical magic technique based off pop culture. Admittedly, in this case, it helped that I'd actually done some research into how comic books are set up via design and narrative, but as a pop culture magician you ideally are doing just that kind of research with any form of pop culture you are interested in. I read books on writing and design, not only to become a better writer, but to also understand how I can take various media and apply them to magic. I also watch commentaries on shows and movies I like because I want to understand the thought process that went into creating those shows, but also because doing so may give me some ideas for magical work. My point is that you want to look outside of books on occultism to get your inspiration for pop culture magic. Certainly you should read books on magic and occultism to learn the principles of magic, but if you want to do pop culture magic don't limit yourself to just those books. Look toward pop culture itself for your inspiration and as you read, watch, and otherwise participate in pop culture keep this question in the back of your mind: "How can I take this pop culture and turn it into a magical working and what would I use that working for?" By keeping that question in the back of your mind, you will be able to discover multiple possible pop culture magic workings. Then you need to design and implement those workings. Remember an idea isn't reality until you make it reality, so if you get inspired to do practical pop culture magic, don't just come up with the idea…experiment with it by actually doing the magical work.

Pop culture abounds with inspiration for practical pop culture magic. For example, the *Harry Potter* series has a variety of ideas that can be applied to practical magic. Do you need a banishing spell? Why not use the Patronus as a spell? All you need to do is come up with a feeling of protection and then channel that feeling into the word Patronus. You can use a wand, if you feel it's necessary, but if you are in touch with that feeling of protection, that should be enough to call forth a Patronus that you can use for banishing purposes. This is an easy example of practical pop culture magic, with the mechanics of the working already explained.

Another *Harry Potter* example is that of the time turner. If you want, you can shell out some money for a time turner collectible item to use in the magic working, but you could also create your own time turner with an hourglass. What you really want to harness is the actual principle being employed. In this case, a time turner magic working could be done for several purposes. You would set it up where the hourglass is turned, and then you go into a meditative state with the purpose either being to work with a future possibility you want to manifest, a past memory you want to change, or to work directly with a younger or older version of yourself for whatever purpose. While you physically won't travel through time, you can project your mind and spirit into the past, future or alternate present. The time turner can be an excellent way to accomplish that, with the hourglass representing the manipulation of time, and the meditation actually helping you connect to a specific moment in time.

The Pensieve, which is a cauldron of memory, is another example of time magic from Harry Potter. You don't necessarily need to pull the memories out of your mind and put them into a cauldron, but the principle of being able to relive your memories can be useful, and you can take it a step further and actually change the memory. The invisibility cloak is also a great example that can be applied. If you need to do an invisibility working, then visualizing the cloak hiding you, your energy and your presence from other people can be quite effective. Doubtless you can think of other examples from Harry Potter that, with some creativity, can actually be turned into practical pop culture magic you can use.

As you start to develop practical pop culture magic workings, there are a couple caveats to keep in mind that can be useful for the pop culture magic workings you do.

Pop Culture Magic Props: Do you need Them?

As you read this chapter, you might wonder if you need to get the various props associated with a given form of pop culture. In the case of *Harry Potter* there are wands, time turners, and other items galore, all of which can help a person get into character, but the real question that should be asked is: "Do I need any of these props to actually do practical pop culture magic?" The answer is that it depends on the practitioner. I don't feel like I need to spend $30 on a Harry Potter wand. I could just as easily make on from some wood I found, or just go without one altogether. What needs to be remembered is that a given tool is just that: a tool.

Your magical artifacts serve a specific purpose. They help you take the conception of a force or aspect and turn it into a manageable and practical reality. However it is possible to do magic without any tools or with tools that aren't overtly associated with magic, but nonetheless can still represent magic. My wand is my paint brush. My cauldron of memory is my actual memories, and my trench coat, on occasion, has doubled as an invisibility cloak. There's nothing wrong with buying collectibles and using them for your magical work, and if you find that buying a collectible wand helps you to effectively practice magic then by all means go for it. However, I would also throw out there that it's possible to do a given practical pop culture magic technique without having to use specific props from the pop culture, and that it's also possible to outgrow the need to use the props.

A few years ago I developed a memory box. The memory box is fairly similar to the memory cauldron. The inside is painted with silver, and the practitioner can use it to visit their memories or the web of time[11]. I used this tool quite a bit when I

[11] For more details, read *Magical Identity*.

first developed it, but as I continued to work with what it represented, I found the need for the tool diminished and now I can access the web of time by altering my state of consciousness, and no longer need the memory box. As you work with a given technique and become familiar with what it does, you'll also find that you don't need to use the tools you previously used. They helped you to initially connect with the concepts they embody, but eventually you learn to embody those concepts directly. Keep that in mind as you develop your pop culture magic techniques, and don't automatically assume you need a given tool to do a magical working.

Special Effects Magic vs Real Magic

Another caveat which needs to be considered is that what you see on television or movies is special effects magic. It's very important not to get attached to special effects magic. While the magic of Harry Potter looks amazing, it's not how magic work. Yes, we can derive practical techniques from it, but we shouldn't fall into the trap of expecting special effects to occur. Instead we should look at what can be derived from pop culture and then do it, with an eye toward manifesting change in our lives. If we get consistent results then we know it works and that is what is most important.

Pop culture is in the business of special effects, so seeing a character fly or levitate an object or do something else in that vein is part and parcel of the entertainment aspect of pop culture. Pop culture magic admittedly does draw inspiration from pop culture, but it does so in relationship to the principles of magic and how magic works. I have yet to toss a fireball or lightning bolt, which falls into special effects magic, but I have been able to do practical pop culture magic that has manifested possibilities into reality. It's not as glamorous or overt, but it still can manifest practical results and that's what you're working toward.

Further Examples of Practical Pop Culture Magic Workings

Something else to be aware of as you develop practical pop culture magic is that in some cases you'll see possible pop culture techniques that other pop culture magicians don't see. You don't all have to agree with each other. It comes down to what works and if it works for you consistently then that's all that matters.

Harry Potter is a softball when it comes to developing practical pop culture magic. You already have the core technique shared as well as an explanation for why and how it works. Another softball is the *Dresden Files* by Jim Butcher. In the various books, Harry Dresden is a magician who has to come up with some techniques for dealing with the various foes he encounters. One that I like and have found useful is how Harry takes his movements and converts the movement into potential energy stored in his rings, which he can then use as a weapon. You don't need to weaponized this concept but it is quite sound and one that I've used for a long time (well before Butcher wrote about it). In my case I've stored the energy expelled by my movement into energetic batteries that I can draw on when doing a magical working or to bolster my health in a time of sickness. For that matter, I could use the energy offensively if I got into a fight. You don't need to have the energy sent to a physical object. My energetic reservoirs are actually energetic, but nonetheless still accessible when I need them.

Another idea I like is the shield bracelet, which is a bracelet imbued with protective magic. The character actually does this with his coat as well. What you'll note is a theme of affixing certain objects with specific traits or characteristics that can be drawn on and used by the magician. I've actually done something similar with my hat. It can either get the attention of people, or it can make me invisible. I have it set up to perform either function as needed. You could take an object you have and imbue it with a specific function, such as protection, invisibility, or temporal manipulation.

Aside from those ideas, one of the key concepts about magic that *The Dresden Files* shares and I agree with is that magic is personalized. In other words, the magician personalizes how they practice magic, and that personalization can differ from person to person. I find this to be true to a certain extent within magical practice, and what I like about the series is that you see how someone personalizes their magical work which can provide some good insights into how personalize your magical work.

You don't need to stick with contemporary fantasy to draw inspiration for your magical work. The Elric saga by Michael Moorcock was written in the 1960's and 70's and has some excellent ideas about magical work. In the first book, *Elric of Melnibone*, the author shares two examples of evocation which could be drawn straight out of a grimoire. He also shares a secret about why the evocations work that can easily be applied to your own magical work. The need the person felt when doing the evocation was what helped to create a bridge from one plane of existence and another. Another aspect the author emphasizes is the importance of the words and how those words reverberate in the consciousness of the practitioner as well as the environment around him. All of this is shared in a fantasy book, which shows that some esoteric secrets can be found in places you wouldn't expect.

The original *Dune* series can also provide some inspiration, particularly with the Mentats and sisterhood, each of which utilize techniques to do what they do. For example, one of the concepts shared is the manipulation of the biochemistry of the body by the sisterhood. They are able to access states of experience such as sickness and make themselves feel that way on purpose. Now you might question why you'd want to induce a state of sickness on purpose, but my point is that what you can learn from this concept is how to work with your body to create different states of experience that can be drawn upon at any time. For example, if you've ever done entheogens, you've experienced an altered state of consciousness. You might think that you could only re-experience that state of consciousness if you do entheogens again, but because you've had the experience you can replicate it without dependence upon a substance. To do it involves cultivating a relationship with your body where you access the stored experience in your body's memory and evoke it into your consciousness. Reinforce that feeling when you meditate, and as you meditate you remember that state of experience and bring it out in your consciousness. This concept hasn't been written about in books on magic other than my own, and I was inspired to experiment with it by reading the *Dune* series and asking myself if it was possible.

There are many sources of inspiration available to you in fantasy books. Even if an idea seems far-fetched, in terms of turning it into practical pop culture magic, give it a try anyway, because you might just be surprised at what you discover as a result. Don't let naysayers tell you what you can't do or shoot your idea down. Chances are they've lost any sense of wonder or imagination they have, and consequently lost a significant connection to magic as well.

You don't need to limit your inspiration for practical pop culture magic to Fantasy books. There is plenty of inspiration that can be found in anime. On Tumblr, I've seen people share *Sailor Moon* magical workings they've done where they've used a wand similar to the Scepter of *Sailor Moon* and come up with a chant for the purpose of directing their intention to manifest a result. I've also seen people use the concept in *Full Metal Alchemist where* the circle of life is used as a way to do energy work and connect with spirits. I got inspiration from *Yu Yu Hakusho* for some ideas on how to work with space and set up specific limitations in the space when working magic in order to limit the field of probabilities.

Exercise

What are some sources of pop culture that are inspirations for your magical practice? What techniques have you developed or would you like to develop? What are the mechanics of those techniques (how and why do they work)?

The Anatomy of a Practical Pop Culture Magic Work

While I've already shared some examples of practical pop culture magic and explored the mechanics of several of those examples, I thought it might be useful to provide a case study of such a working in order to explore in further depth how you can derive a practical pop culture magic working from pop culture. The first key is to pick out the pop culture you'll be drawing inspiration from. Does the pop culture in question actually have specific techniques the characters use, or does it explore magic in some other way that catches your interest? If the pop culture in question doesn't integrate magic, what about it is inspiring possible ideas, and how will those match up with your match up with your magical work?

Next, you want to determine what magical principles will be used in the working. If you're doing an invocation or evocation, then the principle of connection will play a significant role. If you are doing a protection working then the principle of limitation will be an important one to draw. The principles of magic are the fundamental rules of magic that are used in workings. They are the one aspect of magic that isn't optional as they dictate how the magic will manifest[12].

Finally, you need to create and test the actual working. What steps need to occur in order to make the magical working happen? What are the necessary tools that are needed to help pull it off? What's the desired result and how will you know you've achieved it? Once you've answered these questions, you need to do the working and see if it helps you achieve your desired result. If it doesn't, you need to examine the steps and determine what went wrong, what principle of magic wasn't executed, or if something was flawed in your working as it related to the pop culture you derived the working from. All of this explained, let's use an example to illustrate how this process works.

One of my favorite fantasy series is the *Deathgate Cycle,* which was published in the 1990s. Neither of the authors actually practice magic, but in the appendices of each book, they provide detailed explanations of how the systems of magic work. What I found really useful was the focus on the rune magic. There are two races of people who can use rune magic, and they each use it somewhat differently from each other, but ultimately the goal is the same: To access the field of possibilities and turn one into a reality. What I did I was take their explanation of magic and apply it to my practical work. For example, one of the rules in their system is that you need to

---

[12] If you aren't sure what the principles of magic are, I recommend checking out my class the Process of Magic which is on the Magical Experiments website (http://www.magicalexperiments.com)

define the result you want to manifest. Defining that result includes defining the limitations as well as what you don't want. This makes it easier to access the field of probabilities and turn a specific possibility into reality. I've used their theories as part of the foundation for the space/time magic work I do, but also for magical work in general.

I picked Deathgate because I liked the explanation of magic that was provided and how multiple perspectives from each race were shared. I haven't used runes per se, so much as I've taken the concepts and applied them to magical work. I find that the theories match up with magical principles nicely. For example, it is useful to define your result, in order to define your process. It's also useful to define what boundaries and limits are needed in order to refine and focus your magical work. I used the concepts shared to create a technique where you visualize all the possibilities available to you and then you start taking the energy or possibility out of the possibilities you don't and putting that into the one you want to manifest…then taking that possibility and putting into my body, embodying it physically, so that it manifests in this reality. This technique has been tested and worked with by multiple people and consistently it has worked.

Look at your own pop culture magic workings. What made them work? How did you understanding of magic play a role in turning your pop culture technique into something that's viable?

Conclusion

With practical pop culture magic, only the surface has been tapped. There are many possibilities for what you can do with practical pop culture magic. All it requires is that you look at the pop culture you enjoy with a critical eye and ask yourself how you could turn what you see, read, etc., into magical workings. Don't let anyone tell you it isn't possible or that you are reinventing the wheel. All that person is revealing is how uncreative and dull they are. What makes practical pop magic viable is the practitioner's ability to recognize a possible working and turn it into a reality. By looking outside of conventional occultism you will find possibilities and ideas that change how you think of and work with magic, and yet are viable because they nonetheless can adhere to the principles of magic. Something all too many magicians forget is that magic isn't your tools or tradition…magic is a way of relating to the universe, and if you understand that then you can develop techniques outside of conventional occultism.

Chapter 11: How to Build Your Pop Culture Magic System

When I wrote *Pop Culture Magick*, the idea of developing a full blown system of pop culture magic was just being explored by myself and Storm Constantine. At the time, the focus was mostly on just doing pop culture magic to get specific results. But in the past decade pop culture magic has evolved and that's in part due to the practitioners and their own needs, which can and do go beyond just manifesting specific results. While not all pop culture practitioners will necessarily be interested in developing a system of pop culture, for the ones who are, this chapter is written for you.

Developing a system of pop culture magic requires some understanding of how magic works. Also a pop culture system of magic is different from a pop culture magic working. It's much more involved than just doing a working. Understanding that is important, especially if you choose to develop a system of pop culture magic. When you develop a pop culture system of magic, you are developing a framework for working pop culture magic regularly with the pop culture you are drawing from. You aren't just doing a working to solve a problem, but instead are integrating it into your life as a regular practice, a part of your spiritual and/or magical identity.

A system of pop culture magic utilizes the principles of magic in relationship to specific pop culture. It is also the creation of a spirituality rooted in the pop culture that nonetheless may draw upon existing structures of spirituality to create a foundation for the system. There are three types of pop culture systems of magic: Devotional, practical, and a combination of devotional and practical. None of the types are better than the others. What matters is what is most useful for you and what calls to you.

A devotional system of pop culture magic is focused on a relationship with the pop culture spirits, where they are worshipped and any spiritual working is primarily dedicated toward that relationship, as opposed to trying to get something from the spirits. Practitioners in a devotional system may not even feel they are practicing magic. In a sense, such a system is more like a religion than anything else.

A practical system of pop culture magic is the opposite of a devotional system. It's a result based system, which nonetheless focuses on developing a specific relationship with the pop culture spirits. Such a system isn't necessarily devotional so much as it's focused on consistently working with a given pop culture in order to manifest results.

A hybrid system combines the results aspect of practical magic with the devotional aspects in order to create a system where pop culture spirits are honored and worshipped, but also worked with when situations arise where their help is needed. Such a system will draw on aspects of devotion, but still utilizes practical magic as a way of resolving problems.

One question that arises is whether you can develop a system of pop culture magic that mixes different pop culture together. In my opinion, it's not useful to mix and match your pop culture deities in a system because there are specific contexts that they originate from, and those can play a significant role in the system you develop. It may be one thing to do a magical working that involves a variety of pop culture characters, but developing a coherent system ideally draws upon one specific pop culture and sticks with that pop culture. With that said, there's no reason you can't develop multiple systems of pop culture magic for each type of pop culture you like. Just recognize that, as with anything else, the time commitment involved in truly developing such a system can be more intensive then you might initially think.

Another question that arises is whether a pop culture system of magic really needs pop culture deities. I think it depends on the pop culture. Obviously most, if not all, pop culture is character driven, so characters do play a significant role in pop culture, but I think it is possible to develop systems that aren't defined by the characters. Such a system is going to be a very practical, technique oriented system, which nonetheless can be very useful and may at times still draw on characters as spiritual contacts, but not be focused on them as the main part of the system.

When developing a system of pop culture magic there are some variables to consider that will help you pick the pop culture and determine how it fits into a magical and spiritual practice. First, you need to consider what pop culture you will use. Not every pop culture lends itself easily to being used in a system of magic. You want to pick pop culture that resonates with you, but is also something you can graft onto magical principles in a way that makes sense and isn't forced. Additionally, if your pop culture lends itself to fitting into correspondences, this can be helpful in the development of your system. With that said, what can be interesting with a pop culture system of magic is your choice to buck convention and do something different that doesn't necessarily fit into conventional frameworks of magic.

For example, you can easily develop a system of pop culture magic around Pokémon, aligning it to specific elemental attributes and other such systems that provide specific correspondences. On the other hand, it could be hard to develop a system of magic on something as nebulous as the Force in Star Wars (which isn't to say it couldn't be done). Part of what makes a pop culture viable for magic is how that pop culture can be meshed with pre-existing magical correspondences. The correspondences and principals of magic lay out how magic works and a given form of pop culture that is detailed enough in its own way can be meshed with those correspondences and principles because of the components involved.

The mythology of a given pop culture can also be an important aspect of your magical work. The mythology provides a cosmos to work with that helps to flesh out the framework. In fact, you may find that the mythology plays a central role in the development of the magical system. For example, when Storm Constantine and I were developing the Dehara system, part of the work we did involved putting together a mythology that could be integrated into the framework of the Sabbats, and consequently set up a way to meaningfully work with that system of magic year round. Having the mythology in place enhanced the Dehara system of magic and made it something that people could relate to. Many systems of pop culture borrow heavily on pre-existing structures such as the Tree of Life or Wheel of the Year because those structures provide enough grounding to make the pop culture system viable, while also leaving enough space for a person to develop their own variations.

Some pop culture has specific rules, which may consequently effect the system of magic you develop. Remember that the development of a system isn't just what you want in the system, but also whatever else is relevant to the pop culture you are drawing on. For example, if you were to put together a system of pop culture magic based on Once Upon a Time, one rule you'd have to deal with is Magic always has a price. That's an integral rule of the mythology of the show (and in my opinion, makes it less useful as a system of pop culture magic). You can't arbitrarily undo the rules of a given pop culture that you don't agree with, especially if you end up working with the pop culture characters, because those characters will stick to those rules in their interactions with you.

Another variable to consider is complexity or lack thereof with a given pop culture. Some pop culture will be more complex or simple than other pop culture, and consequently a system of pop culture magic based on a given pop culture will also be either complex or simple. If you were to create a system of pop culture magic based on the main characters of Cowboy Bebop, you'd be able to match those characters up the classic five elements, but whether you could develop anything beyond that would probably be a bit of stretch and one that might not be worth the effort. There's also something to be said for not making your system of magic needlessly complex. If you get mired in lots of correspondences or other details, it actually can stop you from doing magic, and the whole point is to actually develop a system you can implement in your life.

In putting together a system of pop culture magic, you also want to consider what physical components you'll integrate into the system. Posters and statuary of the pop culture characters can be useful for both devotional and practical purposes. The props of a given pop culture such as the electronic screwdriver or lightsaber can be useful as ritual components that set up the experience of connecting with a given pop culture. You'll find that pop culture artifacts can fill in for traditional tools and have a deeper connection because of what they represent and how they personalize your system of pop culture magic.

The last variable is very personal, but important because of how personal it is. While you could work with any pop culture you come across, in my experience working with what has meaning to you, especially on an emotional level, is helpful for really connecting with the pop culture spirits you work with. Regardless of whether the magical work is purely practical or devotional, it's something which ought to resonate with you, at least if you're going to make a system out of it. The personal connection provides the foundation for the pop culture magic and spiritual work you'll be engaged in.

In the next section I want to share some examples of pop culture systems of magic that either exist or could exist and what was either done to create them or what would be needed to create them.

Dehara: The Wraeththu System of Pop Culture Magic

Storm Constantine and I created the Dehara[13] system of pop culture magic, along with some other practitioners who helped test what we were doing. We shared the concepts and practices of the system in *Grimoire Kaimana* and we are currently working on a sequel that will hopefully be available in 2016. Storm used the wheel of the year to form the basis of the devotional aspects of Dehara, taking the Pagan holidays and creating equivalents in Dehara along with specific Dehar (deities) that could be worked with for those holidays. My own work in Dehara ventured more toward practical magic, with the creation of a Dehar of Dreams and one of wealth and another used for manifesting specific results. Additionally, I integrated sex magic with Dehar into the system because of the role sex magic plays in the *Wraeththu* series. Storm and I also created elemental Dehar for the purposes of working with the classic five elements and directions, both for ritual magic of a theurgical bent and practical magic of a thaumaturgic bent. In setting up the Dehar in that way, it made it possible for any practitioner to personalize the system to their preferences.

What's made this system effective is the mapping of the Dehar to pre-existing systems such as the Wheel of the Year and

---

[13] A system based off the *Wraeththu* series by Storm Constantine, and working with hermaphroditic godforms.

other classic elements, while also creating specific Dehar for specific purposes. What makes this system unique is that Dehar are created, as opposed to relying on pre-existing characters. In her later books, Storm incorporates some of the Dehara into the book and further illustrates how the system of magic works for her characters, but the system is left open to interpretation to some degree.

A lot of what you would need to make this system work is familiarity with the *Wraeththu* series, as well as a connection to the Dehara. Standard magical tools can be used for ritual purposes. The main challenge is how the practitioner adapts to a gender identity that is hermaphroditic, but I've noticed that most people involved in this system have found it easy to work with. This is a hybrid system of devotional and practical magic.

Harry Potter

With *Harry Potter*, you could come up a devotional or hybrid or practical system of magic. When I created my own system of work with *Harry Potter* it was a hybrid system. We used the four houses of Hogwarts to represent the 4 directions, drawing on characters in the series to be guides to those houses. You'll note that in the books the houses even have specific items linked to them, such as Gryffindor's sword or Ravenclaw's Circlet, which could be used in conjunction with the respective house. In the first book, the author also has specific chants for each house that can be used for calling the quarters.

As I mentioned earlier in the book, you also have the wands and the practical magic associated with them such as the patronus charm. While a lot of the magic in *Harry Potter* isn't something a magician could replicate directly, the concepts are worth exploring in terms of how you might apply them to your magical work, and of course you have access to the teachers of the *Harry Potter* world as spiritual guides.

You might also look at linking specific characters to other structures. For example, using the Tree of Life as a structure, you could associate Ron Weasley with Malkuth, Luna Lovegood with Yesod, Hermione Granger with Hod, Ginny Weasley with Netzach, Harry Potter with Tiphareth, Severus Snape with Geburah, Sirius Black with Chesed, Minerva McGonall with

Binah, Albus Dumbledore with Chockmah, and for Kether, magic itself...mind you this an arbitrary set of associations made as I'm writing this book. Chances are you could come up with your own version that speaks to you, but I'm using it as an example of how characters from Harry Potter could be associated with the different Sephiroth. To determine if the association really works, look at the traditional correspondences associated with the Sephiroth and then at the behavior of the characters to see which characters really fit. You can also do the same with the major trumps of the Tarot deck or any other structure of magic you care to draw on.

If you develop a pop culture magic system around Harry Potter you might also create an altar with the books, movies, and other regalia relevant to the mythology, both for purposes of devotion and practical magic. Creating such a shrine can help you to connect to the characters of *Harry Potter* and provide you a place to make offerings to them.

What I've shared here are some ideas if you wanted to develop a system of magic around Harry Potter. These ideas might from the foundation, but you'll have to be willing to do some experimentation as well to discover what else you can do with this system, and how you might change it to fit your own experiences. The same is true with any system of pop culture magic. No one can hand you a system on a platter. You can get some ideas, but what makes a system is your willingness to create it and implement it as part of your life.

Star Wars

With *Star Wars* you can take two different approaches. One approach involves working with the characters, and the other approach involves working with the Force. You can, of course, combine both approaches, but I also think you can just as easily separate them. If you're working with the characters, then what you're doing is going to be similar to what I described in the Harry Potter example. You'll pick what characters resonate with you and work with them. You might get a lightsaber or blaster replica or make your own, as well as either get or create your own costume. You might create an altar with action figures and set up specific workings around the characters. Basically it's standard pop culture magic, where you apply the characters to whatever structures you are using in order to work with them.

The second approach, however, is a bit more complicated. The idea of working with the Force is somewhat nebulous in no small part because it's based on the emotions, as much as a connection with any external force. If you're going the Jedi route of working with the Force, then part of the work you need to do involves learning not to be attached to anyone or anything. You acknowledge what you feel, but don't let it control you. You learn not to use your emotions as your source of inspiration for working, but instead use the sense of calmness you cultivate to guide you in your work. If you take the Sith route, you draw on your emotions and attachments to drive your workings. Whatever emotions you feel are at the core of your working should guide how you utilize elements of the pop culture. Having worked magic both ways, I can say that each approach has its strengths and weaknesses. Attachment and emotion can provide a lot of oomph to a working, but can also cloud your awareness; while calmness can provide you awareness, but not always the same kind of oomph. As for working with the Force itself…I think of that as magic. I think what practitioners can learn from a Jedi or Sith approach is an appreciation for how different sources of inspiration can direct how you work magic. If you work magic from a place of anger, for example, you'll draw on the feeling of anger and use that feeling to keep yourself focused on your desired result. If, on the other hand, you approach it from a place of calmness, you won't be attached and may consequently change what the priority is based on the big picture awareness you cultivate.

A hybrid of both approaches might have you working with Darth Vader or Sidious as your spiritual contact for a Sith approach, or Yoda or Obi Wan Kenobi for a Jedi approach. For example, a while back I worked with the element of emptiness. For a few months during that process my spiritual mentor was Darth Sidious, and he explained how anger, fear, and other emotions created emptiness and how that feeling of emptiness, of never having enough, could be a powerful inspiration for magical workings, He then showed me how to integrate that feeling into my workings. Now that I'm working with Stillness I may end up going to the opposite end and working with a Jedi as a source of inspiration for Stillness cultivation. By working with a Jedi or Sith as a spiritual mentor you can get some different perspectives on how to work with your emotions when it comes to magic.

Watership Down

Watership Down has always been one of my favorite books, not the least because the author provides a mythology for the characters around the Rabbit prince El-ahrairah, the Prince with a thousand enemies. I've never integrated *Watership Down* into a magical working, but if I ever needed to work with a trickster/strategist El-ahrairah would be definitely be a top contender. If I wanted to develop a pop culture magic system around Watership Down, I would integrate the mythology and the characters from the main story together. Each character would fit a specified role, and I would likely integrate the Wheel of the Year into how I would work with such a system because the roles of the characters could be adapted to the Wheel and the mythology already in the books. I might also look at identifying certain characters with the classic five elements, but in my opinion using the Wheel of the Year would probably be more useful.

Batman

Batman is another pop culture mythology which has taken on a life of its own. If you Google Sons of the Batman, you'll find a website where some people have shared what they've done to work with Batman, although there hasn't been a post on the site in a while. What they share on the site is a combination of practical magical workings and cultural commentary which could be useful for someone wanting to work with the Batman universe as a pop culture magic system.

I have my own ideas around such a system and what it would look like. Part of it would focus on Gotham City as an entity in its own right. I find that Batman is very spatially oriented in terms of the places that exist, and as such those places should play a role in the magical work a person does with the system. Arkham Asylum would be another such place. Both those places have distinctive energy in their own right that can worked with astrally. For example, you might do negative magic in Arkham Asylum.

Then you have the characters themselves. Batman, of course is central to the mythos, but there are also the allies such as Commissioner Gordon, Batgirl, Robin, and others who can be worked with. And there are the villains, such as Joker, Two Face, Dr. Freeze, etc., who also can be worked with (at your own risk). You also have characters who are neutral or who play both sides such as Catwoman or the latest iteration of Red Hood. All of these characters can be worked with individually, but you can also develop a magical system around them.

Don't forget as well the various items and technology Batman has. For example the Bat light can be used as both a summons for Batman and a banishment of negative energies. The Bat claw can be used as a way to get you out of a tough situation or to help you get some perspective. Other gadgets can perform similar roles and consequently be assigned to specific correspondences that fit those roles.

The rituals you develop around this mythos can draw on the roles of the characters. For example, Halloween can be Scarecrow's holy day, while April 1st, April Fool's Day, is Joker's holy day. To do a magical working to Batman, the best time is to work at night, when's already active and solving cases. Similarly his allies can also be found at that time and worked with.

Developing a system of pop culture magic takes time and dedication. I've shared some examples above to hopefully provide you some guidance, but you'll find that ultimately such a system is somewhat personal, based in part on your love of the pop culture and also on your own understanding of how the characters of a given pop culture match up to the structures you want to draw on. I've helped develop two systems of pop culture magic and I'm still working on both. I plan at some point to develop my own system around Batman, but my point is that any system of pop culture magic you develop takes some dedication on your part to make it viable. You develop the concept, then you turn it into actual magical workings and that takes time. So be prepared to invest that time if you want to develop a system as opposed to just doing occasional workings.

Exercise

What's a pop culture system you would like to create? What pop culture would you draw on? What pre-existing structures would you want to use? What tools would you need? What other variables need to be considered? Once you figure that out, create your system, do some magical work based off it and start sharing it with other people.

Conclusion

The examples I've shared above are just examples. Don't limit yourself to those examples (unless you want to). What pop culture do you like? How does that pop culture speak to you? Develop your own systems. I would add that there are already other systems of pop culture magic out there and doing some research can help you find them and establish contact with fellow pop culture magicians. With that said, if a pre-existing system exists for a pop culture you like, don't limit yourself to it. Check it out and see if you feel it fits. Test it out and see what happens, but if you have your own ideas, give those a try as well. Remember that what makes a given system of magic work is the understanding of the principles of magic and how those principles can be integrated into the pop culture you like. You can develop pop culture magic systems based off anime, video games, board games, etc, if the pop culture can be meshed with the principles and structures of magic. If you have that understanding, everything else is optional, unless you feel it's necessary. Happy experimenting!

Conclusion

When I first started writing this book in 2013 I was hoping to initially publish it on 2014, a decade after the first book. But books take on a life of their own and this book has been no exception to that reality. As I began writing this book, it quickly became evident to me that I needed to do some research in pop culture studies, look at what other pop culture magicians and Pagans were doing as well as what challenges they were encountering. It also became obvious that my definition of pop culture had changed quite a bit since I wrote *Pop Culture Magick.*

In researching, experimenting, and writing this book I found that my joy as a pop culture magician was rekindled. For a long time I had been somewhat bitter in regard to pop culture magic, in no small part due to the criticisms I'd received over my work. But in the last two years I saw more and more people embrace pop culture magic, and seeing that has made me feel really good. It's my hope that as you read this book you discover you aren't alone, that there are other pop culture magicians and Pagans, and the naysayers...well they just don't get it and they aren't worth listening to because what they display is a true ignorance of how magic works.

I've written this book to be a practical guide in pop culture magic and Paganism, but I also hope that it's clear that this work is not prescriptive, but rather descriptive. In other words, while I share my own thoughts and experiences on what pop culture magic is, none of what I share is written in stone. Test and question everything you read. Recognize that the best teacher for you is yourself and anyone else is just a guide meant to facilitate your journey in some manner.

Eleven years ago *Pop Culture Magick* was written. It's my hope that none of us will have to wait so long for another book on pop culture magic to be shared. The work is really just beginning and there is so much for all of us to share with each other. I'm already thinking of a new book on this topic, and a correspondence class on pop culture magic, so keep an eye out for both. Keep an open mind, be willing to share, and let's see what we can all learn from each other.

May pop culture be with you!

Taylor Ellwood
Portland, Oregon
June 2015

Appendix 1: Clothing, Magic, and Identity[14]

The saying that clothing makes the person may be clichéd, but there's still some truth to it. The way a person dresses can tell you a lot about how attractive s/he feels, and even the attitude s/he has toward his/her surroundings. Imagine going into an interview with torn up jeans and a t-shirt. It's almost a guarantee you won't get the job, because no matter how professional you sound or how good your resume looks, the interviewer will take one look at your clothing and likely think that you aren't serious about getting the job or that you'll be a slacker at work. Dress in a clean suit, on the other hand, with hair tied back or otherwise tamed, and you have a better chance of getting the job. The impression the interviewer will have is that you want to work there, that you're willing to put effort into the interview, and that you'll be professional.

The sad fact is that image does govern a lot of people's perceptions of others, and clothing is an integral part of that perception. In our media saturated culture, we are bombarded with brand-new fashion media that's considered in, even as we are told that last season's fashion is out and destined for the thrift store. Of course, for the average person, there are also the widely varied ideas of what fashion is to contend with. In one social circle slashed up jeans, leather jackets, and t-shirts might be considered in, while baggy pants and misaligned hats are important for another. To fit into most groups, though, it's expected that a person will dress in a certain manner.

But clothing isn't limited to just the clothing racks themselves. In television and movies, we find actors who dress in clothing that fits established stereotypes that the actors embody. The nerd who has goofy glasses and clothing that doesn't quite fit, the farm boy that wears plaid shirts and jeans, or the prep who wears stylish clothing are all archetypes that rely in part on the clothing to denote what they are. In other words, the costume is a symbol that signifies the expected behavior that those roles will fulfill. Additionally a lot of the

[14]This is revised from its previous publication in Multi-Media Magic.

clothing also denotes the sexiness or attractiveness of the character.

Clothing can be fetishized as well, with an emphasis not only on how a person appears, but also on what the clothing displays or doesn't display of the person's body. It's no coincidence that some fashion ads focus on the appearance of the clothing as it relates to the person's sex. For example, with many ads for men's clothing the focus is on the washboard stomach, the top button of the pants undone and a picture of muscular arms that demonstrate male strength. Ads for women tend to focus on skin tight clothing that shows off the chest and butt of the woman, and sometimes focuses on the face, but only to highlight jewelry, hair or makeup.

With all of these images of how we should dress, it can be intimidating to actually wear clothing for the purpose of your enjoyment and sense of self-image. One person I know wore warm-up pants and sweaters every day. She felt that any time she dressed up the only purpose was to advertise sexuality, as opposed to feeling comfortable and attractive. Rather than risking unwanted attention, she hid her body under layers of baggy clothing. Her desire to feel attractive was taken away by the cultural emphasis that attractive clothing always denotes sexual receptivity. Obviously, people don't always wear clothing that makes them feel sexy in order to find a one-night-stand, but because our culture emphasizes sex it can create an association in the mind of the person that the only purpose for wearing certain kinds of clothing is to accomplish particular goals (as opposed to wearing clothes for simple enjoyment). Sometimes people who have low self-esteem will wear clothing they think is sexy as a way of marketing their bodies, in order to feel appreciated and wanted. The attention, however, rarely boosts their confidence.

So how do we get over our conditioning and become more comfortable with what we wear and the image it portrays? Magic is a good place to start. In the example above, the person *unconsciously* wore the warm-up clothing as a protective shield against unwanted advances. There's nothing wrong in choosing to wear clothing for a specific purpose, so long as you are conscious of that purpose. If you wear certain fashion styles, but don't know why you wear them, try and think about the reasons. Ask yourself how you feel when you look at yourself in the clothing. Usually your feelings can tell you a lot about how your attire makes you feel and why you might've chosen to wear a certain outfit.

Dressing the Part

I personally find it useful to have a conscious purpose for wearing clothing, so that I can act on that purpose. In other words, I purposely cast a glamour with my outfit. This involves consciously being aware of why you are wearing the outfit in the first place. You then externalize that conscious choice into the clothing, by visualizing it becoming imbued with the characteristics that you feel embody your choice. What I usually do is project into my aura the reason I'm wearing the clothing and then visualize the aura merging into my attire.

There are a few factors to consider when preparing to do a clothing glamour. The first factor is attitude. What is your attitude toward the clothing you are wearing? Who are you wearing it for? What is your purpose/goal for wearing it and what will it help you accomplish? For instance, if you're wearing a business suit to an interview, you know that your purpose for wearing it is to help you land a job and also look professional. You are wearing it for you, but also for the interviewer. The accomplishment you hope the suit will help you achieve is making a good impression on the interviewer. You want your attitude toward the business suit to reflect these purposes. When you look at your clothing do you feel a good attitude toward the idea of wearing it? If not, why? What would you rather be wearing?

The second factor is comfort. Are you comfortable in the clothes you wear? Comfort is always foremost in my mind when I choose clothing to wear. I want to feel comfortable and relaxed. I don't want my outfit to distract me because it itches, or is too hot or not warm enough, or is so tight I can't breathe or move. If anything, it should feel like a second skin.

The third factor is attraction, specifically attraction to you. Ideally clothing you wear will make you feel not only comfortable, but attractive, for the sake of feeling attractive (as opposed to just getting laid). I wear clothing that makes me feel good about myself and my appearance. And if I feel good about myself, chances are that other people will notice this and be drawn to me. The principle of attraction, as it applies to clothing, is that you don't seek to please other people first, but rather you please yourself first. When you feel comfortable and attractive in your clothing it's visible to other people. When you feel uncomfortable and unattractive that's also visible.

What I've learned, by keeping these three factors in mind, is that a purposeful choice can make a world of difference in my presentation, appearance, and overall feeling of self-esteem. It's a glamour. When I want to feel protected I visualize my clothing as part of my protection and imprint my aura into it. When I want people to notice me, I also imprint that into my outfit, by visualizing my energy shining on what I'm wearing.

I've been told by some people that I have a unique dress code and that if anyone else tried to pull it off they would fail. At Pagan events, I dress in flamboyant colorful flowing shirts, torn up jeans, pantaloon harem pants, work boots or sandals, and a fedora. This style works for me, but the reason it works involves a few different factors that anyone can use when it comes to casting a clothing glamour. At business events, I dress in a suit, but I wear vests on the suit, and a black leather hat, with a feather in it, all of which is used to get people's attention, because I know I stand out in what I'm wearing.

It's possible that when you first get up the last thing on your mind is what clothing you will wear for the day. You might even throw on anything that's close by and then just head out the door. Or you might plan out your outfit, but not think about why you're wearing the clothing, beyond meeting the initial practical needs that your choice gives you. The problem is that without consideration of the three factors mentioned above you may not feel as good as you could or make the best impression. A clothing glamour involves those three factors and knowing how you can use your clothing to fulfill the purpose you have in mind for it.

When I get up I consider how I'm feeling emotionally--am I feeling attractive, bummy, protective, etc.? I then choose clothing that reflects the feeling. For instance when I feel attractive I'll choose pantaloon harem pants or ripped up jeans or a nice pair of business slacks (depending on where I'm going).

I'll choose a colorful shirt that makes me feel sexy. And once I've put the clothes on I'll evaluate how they feel. If they don't feel comfortable they come off, because it'll be obvious to anyone that I feel uncomfortable. Worse, I'll be the one feeling uncomfortable and not really enjoy the experiences the day has to offer me. I'll know I've hit jackpot when I look and feel good about myself.

I then take that feeling and put it into my aura. I basically consider my clothing part of my aura and my feelings as the director of the aura. So when I feel good I'll seem to glow, because my aura is charged with the feelings of comfort and attractiveness I feel about myself. Those feelings are anchored into my clothing. This brings us to a less energy dependent way of working a clothing glamour, through neuro-linguistic programming (NLP).

NLP has several concepts that are useful for creating a glamour. Anchoring involves associating an emotion or mind set with something that isn't directly related to it. For instance, you might have a physical gesture that you use and don't even think about, such as putting your hand on your chin. If you wanted, you could associate a state of mind with that gesture, so that every time you did that gesture you would evoke that mental state. But anchoring can be applied to clothing as well.

Are there certain colors you associate with your moods? If so, wearing those clothes will probably bring those moods out. Is there a style of fashion you associate with work, or with having fun? Likely wearing one style or another will condition how you approach a situation, as the clothing will remind you of work or play. What happens as well is that you anchor the associations of work or play or happy emotions with physical features of the clothes. The clothes don't actually have the associations fabricated into them, but because you invest meanings with the associations, you can anchor those meanings into the clothing. In turn when you wear that clothing, you can invoke those meanings into yourself. You can always deliberately evoke a particular feeling for the clothing you wear, changing the anchor at will. Simply choose a different perspective or attitude than you normally adopt with the clothing choices and bring yourself to see the clothing fit that new perspective.

Another NLP technique is called modeling, in which you observe a person's actions, clothing choices, speech and other traits. You can then use these observations to assimilate that person's mannerisms into your own. This can include learning that person's sense of fashion, so that you feel confident in what you wear. Just don't imitate the person to the point where you wear the same types of clothes on the same day, to avoiding being accused of exhibiting creepy stalker behavior.

If you don't want to model yourself off of a person you encounter every day, there's still another way to get what you want out of your clothing. Invoke a spirit of the fashion sense you want for yourself. Find images of people you associate wearing the type of clothing you'd like to wear and try to see if you can imitate that feeling and sense of style. Evoke the clothing sense of the model, by dressing up and modeling yourself in front of a mirror, becoming for a time that model. When you are ready, focus on being a version of you that is wearing those clothes. Look at yourself again in the mirror. What, if anything, has changed about your appearance? Do you feel as confident as before? If you don't, ask yourself what precisely is different. Try this exercise each day until you get to a point where you're confident and comfortable without needing to draw on the model to make you feel that way.

You can also choose clothing to get a specific reaction out of people. For instance, if you want to be intimidating wear lots of leather and spikes, or go with black clothing. Then gauge people's reactions to your appearance. The next day go with a style that is sensual or with a professional style and again gauge differences. I always found that people were always put off when I dressed in clothing that was opposite of what I'd usually wear. I made it a point to dress in clothing opposite of how people perceived me, for my own enjoyment, but also to see the reactions of people. This practice taught me a lot about how easily people can be stereotyped.

Sometime, as an experiment, try dressing up in different styles of clothing. How does dressing in a different style feel? Do you notice any changes in your mannerisms or behavior? If you do, note what they are and ask yourself why that particular style brings those mannerisms. What does that clothing represent to you? Look at your current wardrobe and then study the wardrobe of your friends. Does the clothing look similar? If it does, as an experiment, dress in a different style for a couple days to observe how your friends and other people react to you. Then switch back to your regular wardrobe and note the responses again. What you will likely find is that clothing, in part, dictates how people respond to you, because they associate certain styles with certain behaviors and cliques.

At the same time, this type of practice can also be useful for personality aspecting. The clothing you wear is often associated with your personality. For instance, I like to dress in loose, flowing clothing, a lot of it very colorful. More than once my friends have affectionately called me a hippie. But when I had to get a real job, that particular aspect of my personality and the clothing that went with it wasn't going to be helpful if I wanted to land a job that was better than minimum wage. So I decided to do some personality aspecting, calling on an aspect of my identity I hadn't really developed before. I wanted to appear professional and businesslike. To help myself connect to those aspects of my personality, I used business suits, which helped me feel very professional. I certainly looked different and I acted different as well, connected to a part of my personality that was focused on getting a successful job. The professional clothing gave that personality aspect a sense of confidence and a feeling of professional power, which came in handy with job interviews. I've since used that personality aspect in my business and have found it to be helpful there as well. People in a business setting have different expectations about professional clothing and by dressing for the part I meet their expectations but also set up my personality to conform to the occasion, in order to achieve the results I want.

Another way to experiment with character aspecting involves working with deities or pop culture personae. For example, if one of the Greek Gods, Athena, was walking around in the modern world, how would she dress and act? What kind of clothing would you associate with her? If you have a patron deity, invoke him/her and ask them to give you an idea of how they would dress. In this way you can even find clothing that you can use in ritual to help you work more closely with that deity. After all, the gods want to be stylish too. In the process, however, you can also work on assimilating attributes from those deities that help you draw out aspects of your personality that you want to get to know. Want to be more sensual and attractive, work with Aphrodite or a similar deity. The same principle applies to pop culture personae that you want to work with. Find a celebrity whose clothing style and personality is one you want to emulate and work with that persona in the same way you would with a deity.

You can always create an entity to guide you in buying clothing. Base the entity creation off of what you consider stylish. Make the entity out of some spare clothing and jewelry, perhaps creating a pouch to house the entity. When you go to the mall or the thrift store have the entity direct you to the clothes that'll fit your requirements. Call the entity's name and then let your intuition take over. You can make a name for the entity. Take a sentence such as, "I want to have better fashion sense" and get rid of the repeating letters. The result is WBVRF. It may not seem pronounceable, but chances are you can make a name out of the noises. It may sound a little silly, but the benefit is that the name will be unusual enough that it will stick out in your mind. Take your fashion pouch and go shopping, asking WBVRF to aid you in your clothing search. When you find clothing you want, which it's led you to, thank it and buy the clothing. You might even ask the entity for help finding sales and other good bargains.

Conclusion

The clothing you wear can, in part, dictate how you act as well as how others perceive you. Making your clothing work for you involves learning how to make yourself feel comfortable with who you are no matter what you wear. Finding a sense of style involves finding a sense of comfort in how your clothing reflects your personality. Embrace your own style and let your inner self express itself in your clothing choices. You'll weave a glamour that'll dazzle even yourself!

Appendix 2: Fan Culture and the Astral Planes[15]

One aspect of pop culture magic I've observed has been how some pop culture magicians and Pagans have used the astral realm to connect to their pop culture spirits of choice. While the astral plane can be a useful medium, we also need to recognize the potential shortcomings that occur with working on the astral plane. A while back, I read an account where a woman believed she was married to Sephiroth from *Final Fantasy Seven*[16]. Another person claimed she was married to Severus Snape from the *Harry Potter* universe[17]. In both cases the marriages occurred on the astral plane or through dreams. The people involved didn't have a relationship with another person in everyday life. These aren't the only cases either. There are other cases where people have "married" pop culture characters. In almost each of these cases its characters that exhibit negative behaviors and actions, and seem to feed off of the obsessiveness of the fans. Are these marriages real? Perhaps, perhaps not. As I'll show further down there is a case to be made for having a healthy astral marriage with a pop culture (or other) entity, but in some situations, it's a case of taking an interest to the extreme, to the point that it becomes unhealthy for everyone involved. In such cases the entities seem to insist that the person can only have a relationship with them and the person involved with said entity is obsessed to a point that little else seems to matter to him/her, including maintaining relationships (romantic/sexual, or otherwise) with other people in his/her life. The pop culture entity that the person's obsessed with is fed power by the belief and devotion of the person. And that's the real danger of this fixation, because when a person fixates on an entity to the point that s/he thinks it's married to him/her there's the possibility that the entity is feeding off the person. It's similar to the legend

[15] Originally published in Multi-Media Magic and revised for this book.
[16]See http://sephiroth.blogdrive.com/ and http://mrs-sephiroth.livejournal.com/ for more details.
[17] See http://www.journalfen.net/community/fandom_wank/1015949.html for more details.

of the succubus or incubus who comes at night and feeds on its lover, while tantalizing the lover with fantasies.

Sephiroth is a good example of this. He's a vampyric entity that wants to destroy the world and become a god. He may not exist physically in our reality, but the belief in him creates enough energy for him to take form on the astral plane. Now add someone in who believes s/he is married to him and what you get is an entity drawing on that person's life force and at the same time isolating him/her from the people who care about that person. If it seems far-fetched, just consider that some fan forums are obsessive enough about how their favorite characters are treated that they form cults (as is evident by several different LiveJournal communities devoted to the literal worship of Sephiroth[18]). In other cases, some fans actually claim that they have become the character or have bonded with the character to the point that the character has an active presence in their lives[19]. These fans treat a character such as Sephiroth as an active entity that is also part of their existence, to the point that they sometimes let him encompass their existence. As someone who's invoked pop culture entities, I find it very important to recognize that while it can be a very fulfilling relationship to work with such an entity, it's also important to not let yourself obsess over it. Moderation is key in magic…otherwise you can end up fairly delusional.

Fans are rather unique because their interests in particular stories or characters can sometimes provide enough energy to make what they focus on come to life:

> Fans appear to be frighteningly 'out of control,' undisciplined and unrepentant rogue readers. Rejecting 'aesthetic difference,' fans passionately embrace favored texts and attempt to integrate media representations within their own social experience. (Jenkins 2006b, p. 39)

---

[18] See http://community.livejournal.com/sephyism/806.html and http://community.livejournal.com/sephirothism/profile for more details. On an aside these communities could be parodies, but it does seem like they take their beliefs fairly seriously.

[19]See http://community.livejournal.com/soulbonding/275290.html?thread=2951770#t2951770

This integration can be positive and negative. It allows fans to find other people who are part of their subculture and the social experience can even include very spiritual and magic intensive experiences, but it can also lead to such occurrences as the examples mentioned above.

While pop culture can be used as a medium for magical practice, there is the danger of buying into it too much, and this danger is most apparent on the astral plane. As my good friend D. J. Lawrence said, "That's why I recommend against beginners doing astral stuff. It often just becomes fantasy games" (personal communication, September 7, 2005). The astral plane is a subjective reality, which means that it can take what's in your imagination and give it form, especially if you don't have the training needed to control your thought processes. When creating your own model of the astral realm, or for that matter interacting with an entity there, you have to question whether it's a wishful fantasy or reality or a mixture of the two. The way this can really be tested is found in the effects that such interactions have on the physical plane and I'm not talking about finding love hickies on you after a particularly hot and sweaty astral journey with Sephiroth.

Still, while it's evident that some of these relationships can be dangerous, it's also true that others can be healthy, particularly when balanced with relationships with other people and interests in other hobbies, spiritualities, and life in general. The key is to not get obsessed to the point that only the entity matters. A precedent for this can be found in Voodoo. Sometimes the Lwa will demand that a person marry one of them. That person could already be married to a person, but may still have to also marry the Lwa (and sometimes not just one, but at least several in order to provide balance to the relationships). However, there are definite benefits for both/all participants, as opposed to the Lwa being a parasite in the life of the human being. When such a marriage occurs, the person has specific days on which s/he is devoted to the Lwa alone, but s/he is not expected to give his/her entire life to the Lwa-marriage (Filan 2007). While it's not the only religion where marriage to a god or other entity occurs, it's the best-known to Western occultism. This approach can be applied to a pop culture entity.

Let me provide an example of what a healthy astral marriage with an entity can entail. I've worked with the character of Thiede or Aghama quite a lot in the Deharan system of magic created by Storm Constantine. One of the workings I frequently did to contact him is called the gateway ritual. The practitioner astral projects into the astral plane and then rides a spirit beast or Sedim to a palace. In the palace there is a series of mirrors, which act as gateways into the Wraeththu universe. I would usually project myself into that universe and "ride" the body of a Wraeththu so I could interact with Theide.

My workings with this particular god form were focused on an astral marriage with the goal being to create another entity from the union. Over the course of several months I met with Thiede and had what might be considered astral sex, but with the purpose of impregnating the Wraeththu I rode with a pearl or baby. Once this was achieved, my astral workings changed, focusing more on the pregnancy process and eventual birth and hatching of the pearl into a new Dehar, Kiraziel, who became the Dehar of wishes. At this point I began to work with Kiraziel and prepared him for another working I had in mind, which he would help me fulfill. I was and am still married to Thiede to this day and still set aside time which is specifically for him, but at that time the work with Kiraziel took over a lot of my focus, as is often the case with children.

At this point, you may wonder if I'm deluded. However, you will know something is really occurring in the astral when there is a resonance that occurs in the physical realm. As an example, my workings with Thiede were also driven toward learning more about space/time magic and from him I learned the DNA meditation technique (as detailed in *Space/Time Magic*) that I and others have used with good results. This technique was grounded in the physical world when probabilities evoked via it manifested in the physical realm. Likewise my workings with first Thiede and then Kiraziel would also produce resonance (with them) and manifestation of several desired results into my life.

I created Kiraziel with the specific purpose of granting a wish in my life, in this case to find a magical partner. This occurred on the winter solstice of 2003. Shortly after I created him, I met someone who I thought might be my magical partner, but was not. At first I wondered if I had deluded myself, if the astral projection work had just been a fantasy. But then I considered as well that finding such a partner would not occur on my schedule, but would occur in a time and place that was right for finding the person. In the summer of 2005 I met my ex-wife, who became my magical partner. About eight weeks into the relationship, Kiraziel visited me and indicated this was the person I'd been looking for and that he considered the wish fulfilled. It was now up to me to follow through on what I wished for. That relationship didn't work out in the long run, but at the time she was a magical partner to me and fit the bill, so to speak.

Granted it was almost two years before this wish came true, but when I consider the time span of the ritual to create Kiraziel, it took approximately just under two months for the working to occur. I think that the time spans correlated with each other, in the sense that one month of ritual work could represent one year in a person's life[20]. Kiraziel knew that it would take time and effort to find my magical partner. However what really told me that Kiraziel had manifested in my life was a death-rebirth ritual I did shortly after he'd been created. This ritual was focused on inducing a state of near death for several days and then bringing me back to life on the third day. Kiraziel played a role as one of the rebirthers. When the final stage of the working was completed, a witness to it felt his presence very strongly and asked who he was. I explained my previous ritual (which she didn't know about).

It should be borne in mind that I told Kiraziel that I wanted him to find me a magical partner who fit what I was looking for, no matter how long it took. I didn't do other specific rituals afterwards for this purpose, beyond being guided one night in January 2005 to make a collage. Even though that collage was random and unfocused it ironically (or magically) ended up having an unattributed photograph of my magical partner that was printed in a pagan newspaper in it (before I ever met her), as well attributes central to what I was looking for. The guidance I felt was an inspired guidance, a voice that

---

[20] Note: I should mention that from my personal experiences the time span of a ritual usually is echoed to a greater degree by the time span of the results coming from that ritual. 2 months to do a ritual, 2 years of experiencing the results.

said to make a collage and see what would happen. I made the collage to foretell events in my immediate future, but now I suspect that Kiraziel was working through me to use the collage to help with his search.

Although astral projection can be a useful skill to learn and work with you need to keep yourself grounded and focused on living in this reality. An astral marriage is fine and well, if the purpose is to do more than try to live your dream boat fantasies with the entity in question. In Voodoo, as well as in my example, there are some expectations of devotion and focus, but there is also an understanding that the entity doesn't overshadow the life of the person.

It's easy to get caught up in the feeling of being loved by such an entity, but if it doesn't exist in the physical realm and is keeping you focused on itself, chances are it's using you as a source of energy. Certainly Sephiroth would have no problem using a person foolish enough to be in love with him as a sort of battery. And as such you should be doubly careful with who or what you choose to work with on the astral plane, because not only are you giving form and life to such a being, you are also inviting it to that place, where it has some power. If that occurs such a being could easily create problems for you. I recommend banishing in the astral plane using your preferred technique (and if you don't have one yet then you probably shouldn't be doing this sort of work!) and then banishing in the physical world, followed up by getting rid of any paraphernalia associated with the entity. For someone in love with Sephiroth this would mean getting rid of any *Final Fantasy* material associated with him. If that seems extreme, just remember that an entity can and will use any vector that allows it to have a connection with you. By getting rid of the physical objects you cut off the connection.

A better route though is to work with such entity in moderation. I don't work with either Thiede or Kiraziel often. My workings with them are occasional, done with respect, but with an awareness that I also need to attend to matters in this world. By moderating the time I spend working with them I can get what I need from my workings and maintain those relationships, but without compromising my life in other ways. Remember to test these workings as well. Look for physical manifestations of the work and make sure it's goal oriented, as opposed to supporting a non-existent love life that becomes the entity's cash cow. Finally, keep your emotions on a tight rein. Work with the entity, but keep yourself grounded on what you need to accomplish in your everyday life. Remember that the astral plane you work with is your model of that reality and as such can be changed if you so choose. But also remember that because the astral plane is your model of that reality it can become such an ideal model that it sabotages your purpose[21]. Who wouldn't want to live in an ideal world where everything goes right? On the surface, such a reality in the astral plane might seem ideal, but carefully consider that it could also be a delusion fashioned by your desires, but one that doesn't help you meet those desires. Want someone in your life? Sephiroth might seem like the perfect boyfriend on the astral plane, but it's not like you can introduce him to your friends or family or do any of the other fun things you can do with a person on the physical plane. Whatever astral marriages you have are in the end a combination of the product of your mind and your consciousness interacting with other consciousnesses. Recognize that and you will recognize whether what you are doing is a delusion or a means to an end that can help you manifest what you really need in your life.

[21] This is similar to the obsession some people can display with online games.

Appendix 3: Holiday Magic

I always find holidays to be interesting, not only for the dynamics of human behavior that come forth, but also for the presence of the holiday, the energy that courses through it and builds to a quiet but steady hum of tension which then results in behavior where people let out that tension and have fun (though some of how they act might not be appropriate). The 4th of July is a good example of this. The tension starts the day people get out of work early and start driving to visit family, to buy food or to get fireworks. The traffic is heavier than usual, the grocery stores are packed while people try to get food, and there is a simultaneous sense of enjoyment and frustration depending on what happens. The day of the holiday the tension rises through the day until people celebrate the 4th with firecrackers, with parties, with all the excesses people bring to such matters. And then there is what the day means. For the 4th of July it's a day of creation, the celebration of the birth of the U.S. It's also a celebration of the concepts of Freedom, liberation, and other assorted values that a person might associate with this holiday. And to me it makes everything that happens a ritual of sorts, not necessarily religious, but holy nonetheless to the people who celebrate it. Every action taken is part of a ritual that people are unknowingly taking a role in. The pop culture magician, if s/he so chooses, can utilize a given holiday and all the energy and tension around it as part of their own magical workings.

Typically when we think of holiday magic, we think of magic associated with religious holidays, but I don't think we should limit ourselves to any given holiday, and I also think that if you are doing magic on a given holiday you can tap into the energy of that holiday. Going back to the example of the 4th of July there is a lot of energy that goes into that holiday, a lot of emotions, a lot of tradition, and so why not tap into that if it's something you feel inclined to tap into? You could tap into the 4th of July for creative or healing magic. Alternately, you could also tap into it for more destructive magic. It really depends on what you want to do with it, but the point is that the holiday brings with it energy that can be accessed for magical work.

Each holiday we celebrate has its own energy, its own tension and associations as well. Valentine's Day is a holiday about love and lust, while Christmas is a holiday of both greed and giving. Thanksgiving is a day of thanks and a day of gluttony, while Memorial Day is a day of remembrance and honoring the dead. Labor Day honors work and people who work, and those are just the major secular holidays. But although those major holidays are secular there is something to be drawn on. So if you want to draw on the energy of a particular holiday look to what the holiday represents, both to yourself, and to people in general. Then plan your ritual for the day of the holiday. If you were to use the 4th of July you might time the ritual to begin when the fireworks began, using the sounds of the people and the fireworks going off as part of a ritual accompaniment. With Thanksgiving, you could use both the food preparation and the serving of the meal as part of your ritual. If you want to draw on a holiday, you want to tap into the energy of the day by integrating the actual rituals of that day into your own rituals.

In the case of some holidays, what you end up having is an extended period of time for the tension to build up. Christmas is an excellent example. The build up to the Christmas holiday literally starts right after Halloween when stores start to play Christmas music and put up Christmas decorations (even though most people wish they would just wait until after Thanksgiving). The tension continues to build as people start thinking about what gifts they'll get for people, and also what sales opportunities, such as Black Friday, they'll use in order to save money. After Thanksgiving, the tension increases as Christmas movies are shown and music is played around the clock everywhere you go. There are holiday parties to attend, gifts to buy, family relatives to deal with and all of it contributes to the energy of Christmas. You have a two month period of time focused on this holiday and all of that energy can be very useful for a magical working of pretty much any type given the various emotions and experiences people have in respect to the holiday.

With specific holidays you may want to use specific types of magic. Sex magic would be useful on the 4th and Valentine's Day, while candle magic might be useful on Christmas,

Thanksgiving, and Memorial Day. Think about what practical magic techniques you might use for a given day and ask yourself if those techniques are in character with the holiday. That can help you determine if what you'll do will help you draw on the energy of the holiday, or if it'll distract from the energy of the holiday. After all, if you want to draw on the energy of a holiday then you want to do activities that complement the holiday, because it will sync your efforts with the available energy you want to draw on.

Another thing you can do with holiday magic is use the miracle of modern technology to evoke the energy of a given holiday at any time. If you video record your holiday festivities, then you can use the recordings to capture the magic of the moment. And you also don't have to limit yourself to waiting for the time of year to do magical work associated with a holiday. If you want to do wealth magic and draw on the energy of Christmas, why not integrate Christmas carols into your working by popping some Christmas music into your stereo? While I do think you'll get your most potent results during the actual holidays, it certainly doesn't hurt to draw on them at other times of the year if you think it will be useful.

Holidays are holy days, regardless of whether they are associated with a religion or not. They are days where people's energy is focused on ritualistic behavior that otherwise doesn't occur. Draw on them and see how they can empower your magical workings, and don't hesitate to use the pop culture of the holiday as part of your magical work, because there is some potent pop culture to draw on such as the Thanksgiving Turkey or Santa Claus, or the stereotypical couple on Valentine's Day. Just keep in mind that if working with those entities your working should align with their nature.

It's also important to make sure you honor the holiday itself, as it is an entity in its own right. People have put a lot of energy into the holidays over many years and that brings with it a kind of awareness that should be respected. I recommend doing an offering to the holiday on the actual day and possibly before the working, if the working starts before the actual day. That way you honor the spirit of the day and get its blessing for your magical working. You might even make your own celebration of the holiday part of the offering you make.

Holidays are a time of tension and focus. Holiday magic is the recognition that you can harness that tension and focus for your own use. Regardless of what holiday you work with, what you draw on is not just that day, but also the echo of all the other times that day was observed. It's a powerful resonance you can work with that will fuel your magical working.

Appendix 4: Conventions and Pop Culture Magic

For the pop culture magician a convention can be an opportunity to meet your favorite actors, buy pop culture artifacts you enjoy, and share what you love with fellow fans. It can also be a space where you can interact with the attention, emotions, and energy of your favorite pop culture, amplified by the fans at the convention. Conventions are sacred spaces. They are places where lots of fans come together and share their joy, and in the process create a sacred space for the pop culture they love. As a pop culture magician, you can use that in your workings. Carlin does offer a cautionary warning I agree with when she notes the following about the energy of conventions:

> Of course, just because energy is strong and available doesn't necessarily mean it's in tune with your goals. The energy of a bunch of squeevy dudes drooling over pinups probably won't help you ace your feminist theory class and the energy of a vendor arguing with convention staff won't help your prosperity spell. Take your time to walk the floor to feel out the energies. Find the energy that feels most sympathetic to your goals and take a bit from that area. If you're doing a spell on the fly just be sure to walk through that area when you need to gather energy. If you're setting up for a larger rite you can always charge a stone, sigil, or talisman while walking through that area. (2015b)

With that said, you don't necessarily need to do anything at the convention with the energy. You could simply gather up the energy of the convention and save it up for a later time. I've done that myself, and in the process have filtered out anything that didn't fit. There is a lot of energy occurring at a convention, and so it's easy to take some of that energy and store it, either in a ritual object or energetic battery.

If you want to do a magical working at a convention, you can approach it as a solo working or as a group working. In either case the working can be practical or devotional, but in the case of the group working it helps if each person involved actually likes the particular pop culture you might be working with. For example, if you are at a Bronies convention, all of you will likely be working with My Little Pony, but if you are a convention where there are multiple pop culture fandoms it's important that each person in the group knows what pop culture is being worked with and can work with it.

Whether you are doing a solo or group working, one advantage you have at a convention is that you can dress up and use your pop culture gear without much negative attention being directed your way. So if you are doing a magical working related to *Star Wars,* why not dress up as a Storm Trooper, Sith lord, or Jedi knight (depending on the purpose of the working and who/what you want to work with)? The costume work helps you invoke the energy of the pop culture you work with, as does the pop culture artifacts you are using. At a convention you can usually get pop culture artifacts and costumes to relate to your favorite pop culture, or you can make your own ahead of time. Either way, why not take those objects of pop culture devotion and use them in your magical workings? The attention you get for your costume can be drawn on for your working, and it also helps you be more receptive to the pop culture mythology you are working with.

If you are doing a solo working at a convention, you can set the working up to be activated by the energy of the convention, but also by moments that are personally relevant to you such as meeting a favorite actor or getting access to new information about your favorite pop culture. By integrating the personal moments of significance into your working, you are effectively building up and directing the energy toward your specific working. This puts more oomph into your magical working.

If doing a group working, it's important that you do the working in a place that doesn't interfere with the enjoyment other people are having at the convention. You don't want to sour the energy. You might set the working up in a hotel room, or if it's possible in a room not being used at the time for anything else (though you may need to check with hotel and con staff ahead of time). Ideally, you set up the working so that it doesn't interfere with any of the participants' enjoyment of the convention. After all, if one of your members really wants to be at the panel while you are doing a ritual, there focus is distracted even more than it already would be. Set your group working up so that it occurs at a time where it works for everyone. Another possible alternative is to actually do the ritual before the convention or after it, but have everyone visualize they are in the convention.

If you are doing a pop culture magic working for devotional purposes, keep in mind that your pop culture deities will likely want you, as part of that devotion, to engage in activities that honor them. So you may get an intuitive urge to go to a particular panel or buy a particular artifact. Pay close attention to those urges and follow through on them, with an understanding that what you are doing is an act of dedication to your pop culture deity.

Every activity you get involved in can feed your working. If you are playing a game, attending a panel, even having lunch and talking with friends about your activities; all of it can fuel the magical workings you do while at the convention. Most importantly though have fun, for the enjoyment you have while there is also an active part of the magic.

Appendix 5: Board Games, Card Games, and Pop Culture Magic

Board and card games can be another useful source of pop culture magic. While a lot of the principles I've shared in the chapters on RPGs and video games can be applied to magic utilizing board and card games, it's worth noting that board and card games are unique in their own when it comes to pop culture magic. For example, you are playing with (and sometimes against) other people in a face to face to situation. There are also specific rules for each game which can be useful in pop culture magic, in terms of how you use those rules and the limits they embody to your advantage.

There are a decent variety of games and so how you use a given game in your magical working depends in part on the actual game. For example, with *Tri-Ominos,* my friends and I have created sigils out of the shapes that we put together when we played the game. It didn't matter to us who won or didn't win. What mattered was what sigil shape we could create and what we would focus the sigil on. We agree ahead of time about what the sigil should be focused on and then play the game to create the sigil (See below for an example of a *Tri-Ominos* sigil).

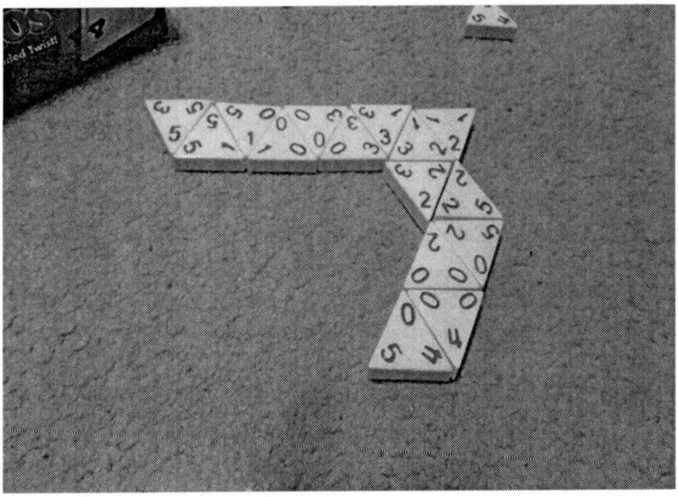

In games where this a sense of competition, you can use the competition and emotions surrounding it as a way to fuel either an individual or group working. If it's a group working, then you set the magic working up ahead of time and prime it with game playing, so that it's released when the game is finished. You can likewise do the same if it's an individual effort on your part. What's important is that you don't get fixated on winning or bothered if you lose. Feel whatever emotions you feel, but focus on channeling them into the working as well as drawing on the experience in general to help with the manifestation of your desired result. I like to use *Risk* games in this capacity because the game is usually a high tension game for everyone involved. As a result, the emotional energy generated can be quite useful for powering a working.

Sometimes what you might use is the sense of accomplishment you feel when achieving a specific action. When I play the game *Sequence* and manage to line up five tiles (which is necessary for winning the game) I feel accomplished for having managed it, especially with other people trying to stop and block me. *Forbidden Island* and *Forbidden Desert* are cooperative games which are similar in that everyone is trying to achieve the same goal, so the principle works the same, in that if you can accomplish those goals, the effort and the consequent feeling of success can be useful fuel for a magical working.

When deciding if you'll use a game for your magical workings, I suggest playing through it a few times just to get a feel for how it works and what it is you're trying to accomplish. Then think about how the gameplay activity and feelings around playing the game can be directed for magical purposes. You want to consider how the rules of the game can factor into your working. For example with *Attika*, you have two ways you can win. You can either build your city from one temple to another temple, or just build the entire city. However part of how you win the game involves picking the correct sequence in which to build your buildings and also involves managing your resources in order to build the city. The rules around the game show you how to do this. Knowing those rules can be helpful in planning how you'll link playing the game to your magical working. You might for example, focus on skillful use of resources and correct sequences as activities that contribute to a magical working for wealth, as those game skills also play a role in how you manage your wealth in your own life. Understanding the rules and activities of game helps you take the activities and turn them into magical actions that help you manifest your goal.

Some games can be adapted to specific magic activities. Felix Warren, for example, uses *Cards Against Humanity* to do accurate divinatory readings for people. The reason CAH works so well with divinatory readings is that the information is contextual enough in regards to people, that if you know anything about those people, you can start to see patterns via the cards you pull. I've actually used the cards from *Dixit* for similar purposes, because they are open enough for interpretation that they can be applied to a person and their respective situation.

The magical aspect of playing games really comes down to understanding how you can take a given activity and link the effort, emotions, etc., into your magical working. You are using your activity and the activity of others as fuel for your magical working. You may do a magical working separate from the game, but what you'll do when you do the working is create a specific connection to the game activity to make sure that activity feeds the working. Or you might use the game activity as the actual working. You set up the desired result ahead of time and as you play you visualize the result and see your efforts, activities, and emotions flow into it, until you've reach saturation and then when a specific activity occurs, you visualize that result merging into reality.

Games, by how they are designed, simultaneously entertain and focus the players. That focus is similar to how a ritual focuses a person and like a ritual the games have specific actions and rules that are followed in order to produce specific results. Look at your board and cards games with that understanding and you'll see how you can apply them to pop culture magic.

Bibliography

Arkenburg, Chris (2006). My lovewar with Fox news. In Jason Louv (ed.). *Generation Hex*. (pp. 203-217). New York: Disinformation Ltd.

Austin, Alec (2013). *The implicit contract*. Retrieved February 2, 2015 from http://spreadablemedia.org/essays/austin/#.VNAp32jF_4t

Barton, Kristin M. (2014). Chuck versus the advertiser: How fan activism and footlong subway sandwiches saved a television series. In Barton and Lampley (eds). Pp. 159-172. *Fan CULTure: Essays on Participatory fandom in the 21st century*. Jefferson: McFarland & Company, Inc., Publishers.

Bowman, Sarah Lynne. (2010). *The functions of role-playing games: How participants create community, solve problems and explore identity*. Jefferson: McFarland & Company, Inc., Publishers.

Bowman, Sarah Lynne (2012). Jungian theory and immersion in role-playing games._In Evan Torner and William White (eds). Pp. 31-51. *Immersive gameplay: essays on participatory media and role-playing*. Jefferson: McFarland and Company Publishers, Inc.

Bey, Hakim. (1991). *T.A.Z. The temporary autonomous zone, ontological anarchy, poetic terrorism*. Brooklyn: Autonomedia.

Brooker, Will (2007). A sort of homecoming: Fan viewing and symbolic pilgrimage. In Gray, Sandvoss, & Harrington (eds). Pp. 149-164. *Fandom, identities and communities in a mediated world*. New York: New York University Press.

Carlin, Emily. (2014a, January 30). *Who's your Doctor?* Retrieved April 15, 2015 from http://blacksunmagick.blogspot.com/2014/01/pop-culture-magick-for-geeks-whos-your.html

Carlin, Emily. (2014b, February 5). *A wretched hive of scum and villainy*. Retrieved April 15, 2015 from http://blacksunmagick.blogspot.com/2014/02/pop-culture-magick-for-geeks-wretched.html

Carlin, Emily. (2015a, February 21). Working with villains. Retrieved April 15, 2015 from http://blacksunmagick.blogspot.com/2015/02/pop-culture-magick-working-with-villains.html

Carlin, Email. (2015b, April 7). *Con-edition part 1.* Retrieved April 15, 2015 from http://blacksunmagick.blogspot.com/2015/04/pop-culture-magick-con-edition-part-i.html

Collins, Jim, and Porras, Jerry I. (1994). *Built to last: Successful habits of visionary companies.* New York: HarperCollins Publishers

Couldry, Nick. (2007). On the set of *The Sopranoes*: 'Inside' a fan's construction of nearness. In Gray, Sandvoss, & Harrington (eds). Pp. 139-48. *Fandom, identities and communities in a mediated world.* New York: New York University Press.

Ellwood, Taylor. (2004). *Pop culture magick.* Stafford: Megalithica Books.

Ellwood, Taylor. (2008). *Multi-media magic: Further explorations of identity and pop culture in magical practice.* Stafford: Megalithica Books.

Ellwood, Taylor. (2012). *Magical identity: An exploration of space/time, neuroscience, and identity*. Stafford: Megalithica Books.

Epstein, Mark. (1995). *Thoughts without a thinker: Psychotherapy from a Buddhist perspective.* Cambridge: Basic Books.

Filan, Kenaz. (2007). *The Haitian Vodou Handbook.* Rochester: Destiny Books.

Fiske, John (1989). *Understanding pop culture.* New York: Routledge, Taylor, & Francis Group.

Fuist, Todd Nicholas. (2012). The agentic imagination: Tabletop role-playing games as a cultural tool. In Evan Torner and William White (eds). Pp. 108-26. *Immersive gameplay: essays on participatory media and role-playing*. Jefferson: McFarland and Company Publishers, Inc.

Gee, James Paul. (2007). *What video games have to teach us about learning and literacy.* New York: Palgrave Macmillan.

Gee, James Paul. (2013). *Good video games + good learning: Collected essays on video games, learning and literacy*. New York: Peter Lang.

Grabill, Jeffery. (2001). *Community literacy programs and the politics of change.* Albany: State University of New York Press.

Grabmeier, Jeff. (2012, May 7). *"Losing yourself" in a Fictional Character can Affect Your Real Life*. Retrieved December 3, 2013, from http://researchnews.osu.edu/archive/exptaking.htm

Graham, Anissa M. (2014). A new kind of pandering: Supernatural and the world of fanfiction. In Barton and Lampley (eds). Pp. 131-146. *Fan CULTure: Essays on Participatory fandom in the 21st century*. Jefferson: McFarland & Company, Inc., Publishers.

Gray, William G. (1970). *Inner traditions of magic*. York Beach: Samuel Weiser, Inc.

Gwynne, Owain. (2014). Fan-made time: The lord of the rings and the hobbit. In Barton and Lampley (eds). Pp. 76-91. *Fan CULTure: Essays on Participatory fandom in the 21st century*. Jefferson: McFarland & Company, Inc., Publishers.

Halloran, Tim. (2014). *Romancing the brand: How brands create strong, intimate relationships with customers*. San Francisco: Jossey-Bass.

Harpur, Patrick. (2002). *The philosophers' secret fire: A history of the imagination*. Chicago: Ivan R. Dee

Harpur, Patrick. (2003). *Daimonic reality: A field guide to the otherworld*. Ravensdale: Pine Winds Press.

Harpur, Patrick. (2011). *The secret tradition of the soul*. Berkeley: Evolver Editions.

Henderson, W. M. (1997). *I, Elvis: Confessions of a counterfeit king*. New York: Boulevard Books.

Hibbard, Allen. (1999). *Conversations with William S. Burroughs*. Jackson: University Press of Mississippi.

Hill, Annette. (2011). *Paranormal media: Audiences, spirits and magic in popular culture*. New York: Routledge, Taylor & Francis Group.

Hills, Matt. (2002). *Fan cultures*. New York: Routledge, Taylor & Francis Group.

Hoffman, Donald D. (1998). *Visual Intelligence*. New York: W.W. Norton and Company.

Hook, Nathan. (2012). Circles and frames: The games social scientists play. In Evan Torner and William White (eds). Pp. 52-70. *Immersive gameplay: essays on participatory media and role-playing*. Jefferson: McFarland and Company Publishers, Inc.

Jenkins, Henry. (2006a). *Convergence culture: Where old and the new media collide.* New York: New York University.

Jenkins, Henry. (2006b). *Fans, bloggers, and gamers: Exploring participatory culture.* New York: New York University Press.

Jenkins, Henry. (2013). *Textual poachers: Television fans and participatory culture.* New York: Routledge, Taylor, and Francis Group.

Jenkins, Henry, Ford, Sam, and Joshua Green. (2013). Spreadable media: Creating value and meaning in a networked culture. New York: New York University.

Johnson, Derek (2007). Fan-tagonism: Factions, institutions, and constitutive, hegemonies of fandom. In Gray, Sandvoss, & Harrington (eds). Pp. 285-300. *Fandom, identities and communities in a mediated world.* New York: New York University Press.

Jung, C.G. (1990). *The archetypes and the collective unconscious.* Princeton: Princeton University Press.

Koren-Kuik, Meyrav. (2014). Desiring the tangible: Disneyland, fandom and spatial immersion. In Barton and Lampley (eds). Pp. 146-158. *Fan CULTure: Essays on Participatory fandom in the 21st century.* Jefferson: McFarland & Company, Inc., Publishers.

Kozinets, Robert V. (2013). *Retrobrands and retromarketing.* Retrieved February 11, 2015 from http://spreadablemedia.org/essays/kozinets/#.VNw0w_nF_4t

Lakoff, George, and Johnson, Mark. (1980). *Metaphors we live by.* Chicago: The University of Chicago Press.

Lisiewski, Joseph C. (2004). *Ceremonial magic & the power of evocation.* Tempe: New Falcon Press.

Lukka, Laura (2014). The psychology of immersion. In Back (ed). The Cutting Edge of Nordic Larp Knutpunkt 2014. Retrieved May 15, 2015 from http://nordiclarp.org/w/images/e/e8/2014_The_Cutting_Edge_of_Nordic_Larp.pdf

McCloud, Scott. (1993). *Understanding Comics: The Invisible Art.* New York: Paradox Press.

McCloud, Scott. (2006). *Making comics: Storytelling secrets of comics, manga, and graphic arts*. New York: Harper Collins Books.

Sandvoss, Cornel (2007). The death of the reader? Literary theory and the study of texts in popular culture. In Gray, Sandvoss, & Harrington (eds). Pp. 19-32. *Fandom, identities and communities in a mediated world*. New York: New York University Press.

Schiappa, Edward. (2003). *Defining reality: Definitions and the politics of meaning*. Carbondale: Southern Illinois University Press.

Scott, Eric. (2014, February 6). Why you should read LOKI: AGENT OF ASGARD. Retrieved February 8, 2014 from http://witchesandpagans.com/Pagan-Culture-Blogs/why-you-should-read-loki-agent-of-asgard.html

Stewart, R. J. (1990). *The underworld initiation: A journey toward psychic transformation*. Lake Toxaway: Mercury Publishing Inc.

Stewart. R. J. (2006). *The spirit cord*. Boulder: R. J. Stewart Books.

Stribling, Eleanor Baird. (2013). *Valuing Fans*. Retrieved February 2, 2015 from http://spreadablemedia.org/essays/stribling/#.VNA4RWjF_4t

Theodoropoulou, Vivi. (2007). The anti-fan within the fan: Awe and envy in sport fandom. In Gray, Sandvoss, & Harrington (eds). Pp. 316-327. *Fandom, identities and communities in a mediated world*. New York: New York University Press.

The Pagan Study Group Page. (2014, Feb 04). *Pop-Culture Paganism: An Introduction*. Retrieved November 26, 2014 from http://thepaganstudygrouppage.tumblr.com/post/75580019817/pop-culture-paganism-an-introduction

Torner, Evan, and White, J. William (2012). Introduction. In Evan Torner and William White (eds). Pp. 3-11. *Immersive gameplay: essays on participatory media and role-playing*. Jefferson: McFarland and Company Publishers, Inc.

Unsane, Prenna. (2007). Emerging from the age of the chalice and wand. In Ellwood (ed.). *Magick on the edge: An anthology in experimental occultism.* (pp.131-141). Stafford: Megalithica Books.

Walters, Zachary. (2007). Experiments in dynamic body magic. In Ellwood (ed.). *Magick on the edge: An anthology in experimental occultism.* (pp.67-77). Stafford: Megalithica Books.

Ward, Terence P. (2015). *Percy Jackson: A hellenic hero or a heel? Kids speak out.* Retrieved March 3, 2015 from http://wildhunt.org/2015/03/percy-jackson-a-hellenic-hero-or-a-heel-kids-speak-out.html

Wenger, Etienne. (1998). *Communities of practice: Learning, meaning, and identity.* Cambridge: Cambridge University Press.

White, William, Harviainen, J., & Emily Boss (2012). Role-playing communities, cultures of play and the discourse of immersion. In Evan Torner and William White (eds). Pp. 71-86. *Immersive gameplay: essays on participatory media and role-playing.* Jefferson: McFarland and Company Publishers, Inc.

Wu (2004). Magical Assault on corporations (Version 2.35). (2004, April 13). Retrieved January 15, 2007), from http://www.technoccult.com/archives/2004/04/13/magical-assault-on-corporations-version-235/#more-456

About the Author

Taylor Ellwood is the managing non-fiction Editor for Immanion Press, as well as the author of over twenty books, including Pop Culture Magick, Manifesting Wealth and Magical Identity. When Taylor isn't working on his latest experiment or writing his latest book, he's avidly reading books on a variety of topics, hiking, and playing lots of board and video games. He lives in Portland, Oregon with his wife, two kids, and six cats, and also hosts the Magical Experiments meet up. For more information about his latest work, visit:
http://www.magicalexperiments.com

The Way of the Magician Mystery School

The Way of the Magician is a Mystery School that I have developed to formalize and improve on the work that I have written about in my books. It is a fusion of Western magical practices and Eastern mystical practices, with an emphasis on creating a balanced approach to doing internal work for spiritual and personal growth, while also doing practical workings to solve problems and improve the quality of your life. The Way of the Magician is designed to supplement and enhance any spiritual work you are doing in other magical traditions while still presenting a unique perspective and approach to magical work.

What makes the Way of the Magician Mystery School unique is the integration of modern disciplines and cultural studies into your spiritual work. I think it is important for magic, as a discipline and spiritual practice, to evolve with the times, and part of this is done by exploring how other disciplines such as neuroscience, rhetoric, literacy, etc. can be meaningfully applied to spiritual practices.

I offer correspondence courses on the Process of Magic, Space/Time Magic Foundations, Inner Alchemy Foundations, and Pop Culture Magic Foundations. I also teach teleclasses on intermediate to advanced topics. I offer a magical apprentice program for anyone who wishes to work one on one with me.

If you would like to learn more about available classes at The Way of the Magician Mystery School, please visit http://www.magicalexperiments.com/way-of-the-magician/

Get More at Immanion Press

Visit us online to browse our books, sign-up for our e-newsletter and find out about upcoming events for our authors, as well as interviews with them. Visit us at http://www.immanion-press.com and visit our publicity blog at:
http://ipmbblog.wordpress.com/

Get Social with Immanion Press

Find us on Facebook at:
http://www.facebook.com/immanionpress

Follow us on Twitter at
http://www.twitter.com/immanionpress

Find us on Google Plus at
https://plus.google.com/u/0/b/104674738262224210355/

Lightning Source UK Ltd.
Milton Keynes UK
UKOW04f2324121015

260413UK00002B/33/P

9 780993 237126